Dark Houses

Book One of the Nomads' Land Series

By Catherine Dale

Dark Houses is a work of fiction. Names, places, characters and events are the products of the author's imagination. Any resemblance to actual people, places, people or events is entirely coincidental.

Copyright © 2012 by Catherine Dale

CHAPTER 1

The forest was noisy. Wind ruffled the leaves, birds sang, and something small and innocent scurried through the dry leaves. Caylen liked a noisy forest; it was when things got quiet that she started to worry.

She moved forward quickly but carefully, being sure not to add any sounds of her own to the din around her. A flash of motion off to the right barely caught her attention; small, moving parallel to her path—just a bird. She could make out a shape up ahead, though, something strange about it, almost blending in to the shadow of a large oak, but not quite... something just not right. She raised her left fist in the air, waited long enough to be sure that the signal had been seen by those traveling behind her, and then lowered herself closer to the ground and moved off the path into the undergrowth. It was tougher going, there; she could feel the forest start to notice her. Still not alarmed enough to be silent, but watching.

She crept on, and by about ten strides from the object her brain finally started to process the shape. She could make out a leg, covered in a dark fabric, stretched out from the larger bulk resting against the tree. There was a boot on the foot, nothing fancy. It looked much the same as the boots on Caylen's own feet, although hers were more worn. She eased closer, looking for a trap, ears and eyes open for any changes or danger. Her bow was a nuisance, the only part of her that wouldn't bend, wouldn't mold itself to the forest floor, but she needed it; there was no point in getting somewhere quietly if she were unarmed when she arrived. A little nearer, and a little further around the side, and it became clear that the body slumped against the tree was no danger to her, and would never be a danger to anyone again. She had to be sure, though, so she found a fist-sized rock in the undergrowth and lifted herself up just long enough to throw it, hard, at the body.

The rock hit with a soft sound, tumbling to the ground rather than bouncing off the hard muscle of a living shoulder, and the body didn't move. Caylen had her answer, even before she saw the dark putrescence spreading out from where her stone had broken the body's swelling, rotting skin. She eased out toward the path, still cautious, but not alarmed, and when she got back into sight of those following her she raised her arm again, this time with a flat hand that she jerked forward. *Come on.*

She walked over to the body. It had been there at least a few days, from the look of it. No animals seemed to have found it yet, which was strange, but a careful sniff confirmed that the corpse was just starting to smell. The clothes were nothing special, but there could be something useful on the body. Caylen made sure she kept the smile from her face as she turned to greet

Connell, the band's second-in-command. "I'd check it out, but I'm on point."

Connell peered down at the dead body. "Looks like one of us." One of them. A Nomad, he meant. Connell crouched to get a better look at the face, then shook his head. "Hard to tell, now, but he doesn't look familiar." He glanced back at the group of nomads gathering behind him. "Romy, check him out." He jerked his head down the path. "And you, Cay—if you're on point, get your ass *on point.*"

Caylen moved forward quickly. Once she was a few strides away, she took a moment to re-center herself, getting back into the right mindset. Alert, but relaxed. Hearing and seeing everything, without letting herself be distracted by unimportant details. It had taken a long time to develop this skill, and she was proud that she was being given the responsibility of scouting ahead more and more often. Nora, the leader of their band, was a hard woman, and not easily impressed, or even satisfied. She expected discipline and skill from everyone on the team, and it made no difference to her that Caylen was young. Made no difference that she was Nora's daughter.

Caylen didn't think it would take long for Romy to search the body, so she didn't bother slowing down to wait for him. She moved forward along the side of the path, not creeping, but not strutting along like she'd seen people doing in the cities. She was part of the forest, but she didn't own it. She wasn't arrogant enough to think that she was ever totally safe, or totally in control.

The next body was lying face down in the middle of the path. Caylen hadn't stayed around long enough to see what had killed the last one, but this time it was pretty obvious; three arrows stuck out of the corpse's back. Caylen didn't bother creeping up on this one. She found another stone, made another hard throw, and was satisfied with another lifeless thud. She moved up to stand near the body, but stayed on alert, waiting for Connell to come for a closer look. Whoever had killed these men was likely long gone, but that didn't mean that there weren't other possible threats.

When Connell came to join her, Nora was with him, and Caylen fought to keep herself from tensing. She was doing everything right, following procedure exactly; there was no room for criticism. Nora just ignored her, crouching down next to the body, and Caylen relaxed. The absence of fault-finding was about as close to praise as Nora ever got.

"Soldier," Nora grunted to Connell, and Caylen let herself take a quick glance down. She saw what looked like a blue uniform before snapping her eyes back up to continue scanning the forest.

"Where's the rest of them, then?" Connell loved to think out loud, and it was always nice for Caylen to be able to listen to him. It was about the only way she had of finding out what was going on. "They don't usually leave their dead. And they don't travel alone."

Nora nodded grimly. "Caylen, right point, take it slow and careful. I'll take left. Connell, put the crew on full alert." She glanced down. "Romy's hands are already dirty. He might as well pick over this one, as well."

"I'll tell him. Better chance of finding something good on a soldier, at least." Connell waited by the body for the rest of the band to catch up to him, while Nora and Caylen moved into position.

It was nerve-wracking to work with Nora, but a part of Caylen loved it. Nora was so perfect, so effortlessly alert, and Caylen didn't think she was flattering herself to believe that the two of them worked well together. It felt good, knowing that she could absolutely trust the ability of her partner, and that Nora trusted her in return. And it was certainly easier to only keep track of half as much forest as usual.

She didn't have long to enjoy the experience, though. They'd only been working their way forward for a few minutes when she spotted the next body. In her peripheral vision she could see Nora's arm lift up at the exact same time that Caylen lifted her own, like the choreography of some macabre dance. It was more than one body, Caylen quickly realized, her eyes finding shape after shape, hunched over on the ground or sprawled in the edges of the forest, trying to get away, and two of them locked together, as if they had died simultaneously, mid-fight. There were probably twenty corpses, at least.

It wasn't her job to investigate, though, just to watch for potential danger. She glanced over at Nora, looking for orders. The older woman was still surveying the scene, so Caylen resumed her own watchfulness. She stepped forward cautiously into the clearing where the battle had occurred, looking for anything moving in the tree line, anything threatening. She saw something flicker in the undergrowth on the far side of the open space, and crouched down, making a smaller target and trying to get a better view. Another flash of movement, and she saw that it was just a squirrel, hopping to a new branch.

She stayed crouched down, looking for a new perspective, her back to the undergrowth at the side of the clearing. She slowly scanned the scene, and saw nothing new, nothing moving. She began to straighten up, and it was only then that she noticed the faint trail on the ground. It was barely there, just a few twigs facing directions they shouldn't be, a scuff of dirt exposed... and when she looked closer, a smear of dark brown, and then another. The trail came from near the center of the clearing. It could have been left by a scavenger, dragging a body away, or it could have been a body dragging *itself* away. She could see a few spots where the dark brown stain was more obvious, as if whoever was bleeding had rested there, while the blood kept flowing. The trail led into the undergrowth, a few strides from where Caylen was standing. She shifted a little, looking to see if she could spot anything, and moved closer. It was only because of years of discipline and training that she was able to keep herself from yelping when a hand shot out of the bushes and grabbed hold of her ankle.

CHAPTER 2

Caylen wrenched her leg back, her dagger in her hand before she was even conscious of wanting it. There was no strength in the grip on her ankle, though, and she stepped away easily. Her heart was racing. Stupid, *stupid*—making assumptions, getting careless! She glanced over to see if Nora had noticed; there was no reaction from the older woman, but that didn't meant too much. Nora was fully capable of storing a mistake like this away for months, pulling it out as ammunition in some future battle that Caylen hadn't even begun thinking about yet. But that was another distraction, worrying about Nora when she should be focusing on the job at hand.

She bent down to see beneath the thick branches of the shrub she had been standing near, this time careful to keep her distance. She still couldn't see much, just a few flashes of pale skin and some dark blue fabric. There was no sign of attack, or any motion at all, since the initial grab.

"Live one," she hissed, just loud enough for Nora to hear.

"Wait for Connell." Nora didn't even glance over.

Caylen stepped back further and waited. She wondered how long it had taken him, this survivor, to drag himself from the middle of the clearing, and how long he'd been lying there in the undergrowth, too hurt to help himself, but not hurt enough to die. She wondered how much longer it would be before Connell arrived and put the man out of his misery, one way or the other.

And then Connell was there, with the rest of the band close at his heels. Nora's orders weren't loud, but they didn't have to be; everyone was waiting, silently alert. "Forward team, set up a perimeter. Back team, check the bodies. Connell, Caylen's got a live one." The band moved quickly and efficiently into their assigned tasks, Connell coming to stand by Caylen. She nodded to show where the man was hiding, and they moved forward together.

Connell crouched down and peered cautiously into the undergrowth. "He's got himself wedged in there pretty well. Good spot." His eyebrows creased. "Could be a bit tricky getting him out." He pulled his shotgun from the scabbard on his back, and for a moment Caylen thought that he'd decided not to even bother trying to help, and was just going to shoot the man and be done with it. It wasn't unheard of for the nomads to practice mercy killing, but they usually didn't do it without a bit more of an effort to save the patient.

Connell crouched down and guided the gun's barrel in through the twigs toward the body. Caylen had heard it so many times: a gun's a distance weapon, there's no point in getting it close to the target; that just gives your enemy a chance to take it from you. So

Connell wouldn't be getting so close if he was planning on shooting. And he wouldn't want to waste precious ammunition on a job like this. But she noticed that his finger was near the trigger, ready to fire if needed.

Connell nudged the body gently with the barrel, and then a bit harder. The soldier shifted slightly and made a pained, breathy sound. His head trembled. It seemed like he was trying to lift it. Caylen remembered how weak the grip had been around her ankle, and wondered if that one effort had exhausted whatever strength the man had left.

Connell frowned at her. "Gonna be a pain to get him out if he can't help."

"We sure he's not playing possum?"

"Nope, not sure." Connell flashed her a quick grin. "Wanna find out?"

Caylen sighed. "By crawling in there?"

"Yup." He gestured with the barrel of his gun. "I'll cover you. I'd do it myself, but I'm wearing my good suit."

Caylen cast a scornful look at his clothes, just as weathered and worn as her own. "Yeah, right. You're just too old to manage it, you mean. Not mobile enough."

Connell smiled. "Call it that if you want to. Now, crawl your ass into that scratchy pit, there, and grab us some live soldier."

Caylen surveyed the situation. Connell was right, there was no way to get at the soldier from outside of the little brush-cave he'd found. And they couldn't just leave him in there. Well, they could, and a lot of nomads would, she knew. But Nora's band wasn't quite that merciless; they were tough, but not as hard as Nora pretended. And Caylen liked it that way, so she crouched down again and tried to figure out a plan.

"Once I get in, there's a fair bit of room. I could crawl in, figure out where he's hurt, and do a field dressing before we try to move him?"

"Not until you're sure he's unarmed." Nora had crept up on them in her usual silent way. Caylen consoled herself by noting that Connell looked a bit surprised by the new voice, as well, so Caylen wasn't the only one not paying proper attention. And Nora was right—one of the soldier's arms was still stretched out as it had been when he'd grabbed Caylen's ankle, but the other was hidden. Who knew what kind of weapon it could be holding?

"I could..." Caylen felt the weight of her wooden bow, strung across her back. It would work, but until she earned the right to carry one of the band's few guns, her bow was her best distance weapon, and she treated it with proper respect. Someone else's, though...

She crossed to the nearest fallen nomad and rolled him a little, wiggling the bow out from under him. It was roughly made, not nearly as balanced as her own, and she had no hesitation about using it for a purpose other than shooting. She tossed it in her hand, feeling its unwieldiness—she'd have no hesitation about using *this* bow for firewood. She crouched down at the opening to the injured man's retreat, and slid the weapon in along the ground. Connell saw what she was doing and shifted around, lining his gun up to have a clear shot if the soldier became a threat.

There was no movement, though, except for Caylen's. She wiggled the weapon in beside the man's body, trying to grab his hidden arm. It took several tries; the bow was recurved, so it wasn't impossible to use it as a hook, but it certainly wasn't easy.

Finally, she managed to get a good hold of the soldier's arm and pulled it out toward her. Once it started moving, it was fairly easy to keep it going, and she was reasonably sure she felt the weight lessen a few times, as if the soldier was trying to help. It wasn't long before she had both hands lined up next to each other, stretched over his head, empty of weapons. She glanced at Nora, who had watched the whole process without comment, but got no reaction. "I'll tie them, as soon as I go in," she tried, and Nora nodded, then turned and headed back to the center of the clearing where the other nomads were collecting whatever they'd scavenged from the dead.

"Good job," Connell said. "Have you got something to tie him with?" Caylen reached into the pack that she'd left on the ground and pulled out a ball of light rope. "Okay, then, in you go."

She slid down on her belly and wormed forward. It wasn't easy, with sharp twigs stabbing her and branches getting in her way, but she made it. She reached out and lifted the soldier's hands in order to tie them, and they were cold. She wondered if they'd found him too late, but then she felt a weak, hesitant pulse under her fingers. Still a little life, then.

"I changed my mind," she called back to Connell after she'd secured the man's hands. "It's pretty crowded in here. I'm gonna drag him out, okay?" Crowded and smelly. The soldier had apparently been in there for a while. And Connell was a much better medic than she was, anyhow.

"Your call."

"Yeah." She wormed her way back a little, then grabbed the soldier's hands and pulled. He outweighed her, and she wasn't at a great angle, but she managed to move him a little, and then a little more. He wasn't doing anything to help her, this time; she was pretty sure he had passed out. Connell reached in to assist, at first dragging her, and then dragging the soldier, once he was far enough out for Connell to get a grip.

They laid him out on the ground and Connell began his assessment. As usual, he spoke as he worked. "Got a lump on his head... probably concussion. And then... cut that jacket off, will you? And the shirt. We need to see where this blood came from." Caylen did as she was told, her dagger sharp enough to make quick work of the heavy wool jacket and thin shirt, and then pushed the soiled fabric to the sides to expose the man's back. The skin was filthy, mostly with dried blood, but there were no visible injuries. Connell said, "Let's roll him, then."

They worked together to make it as smooth as possible. The front of the soldier's shirt was darker than the back, and the bloodstains there were fresh and wet. Caylen wished she'd done an assessment before dragging him; if she'd flipped him over onto his uninjured back, it would have been a lot easier on his wounds. She didn't have time to worry about that, though, so she filed it away as another thing to learn from, to remember the next time she had to make a similar decision.

"Lift the jacket off... good. Now peel the shirt away." Connell said. "No, wait... damn, it's stuck here... okay, cut it again, and we'll soak it later... yeah, get some water, let's get this mess cleaned up a bit. And get a rag for his face, see what all that blood's covering." Caylen followed the instructions. As she cleaned, she saw her patient clearly for the first time, and wondered whether she'd been right to be thinking of him as a man, rather than a boy. His face, still unconscious, was pale and drawn, so it was hard to be sure, but she didn't think he looked much older than she was. He had stubble on his cheeks, and he was filled out, wasn't a scrawny kid, but she seriously doubted that he'd seen his twentieth year. Connell poured a bit of the water directly onto the soldier's chest, and then wet a rag and sponged a few areas off.

"Huh." Connell seemed almost amused, drawing her attention back to the injuries. "We've got quite a variety, here." He pointed as he spoke. "Graze from a bullet, there along his shoulder, and again on his side, here. And a few shotgun pellets, from the look of things— he probably wasn't the target, just ended up in the scatter zone. But this one," he pointed at an angry-looking gash just below the collarbone, "this is the big problem. Looks like he got stabbed there." He leaned down a put his ear to the man's chest. "Didn't hit the lung, doesn't sound like. Didn't hit the heart, or he'd be long dead. Just bled a lot." He looked up at Caylen. "How the hell does a man get shot three times, plus stabbed in the chest, and then lie in the dirt for who knows how long, and not die? He's either damn tough or damn lucky."

"So now that we've got him—he's going to be okay?" Caylen found herself strangely interested in this stranger's fate. Maybe it was the way he had dragged himself away from the carnage in the middle of the clearing, trying to find refuge in the forest as she had so often done herself. Or just the fact that he had held on for as long as he had. It would seem like a waste of his efforts for him to die now.

"I don't know... how much blood has he got left in him?" Connell mopped up around the stab wound, which was still slowly oozing blood. "Less now, that's for sure." He rose to his feet gracefully. "The grazes are fine—the bullets cauterized them pretty well. And the shot holes aren't serious, although we might as well poke around a bit and see if the pellets are still in there. The stab hole's the problem, and it looks like it's starting to run a bit of an infection... that'll be the test." He glanced around the clearing. "Doesn't look like anybody else is still kicking. I'll get a blanket. We can keep him warm, get some medicine, some water in him... see what happens."

When Connell returned with the blanket, he also had some clean rags for bandages, and his treasured bag of medicine. Nora came with him, carrying the canvas and two poles that the band used as a stretcher. She nudged the soldier with her foot. "It'd be good to hear his story. Gonna be a pain in the ass to deal with him, though, if he makes it through the night."

Connell didn't respond immediately. When he was finished setting up the bandages, he glanced up at his leader. "We could take him to a waypost," he suggested. "We don't have to take him all the way to Yorkton."

Caylen was suddenly more interested. "Yorkton? Really? Is that where the soldiers are from?" It was the biggest city in the region, the only one she'd never visited.

Nora ignored her. "Even a waypost is a nuisance. Don't be too gentle when you move him."

Connell shook his head disapprovingly, but didn't respond. Instead, he gripped the man's shoulder and hip, and nodded to Caylen. "I'll roll him toward me, you slide the stretcher under him, I'll roll him back. Ready?" He glanced up at Nora, then back at Caylen. "Be gentle."

Caylen didn't need the extra instruction, and for once, she wasn't worried about disobeying Nora. For one thing, she had Connell on her side, and for another, Caylen really didn't believe that Nora wanted the soldier dead. Not because Nora was secretly soft and kind, but because Caylen knew that her mother was more than capable of reaching down and slitting the man's throat, if she decided it was in the best interest of her band. Nora could be cunning when she had to be, but for the security of her own people, she preferred the direct approach. No, if Nora wanted the soldier dead, she wouldn't wait around for a three-day-old knife wound to claim him.

While Caylen and Connell were working, Nora was poking around with the jacket they'd cut off the patient. By the time the man was safely on the stretcher, Nora had the jacket stretched out, and was looking at the decorations on the front. Caylen followed her mother's eyes, and saw what had drawn the older woman's attention. Caylen wasn't familiar with the Yorkton uniforms, but the man-boy's jacket seemed more ornate than other military tunics she had seen. It had gold-colored decorations embroidered down the front, and some sort of seal over the heart—a cougar and a deer, it looked like, also in gold.

"Damn it." Nora's voice was lifeless, and Connell stopped fussing with the bandages and took a moment to look at the uniform.

When he looked back up at Nora, his face was tight. "Well, that complicates things."

Caylen swiveled her head from one to the other, trying to understand. "He's highborn, is he? Is that it?" She didn't really see the problem. "Couldn't that mean there's a reward, if we get him back safely? I mean, his family must be looking for him, right?"

Nora looked like she was just going to turn and leave, but then stopped. Still, she wouldn't look at either of them. She stared into the forest as if gathering strength, and then snorted a bitter laugh. "I don't know exactly who he is, but based on that crest...." She finally looked down at Caylen. "Based on that crest, his family's already found him."

CHAPTER 3

Caylen was long past expecting her mother to explain herself, but even for Nora, that was a baffling statement. Caylen tried to sort it out. "He's... he's one of us?" She looked at the young man more closely. His hair was long, in the manner of the cities, and the fabric of his clothes, though dirty and bloodstained, seemed softer than the nomads would have any use for. Still, that was all cosmetic, and it wasn't unheard of for nomads to move into towns. Not exactly usual for them to turn into fancy soldiers, though.

Nora pursed her lips. "More like *you're* one of *them.*" She looked angry, as if Caylen had disappointed her somehow. She stared at her daughter, and then her face softened, at least a little. "No, that's not right. You're one of us. To the bone." She turned to Connell, back to her businesslike self. "Leave him with her—you need to look over the gear we found, decide who takes what. Caylen, get someone to help you carry him. We aren't going too far before camping."

Connell obediently started off, calling back over his shoulder. "Get the red bottle out of the pack—give him a capful of water from your canteen, mixed half with syrup from the bottle. If that doesn't kill him, we'll go from there."

It wasn't obvious whether he was avoiding a deeper conversation with Caylen or just taking care of the most important things first, and it didn't really matter. Connell was usually happy to talk, but if he decided to keep quiet or avoid a subject, he was just as stubborn as Nora. So Caylen went to the pack and found the red bottle, carefully wrapped in fabric to keep its fragile glass safe, and to protect the even more vital syrup inside. It was Connell's secret recipe, this stuff. Caylen had seen it perform near-miracles on injured nomads. She'd never seen Connell part with any of it for a stranger's benefit, though.

Caylen brought the bottle back with her and mixed a bit of it with water as Connell had instructed. She sat down beside the soldier and gently lifted his head, bracing it against her thigh. Then she dipped her finger in the water and let a drop fall onto his chapped lips. She changed the angle, then re-wet her finger and dripped into his mouth. She was so focused on her task that it took her an extra second to notice that his eyes had fluttered open, and he was staring at her. He looked confused, and maybe afraid.

"Hey. You're going to be fine." That might be a bit more than she could say confidently, but it wasn't absolutely a lie. "You need to drink this, okay? But you shouldn't sit up, your chest is cut." Caylen frowned, and then shifted his head up a little more. "Hey, you can drink, right?"

The stranger was still staring at her, and she felt a flash of anger. She'd forgotten about these city people, with their safe lives and perfect faces. Her hand itched to reach for her cheek, to feel the long scar that stretched from her temple to below her jaw, but she refused to give him the satisfaction. "Look, drink or don't, I don't care. I have things to do, if you're not interested in helping yourself."

He looked confused, and then his head jogged in what she supposed was an invitation. Hell, if he was so fancy, maybe he was used to people hand-feeding him. She lowered the cap down to his mouth and he leaned forward a little, enough for her to be able to pour a sip in. He closed his lips and swallowed carefully, then looked back up at her. He wasn't looking at her scar, now, though, just making eye contact, ready for her to continue. She tried to be gentler when she brought the cap down again. They repeated the process three more times until the cap was drained. It wasn't nearly enough, not after however long with nothing but whatever had been left in his canteen to drink, but it was a start. And she'd gotten a bit of Connell's medicine into him, too.

The nomads were starting to pack up, ready to leave the clearing behind. Caylen hoped that the band wouldn't need to come back this way anytime soon. The nomads weren't the first scavengers to have found the bodies, and they wouldn't be the last; the forest would absorb the dead, but it would take a while. And parts of the process were pretty messy.

"We need to move you now," Caylen told the soldier. Or whatever he was. She surveyed the nomads who were working near her, and called to one who was about her height. "Pim, can you give me a hand?"

"Screw you, Caylen, I'm not busting my ass for some soldier—he's not one of us."

"It's not for a soldier, Pim, it's for me. *I'm* the one asking." She paused long enough to let him think about that. "Now get over here and grab an end."

Pim scowled, but complied, grumbling. "You're as bossy as she is."

Caylen ignored him. The soldier was still conscious, and was trying to get her attention. He seemed to be attempting to speak, but was having trouble making much sound. Caylen leaned over to hear. "Need...can't leave..." He nodded his head feebly in the direction of the nest where he'd been hiding.

"What, you want to go back in? You don't want to come with us?" Caylen was ready to ignore that request, but he shook his head slightly, and feebly shifted his hand back toward the undergrowth. "You left something in there? There's something you need?" She tried not to groan. "I've already been in there once today...how important is this?"

He made another attempted gesture and then his whole body moved, as if he was trying to crawl off the stretcher and go himself. Caylen quickly put her hand on his chest, being careful to avoid the knife wound. "Okay,

okay, I'll get it. Damn it." She glanced around the clearing. The nomads were starting to move, and she didn't want to get left behind. She dropped to the ground and scurried along on her belly, quicker now that she didn't have to worry about keeping her eyes on the soldier. She got into the space where he'd been lying and looked around, the sun shining dim and green through the leaves above her.

The gun was lying in the duff, near where the soldier's right hand would have been. As soon as she saw it, she understood why the soldier had been so insistent. Guns of any sort were rare, but even in the dim light she could tell that this was a finely-crafted treasure from the Time Before, not one of the rough versions that the smiths in the cities sometimes managed to cobble together. She grabbed it, felt the way it fit in her hand, a balanced, solid weight, and found enough room to turn around so she could crawl out frontward.

When she emerged from the green tunnel, she saw the soldier watching her, and held up the weapon reassuringly. His body relaxed back into the stretcher when he saw it in her hand, but his eyes still held hers, and she thought she understood. Just because she had the gun, it didn't mean he was getting it back. She looked at the pistol in her hands, and in the brighter light, she saw it clearly and was stunned.

Pim came closer, squinting at the gun, and she reflexively pulled it back, hiding it half-behind her back.

"No way, Caylen." Pim sounded outraged. "You don't get to keep it, that's not the way it works!"

"Shut up, Pim, I'm not keeping it, I'm taking it to Nora."

"So why can't I see it? It looks good, Cay...who you think she's gonna give it to?" Pim was pushing middle-age, but he was bouncing around like a little kid. "Don't just assume it's going to you, Cay, you're low on the list—I don't care if she *does* put you on point."

"I'm not assuming anything." Her mind was racing in circles, trying to fit too much information into too little of a pattern. "I'm going to go give it to her—you wait here and I'll be right back." She ignored the injured soldier, wouldn't let herself see the way his hand lifted off the stretcher and reached plaintively for the gun in her hand.

Nora was at the front of the band, ready to take point. She turned when Caylen approached. "Yes?" She sounded impatient, but for once, Caylen didn't care.

"The soldier had a gun." Caylen kept her voice quiet.

Nora lifted an eyebrow. "Really? And you didn't find it earlier?"

"He left it in the bushes. I went back and got it." Caylen lifted her hand up, showed the gun to her mother, holding it so as to display the carved ivory on the handles, the familiar scrollwork that Caylen had been staring at since she was a child. "Strange thing, you saying he's family, and him carrying a gun that's an exact match to yours."

Nora traced the ivory almost reverentially with her finger tips, but her hand was strong and steady when she closed her fingers around the grip and took the pistol from Caylen. "You have work to do." She didn't even watch to see if Caylen obeyed, just bent over and pulled a shirt out of her pack and began wrapping the soldier's gun up carefully.

Caylen paused. She knew better, knew that there was no way Nora would talk if she didn't want to, and that also no way Nora would tolerate Caylen's insubordination. Still, she had to try. "Is there anything I need to know? If I'm the one watching the soldier..."

Nora shoved the gun into her pack with a little extra force, but when she spoke her voice was calm and mocking. "He's unarmed and seriously injured. You're not confident that you can handle him without studying his history?" She straightened and heaved her pack up. "Darton," she called to a nearby nomad, "go help with the soldier. Caylen will take your packs." She still didn't look at Caylen, and didn't wait to see that she was obeyed.

Caylen wondered whether she'd ever learn to keep her mouth shut. Darton was the largest of the nomads, slow and hulking and generally used as a sort of pack horse, carrying all the extra equipment that no one else could manage. He'd been with the band as long as Caylen remembered, and had carried her, even, when she was younger and would get tired on the trail. He watched her sadly as he started shrugging his packs off his shoulders onto the ground, but he knew better than to try to keep any of his original burden. This wasn't the first time Caylen had been assigned to carry his bundles as a punishment, and Nora always checked to make sure she bore the full weight.

There was no way around it, so Caylen trudged over and started figuring out the best way to balance Dart's packs on her much smaller frame. Once she had a strategy, he helped her get loaded up, and then stayed and watched her first few steps to make sure she didn't tip right over, as she had once before when given this job. "At least we aren't going far," he whispered with a furtive look toward Nora.

"Unless she decides that it wasn't far enough, and makes me do it all day tomorrow, too."

Darton looked startled at the possibility, and then shrugged his huge shoulders. "Just stop arguing with her, little Cay."

Caylen bit her tongue against justifying herself to her friend—there was no point in dragging him into the situation. He gave her a quick clap on the shoulder for encouragement, gentle for him but still almost enough to knock her over, then lumbered off toward the stretcher.

The band started down the path, and Cay stumbled forward to keep up with them. It took all of her concentration just to move in the right direction and stay upright, and she had no energy left to be aware of the forest or the other nomads or any of the details that normally kept her attention. She felt blind and deaf, slow and unbalanced, and she hated it. And all because some boy with a fancy gun didn't have the courtesy to stay in the city where he belonged. Or the sense to go ahead and die after being shot and stabbed and left for dead.

She took a clumsy step and fell forward onto her knees, just managing to catch herself before sprawling face first onto the forest floor. It took all her strength to get herself back upright, and none of the nomads near her dared earn Nora's wrath by helping. Not that Nora ever punished anyone else as hard as she punished her own daughter. Caylen sighed, and thought of the city boy. Maybe they had something in common, she decided as she laboriously moved forward—they were both too stubborn to quit.

CHAPTER 4

Caylen lost track of time. That was the only good thing about work like this, the ability, the necessity, to turn off all her brain's higher functions and focus on the simple things. All of her attention was spent following the back of the nomad she was following, lifting her foot and bringing it forward, repeating, repeating....

She stopped when the person in front stopped, and stood there, waiting for the order to continue. The command didn't come. Instead, she felt one of the packs lifted off her back, and then another, and turned to see Darton's deliberately cheerful face. "There, not so bad, huh?" He set the packs on the ground and straightened up. "And we went extra-far tonight, so she won't make you do it tomorrow, probably, right?"

Caylen was having a little trouble snapping out of her work-fog, but Nora's call, strong but not loud, cut right through. "Caylen, perimeter scout."

Darton grimaced sympathetically. Apparently the punishment wasn't quite over. Not that scouting the perimeter of their camp was bad; usually, Caylen was happy for the opportunity to go creeping through her forest, looking for anything unusual. But tonight, with her muscles already in revolt, and her brain dulled by the repetition of her earlier labor...tonight, it was going to be torture. She shrugged off the last pack and tried to roll her shoulders as she moved creakily toward the forest edge, making it clear that she was obeying, before she stopped and tried to get her brain back where it should be. There was no point in scouting if she was too dazed to notice anything. A few quick stretching poses helped re-center her body and mind, although she still wasn't at her best. And this job, while routine, was important to the safety of the camp, so she needed to be paying attention.

When she was as good as she was going to get, she let her body flow out into the forest, rippling around obstacles, slow and silent and careful. She saw where other nomads were setting up their watch posts for the night, felt the moisture in the cool breeze that would have the people at the camp stringing tarps against the possibility of rain, smelled the fresh, pungent aroma of the wild leeks as she brushed through a patch of their bright green shoots. And she heard...she heard everything. All the sounds of a busy, peaceful forest, all the sounds of home.

She came out of the undergrowth at the same spot she had entered, after circling the camp. Nora was conferencing with Connell, their heads bent and their voices hushed. Caylen moved close enough so that it would be clear that she was ready to report, but not so close that she could be accused of eavesdropping. Her efforts to gain information had already gotten her into enough trouble for one day.

It wasn't long before Nora waved her over, and impatiently gestured for her to speak.

"Nothing alarming. Bear tracks to the southwest, but they look a couple days old. No signs of recent human activity."

Nora nodded, but didn't dismiss Caylen, so she stood waiting. Finally, Nora sighed, and sank down to sit on a half-rotted log. She gestured to Connell and Caylen, and they crouched down on the forest floor. Nora took a moment to collect her thoughts, then nodded to Connell. "Catch her up. Just today." The last words were said with a note of warning.

Connell rubbed the back of his neck. "That scene earlier—you were with the soldier, you wouldn't have had the chance to notice, but...it was all wrong." Caylen restrained herself, didn't point out that *obviously* there was something wrong with twenty or so men killing each other in the middle of a peaceful forest. Connell continued. "The soldiers—they were..." He frowns as if he's still trying to figure the situation out. "They were shot. Almost all bullets. And, really bad shots. I mean, not bad, maybe, but...not careful. Not like we shoot." Not like nomads, Caylen understood. Nomads who treasured each round, saving bullets carefully, using them only for sure things. Sure kills. She thought of the two graze wounds on the soldier's torso. Two wasted bullets.

"And other stuff, too. Their bows—they were garbage." Connell was the best archer in the band and was known to be a perfectionist about his equipment, but Nora nodded in support of his assessment. Caylen remembered the bow she had used to pull the soldier's arm free, and she had to agree. If all the bows had all been that rough and unbalanced, there was something very strange. Bows were the everyday weapon for nomads, and even if they had guns, they'd still want good quality bows.

"And for all the gunshots, there were no guns left behind. So that means that somebody walked away from that mess. If it had been soldiers that survived, they would have buried their dead, or at least taken the crests back to the families." Caylen nodded, thinking of the golden cougar and deer that had remained on the injured soldier's chest. That shouldn't have been there. Well, the soldier himself shouldn't have been there, since the survivors should have discovered his injury and helped him. "So maybe it was the nomads that won, but..." Connell turned his head and spat in disgust. "The trail we've been following? It's...it's like a herd of cattle went through."

Caylen hadn't even known they were following a trail, lost in her own punishment as she had been. But if they were following nomads, after several days, and on a path that saw enough travel to be generally worn down— there shouldn't be any trail left at all. She frowned, trying to sort things out. "So...it's like both sides were soldiers?"

Nora nodded in grim satisfaction, but it was Connell who answered. "That's what we're wondering. They could just be outlaws, but they seem too organized to be rogues, and if they're coming from one of the bandit camps—well, unless standards have gone a long way down, this raid was too sloppy for them. And they left some pretty good stuff behind, stuff bandits would have taken for sure. We can't quite figure it out...but who knows what the cities are up to? They're always planning something."

"But they should leave us out of it!" Caylen's indignation drew a rueful chuckle from Connell and a wry twitch of Nora's eyebrows. She tried to subdue herself. "What are we going to do?"

Nora leaned back and looked up at the dark sky. "What *can* we do? Same as always—keep our eyes and ears open, and stay the hell away from city people." She frowned over at the injured soldier. "He going to make it?"

Connell shrugged. "Still on the edge. The traveling wasn't really good for him, but he's getting some fluids down, getting some medicine in."

Nora looked disgusted. "He needs to make up his damn mind."

"I'd say he has. If it's a question of will, he's staying with us. He just has to hope his body can find a way to do what he wants." Connell's medical opinions were usually a bit more practical than that, and Caylen and Nora both looked at him quizzically. He just shrugged. "Kid's got heart, that's all I'm saying." He looked at Nora. "Say what you want to about the family, but you can't say they were cowards."

And just as Caylen was hoping to hear a little more about whatever Nora's connection to the city family was, they all heard the whistle sound to warn that someone was approaching. The nomads were never far from their weapons, so no scrambling was required. They all calmly set down what they had been working on and fell into position, distance weapons in their hands. Being in position meant being near the edges of the clearing, ready to fade into the undergrowth as needed; their distance weapons were mostly bows, although those who owned guns had them ready. Nora jerked her head at Caylen and she melted into the forest, moving to circle around whomever was coming.

Caylen could hear the approaching group, now. They weren't loud, no clang of metal against metal like she'd often heard from soldiers, but they weren't quiet enough to be nomads. Not true nomads, at least. There was another sensation, not quite a sound, more like a vibration, and she knew that they had at least one horse with them. Definitely not nomads, then—horses were creatures of the plains, and of the cities; there wasn't enough of their preferred forage in the forest to keep them fed, and they weren't nearly as useful in the closer quarters and rougher ground.

She circled around carefully, made sure that Romy saw her before she got too close to his guard position. He barely inclined his head, nodding her forward, and she eased past him, working her way closer to the path. It was full night now, but there were stars and a bright moon, so even in the shadows of the forest Caylen had a fairly clear view.

There were nine of them. They were well-armed, all good-sized men, with one riding, the rest on foot, all wearing dark uniforms that would probably be blue in better light. Yorkton soldiers. They had guns, but the nomads had them outnumbered, and this was the nomads' terrain. The soldiers would be fools to fight, and the nomads weren't looking for trouble. Hopefully, this would all blow over.

Caylen found a good spot to shoot from, just in case. As Connell had said, you could never predict what city people would do.

The lead soldier raised a hand to stop the squad behind him, and they fanned out into a reasonable version of a defensive formation for woodland fighting. Not perfect, by any means, but better than Caylen had generally seen from city dwellers.

Then Nora came into view in front of the soldiers, proud and confident, with just Connell standing beside and a little behind her. They both had their guns ready, Nora's still in its holster but with the safety strap unbuckled, Connell's shotgun held in front of him, pointing toward the ground in front of the intruders.

Nora paused, and then said, "Just passing through?" She made it sound like a question, but Caylen hoped the soldiers didn't think they had any options about what the right answer was.

The soldier in front didn't say anything, apparently waiting for whomever was in charge to step forward and speak for them. The pause lengthened, and then the rider swung down off his horse and took a half-step, holding the reins loosely in his right hand. He was facing away from Caylen, but she could see that his hair shone silver and black in the moonlight—just starting to grey, but he stood as tall and strong as a younger man. "Is that any way to greet an old friend, Nora?"

If Nora was surprised, she hid it well. "Jonah. What brings you out into the wilds?"

The man half-turned, as if he'd seen something interesting on the forest floor, and then looked back up at Nora. "Well, maybe you can help us with that, actually. We're looking for some travelers—they're a couple days late, so we thought we'd see if they needed a hand."

"Travelers, huh?" Nora shook her head. "Nope, haven't seen anything like that." She shifted a little, and Caylen could see that she was keeping herself lined up with Jonah, ready to draw if needed. "Saw quite a few dead soldiers, a ways back, wearing Yorkton uniforms. But...no, no travelers."

A couple of the soldiers reacted when they heard about their dead comrades, but their discipline held, and when Jonah spoke, his voice was cool and calm. "All dead? How many?"

"Twelve." Nora's voice was firm.

Jonah was watching her closely. "Twelve. *All* dead?" he repeated.

Nora looked like she was deciding something. Caylen had no idea what—Nora had wanted to get rid of the injured soldier, so why didn't she just give him to the man from the city and forget about it?

"Eleven dead," Nora finally admitted. "The survivor's in our camp."

Jonah didn't react, just kept watching Nora. "And is he the one I'm looking for?"

She snorted a bitter laugh, and didn't even try to pretend that she didn't know what the man was talking about. "Yes. He's the one. So get him and get out." She turned abruptly and strode back toward camp, calling out over her shoulder, "Nomads, maintain your positions."

Great. So Caylen was going to be stuck in the forest, watching, while Nora and the mysterious stranger went and picked up the *other* mysterious stranger and got rid of him. And Caylen would be left with a quiver of questions and no target to shoot them at. She sighed in frustration and slumped against the tree she was hiding behind. She wondered how long Nora was going to keep her out there in the dark.

CHAPTER 5

Caylen did what she could to make herself comfortable. Normally, it wouldn't be a problem for her to crouch in the forest for hours on end, but her muscles were still complaining from the weight she'd been carrying earlier, and she knew that if she stayed still too long, they'd stiffen up. Still, Nora didn't leave people on guard for no reason, so if Caylen was out there she had a job to do, and she needed to focus on that, not on her own discomfort. At the same time, if something did happen and she needed to move, her body had to be in condition to respond. She compromised, alternating between scanning the forest and doing long, slow stretches to help her muscles.

Her next challenge was her stomach. She had jerky in her small pack, the one that was always with her, and some dried fruit, too, so she wouldn't starve. But there'd be hot food back in camp; she'd smelled it before she was sent out, and a faint scent was still wafting out to her occasionally. She didn't want to waste her appetite on trail food if there was a chance of something better. How long was Nora going to keep her out there?

She sensed the horse before she saw it, that same dull thudding of hard hooves against the soft forest floor. It was heading out of camp at a trot, the rider hunched over and looking nervous about being sent out into the forest alone. Caylen didn't interfere—if Nora had wanted the horse stopped, it would never have gotten past the edge of the camp.

It wasn't too long after that there was more movement from the same direction, and Caylen saw Connell heading down the path toward her. He paused at one point and cut into the undergrowth, and Caylen knew that he was conveying orders to the nomad on guard there. He came back out and continued down the path in Caylen's direction; she let him get a few strides past her hiding spot before grunting his name.

He turned calmly and peered in at her. She had found a spot about five feet up a big maple tree, nestled in to the spot where a huge branch came off the main trunk. It was far enough off the ground to confuse attackers and make it hard for them to reach her, but still close enough that she could jump down and run if needed. And the big branch was between her and the road, making it a perfect shield from eyes and from projectiles.

"There you are," Connell said. "The soldiers are staying the night—they don't want to move the young fellow, and I don't blame them." As Connell talked, Caylen paid attention to what he was saying, but kept scanning the forest behind him, as well. His voice wasn't loud, but it could be enough to alert people to her location, and she didn't want to be caught unaware. "They sent a messenger for reinforcements—they've got half the army camped at Burth's Waypoint, from the sound of it. Nora's agreed to guard this bunch until the troops arrive."

That was a little surprising. The nomads made most of their money by guarding townsfolk who were forced to travel through the Wildlands, but they didn't usually perform the service for soldiers. It wasn't usually necessary. "They expecting more trouble?"

Connell shrugged. "If they know what to expect, they're not sharing the information with us." His grin was sudden. "But they're paying damn well, so they're either stupid or desperate."

"Or both..."

"Yeah, that's always an option. Anyway, Nora doesn't know what's up, so she wants you to stay out here. Let the sentries do the guarding, we'll shift them off and on. So, you can sleep, just stay in place so you're ready if something happens."

"I could just sneak back out, like I did last time..." Caylen didn't want a cold night alone in the forest with her aching muscles, not if she could have a warm bed by the fire with a hot meal in her belly.

"Orders have been given, Cay." Connell rarely got angry about Caylen's questions, not like Nora did, but that didn't mean he was willing to give in to her.

But since he didn't seem too impatient, maybe she had an opportunity. "So, how does Nora know these people, anyhow?" She hoped it sounded like a casual question.

Connell's quick eyes showed that he wasn't fooled. "She's been around a lot longer than you, kid. You'd be surprised by how many people she knows."

"Yeah, but...city people? And she said the injured soldier was family." That was sticking out in Caylen's mind. She'd never met anyone but Nora that shared her blood.

"*We're* your family, Caylen."

"No, I know that! I just...why did Nora say it, then?"

"That's a question for you and Nora, I guess." Connell sounded like he knew how likely it was that Caylen would ever be able to have that conversation. "For now, get some sleep, but stay ready...you going to be able to sleep up there? Excellent spot." Caylen was gratified to hear the admiration in his voice.

"Yeah, I can wedge in. Won't be as comfortable as my blankets by the fire..."

"Well, maybe you should have thought about that before you got so good at sneaking around and hiding in the trees. Everyone else is going to have a nice sleep, for at least part of the night, but, hey, you wanted to be a show-off."

Caylen's snort of disgust was all the acknowledgment Connell needed, and he gave her a cocky smile before turning and heading back to camp. Caylen pulled a strip of jerky out of her pack and glumly took a bite. She was pretty sure it was Taryn's turn to cook that night, which made it even worse that Caylen was missing the meal. Taryn, the only female in the band other than Nora and Caylen, fought the pressure to do 'women's work', but there was no way to deny that she was the best cook they had. Taryn was happy to point out that both Nora and Caylen were terrible cooks, so obviously being a woman had nothing to do with it. Caylen generally left the bickering to the others; she didn't care *why* Taryn's food was so good, as long as it kept coming. But that night, she was only going to get jerky.

She did manage to find a way to wedge herself into the tree, and she slept a little, although not too soundly. She was awakened around dawn by the faint sounds of something moving in the forest ahead of her. She opened her eyes carefully and saw nothing, at first, but her ears insisted that something was happening, and she trusted them. When she saw the scout, then, she wasn't really surprised. He was about ten paces from her, creeping through the woods toward the nomads' camp.

The man eased forward, carefully moving a small branch aside rather than brushing past it, putting his foot down gradually, feeling for his balance before moving forward. When he shifted his weight, Caylen barely heard the twig he was standing on as it broke. But that was the problem—she shouldn't have heard it at all. The man was dressed as a nomad, but Nora and Connell were right, he was acting more like a soldier. A good soldier, one trained to work in the forest, but not as good as a nomad scout should be. And he was well armed, with a pistol at his side and what looked like a rifle bundled up and slung across his back. A nomad good enough to have earned those weapons should be good enough to sneak past a sleeping guard.

The intruder was moving steadily, and Caylen watched silently as he slipped by her. She waited until he was several steps away before she eased her bow up from the branch it had rested on as she slept. She wasn't sure who was on watch in this zone, but she couldn't imagine any of the band having trouble with this intruder, especially not with the element of surprise on the nomad's side. But Nora would want the man taken alive, and it could be a lot a trickier to subdue someone than to just kill him. Caylen's help wouldn't likely be necessary, but it couldn't hurt to be prepared.

She whispered an arrow out of her quiver and ran her fingers over the feathers of the fletching, then down to check the arrowhead. She had time to sight along the arrow, making sure the shaft was straight; she'd checked all these things before putting the arrows in her quiver, but sometimes they could be damaged even in the safety of their leather case. She leaned around the tree and raised the bow, lined up the arrow, and waited. Caylen wasn't sure where the nomad guard was; there was a big tree that would be easy to hide behind, but there was also a fallen log with a sort of dip in the ground behind it, where someone could find a spot. The interloper didn't seem too worried about either of those locations, though, didn't seem aware of their potential as hiding places, and Caylen had a little more evidence for the 'not a nomad' theory. He was a few paces from the big tree, and Caylen saw Pim's head peer out from the side opposite the intruder, looking for Caylen. She moved her bow just enough to get his attention, and he nodded at her, then carefully tapped his thigh and looked in the direction of the scout.

That was clear enough, and it made sense. If the man had come closer to the hiding spot, Pim could have taken care of him no problem, but if Pim had to break cover while the man was several strides away, it would increase the intruder's chance to draw his weapon and fire a shot in defense. It wasn't a sure thing, but it was an unnecessary risk. Caylen braced her foot on a branch and leaned fluidly away from the main trunk. She aimed carefully and let her arrow fly, straight into the intruder's thigh as Pim had suggested.

Pim moved at the same time as the arrow, and he reached the intruder before the man hit the ground. Caylen had instantly readied another arrow, but it didn't look like it was going to be necessary; the man was lying on his side on the ground, moaning and grabbing his leg. Pim wasn't gentle as he grabbed the intruder's hands and quickly and efficiently tied them together. Then he pursed his lips and gave a loud whistle, the distinctive one that called for Nora and Connell. Only then did Pim look over at Caylen.

"Nice shot." His hands were searching as he spoke, pulling the scout's pistol and rifle away and looking for more weapons.

Pim bent down and pulled his knife out, holding it so the tip was right in front of the man's eyes. "We need you to be able to use your mouth, but we don't care if you can use your eyes. You cooperate, you won't see the knife again. You give me trouble, and it'll be the last thing you ever do see. Clear?" The man nodded carefully, and Pim shifted his weight to a more balanced position. "What are you doing out here, anyway? Sneaking up on people?" Pim didn't really seem to expect an answer, but that didn't keep him from talking. "It's not neighborly, not at all. And if you're gonna do it," and he nudged the man's thigh with the point of his boot, not hard, but close enough to the arrow to make the man gasp in pain, "do it better."

Caylen caught Pim's eyes and nodded in the direction of the camp, warning him that Nora was coming. Questioning prisoners was Nora's responsibility, and while Caylen didn't see anything wrong with Pim getting a head start, there was no telling if Nora would agree. Pim nodded back and stepped away from the prisoner. He turned with a broad smile to greet his leaders. "Caught something for ya!"

Nora closed the remaining distance swiftly, but without seeming hurried. "And told the whole forest about it, with all your racket." She glanced at the body on the ground, then turned to Connell, who was, as usual, right behind her. "Can we leave the arrow in? We might like to have a handle."

Connell nodded. "Sure. No point in doctoring him up if we're just gonna kill him anyway. We can wait and see if he cooperates, then decide?" Caylen appreciated their performance. Nora had asked a real question, but the tone of it and of Connell's reply had all been designed to intimidate the prisoner.

Caylen couldn't say what it was that she heard or saw, but her head swiveled at the same time as Nora's, both of them turning away from the camp to see yet another stranger, maybe twenty paces away through the forest, frozen for a moment as he absorbed the scene in front of him. He turned as soon as he realized that Nora and Caylen had noticed him, and he was half a step away when Caylen's arrow found him.

She had aimed for middle of his back, and was pleased to see that her aim was good, but the man must have been wearing some sort of armor, maybe just hardened leather, because he stumbled forward, fell to his hands and knees, but was still moving. And yelling. "Nomads! Nomads! They have Campbell! Help me!"

Nora acted quickly. She sounded the whistle to warn of attack, sending everyone back at camp to their defensive positions. She took a second to think about the prisoner, then looked at Connell and Pim. "Drag him back a ways, but leave him if the attack comes. If there's time, question him." She turned to Caylen. "Scout."

It was a simple order, and one that Caylen welcomed. She was tired of not knowing anything, and scouting would be a chance to get some answers. And if the intruders did press an attack, she'd be close enough to them to do some damage from a direction they wouldn't be expecting. It was perfect. She knew she was smiling as she got to work, but she didn't worry about explaining. If any nomad saw her, they'd know her well enough to understand. And she had no intention of being seen by anyone else.

She headed out into the forest, angling away from the direction that the attackers seemed to be coming from, and then cutting back in, moving more carefully, but keeping her speed up. The man with her arrow in his back was still yelling, and it was annoying because it made it harder for her to hear anything else, but it also covered any sound she might make. And he was crawling back to his group, she expected, so she could judge their placement by the direction in which he was moving. When his noise stopped, she assumed that he had reached them.

That gave her a good idea of their primary location, but she still had to watch out for sentries, or scouts coming out to find her own group. She crept forward, more slowly now, working her way carefully toward her target. There was no sign of an impending attack, although as she got closer she could hear voices, heated but trying to be quiet. She was still too far away to make out exact words.

She spotted the first sentry crouched in a narrow overhang by a large boulder. It wasn't a *terrible* spot, but wasn't as maneuverable as Caylen would have liked and her estimation of these so-called nomads went down another notch. She had to remind herself that, skilled or not, they were definitely well-armed, and even a panicked amateur could kill with a gun. She skirted past the area where the sentry was keeping watch, and tried to find another way to get closer to the camp.

She saw her opportunity when she found a spot where the forest floor sloped into a steep hill, almost a cliff, with the group of strangers near the bottom. She started up the hill, moving extra carefully to avoid a slip on the loose soil. When she reached the top, she kept going enough that she wouldn't be silhouetted above the crest, and then crept sideways near the ridge, working her way toward the strangers. The vegetation was sparser on the slope, easier to see through, and if she was spotted, it would be easy for her to duck back over the peak and be sheltered from their aim. By the time they fought their way up the hill, she'd be long gone. Nora would never have let her band stop in such a vulnerable location.

Caylen got as close as she could to where the sound was coming from and then eased her way forward. She spotted the sentry against the tree trunk half-way down the slope, and made sure that she was well hidden. Caylen's clothes were the colors of the forest; even her body cooperated, with her brown hair and green eyes, her skin tanned and dirty enough to pass for fallen leaves. As long as she kept her eyes squinted to hide the whites, and her mouth closed to cover her teeth, she was just part of the scenery. Sudden movement would catch the sentry's eye, but she was trained to move slowly when necessary.

She kept herself partly aware of the sentry, but allowed her vision to extend beyond him. The branches of the trees kept her from seeing heads, but down low where the branches were thin she could see more clearly, and she counted the legs. She was tempted to creep closer, try to hear what they were saying, but it was an unacceptable risk; if she was killed or captured, Nora wouldn't get the information she had gathered. Caylen would make her report, and then request permission to come back out.

She eased backward, and then swung out wide on her way back to the nomad's camp. It took longer, but was safer. And now that they were finally getting some information about these intruders, she absolutely wanted to be sure that it was all shared. Maybe that would earn her the right to learn a little more about Nora's secrets.

CHAPTER 6

When Caylen arrived back in camp, it was almost empty; the nomads must have all been sent out on guard. The soldiers were still there, though, set up in a defensive position around their injured comrade, and Nora and Connell were standing over the body of the scout Caylen had injured. He wasn't moving.

"What happened?" She wasn't sure she wanted to know.

Connell shook his head. "Bled out. The arrow must have nicked the artery...it blocked the flow for a while, but when we moved him, it jiggled loose."

Caylen stared down at the body. She had killed before, but this seemed different. In battle, she was so full of adrenaline, so busy trying to stay alive, that she didn't really have time to reflect. Didn't have time to stand and stare at the body, wondering about the life she had ended. The scout wasn't that old, maybe in his late twenties—old enough to have young ones at home, but not old enough for them to be able to look after themselves without a father.

Nora's voice broke through Caylen's thoughts. "It was a good shot. Things just go wrong sometimes." That was more understanding than Caylen had expected, and apparently all that Nora planned to share. "What did you find?"

Caylen forced her mind back to the business at hand. "I couldn't get close enough to hear them, but there were thirty-four men in camp, and I saw two sentries, would expect at least three more, from the spacing. I couldn' t see weapons." She glanced over toward the soldiers, then back at Nora. "And they had the messenger's horse. I didn't see him anywhere."

Nora's lips were a thin line. "Damn." There were only eleven nomads in the band, so even with the eight soldiers, they were outnumbered. And they were certainly out-armed. "We can't afford to play around with this." Norah took a deep breath. "Jonah...Jonah knew your father. And you look a lot like him, so Jonah will probably recognize you. Just ignore him, focus on the job at hand. Understood?"

Caylen nodded blankly. That was a lot of information in a few words, but it still wasn't enough to give her the whole story, just a few more tantalizing glimpses. Still, Nora was right—they really didn't have time for a long conversation.

Nora gave her a careful, assessing look, then turned and called, "Jonah? We have news."

The man had been crouching next to his injured friend, but he rose gracefully to his feet at Nora's voice. He approached them casually, giving Caylen a quick once over before doing a clear, almost comical double take. Caylen focused on keeping her hands from covering her scar as Jonah's eyes swept over her from head to foot before focusing on Nora.

"Damn it, Nora. I'd heard rumors, but I didn't believe them..." It wasn't clear what he was feeling, besides surprise.

"Not now." Her voice left no room for argument. "Your messenger didn't make it through, and we're outnumbered at least two to one." She paused for a moment, to allow that information to sink in. "Our best chance is to get around them, and keep moving." Another pause, and then a calculating look. "Just how important is your boy, there? Because he's going to be a problem, if we try to move fast and light."

Jonah looked confused, and then outraged. "We're not leaving him behind. He's...Logan's the point of all this!" He cast a quick look at Caylen. "Now, that may have changed a bit, but he's still our best bet. Or at least...Damn it, Nora, how could you hide her from us?"

"It was easy." Nora's voice was flat. She turned to Connell. "Ideas?"

"We still don't know who they are, or what they want," Connell said. "Makes it hard to know how they'll play it."

"I could go back out." Caylen knew she shouldn't be jumping in, but she wanted to make sure they understood. "I came back to tell you how many there were, and about the messenger, but I could try to get closer. Close enough to hear them. I think I know how I could do it..."

"No!" Jonah sounded outraged, and he addressed himself to Nora, not Caylen. "You can't send her out into danger! She's—"

"She's part of my band, and she'll do her job." Nora's tone was cold. "She's not for you to play with." Nora waved an arm in the direction of the injured soldier and spoke to Jonah. "You and your men get him packed up and moving...back the way we came from." She looked at Connell. "We'll just have to hope there's only one group of them. You and Caylen, hit the woods, circle around behind them. The rest of us will flank the path here, ready for when they come through."

Jonah looked uncertain. "Is it safe to move him?" he asked Connell.

The nomad shrugged. "Hell of a lot safer than it'd be to leave him here."

It had been a stupid question, with an obvious answer; it seemed like Jonah was just looking for ways to resist Nora's plan. Resist her authority. Caylen wondered again how the two knew each other, but she didn't really have time to speculate. She needed to get moving.

She took a moment to glance at the dead scout. "Did the arrow break?" she asked Connell. She caught Jonah's look of surprise at the question, but Connell seemed to know what she was after.

"No, it's good. I put it with my pack—do you have enough for now, or should we find it?"

She checked her quiver, although she knew perfectly well what she'd find. "Eighteen. Should be lots, right?" She grinned, and gave him a quick hip check. "Unless you're planning on slacking, not getting your share..." She could tell that Jonah was still staring at her, probably thinking that she was a bloodthirsty savage; that's what city people usually thought about nomads. She refused to let herself care, though, not about some stranger's opinion, and not about the dead scout at her feet.

Connell was smiling indulgently at her. "I'll get mine, Cay, don't worry about that." He checked his own quiver, as well as his shotgun. "Alright, then...you've already been out, so you can lead." He glanced over at Nora to be sure there were no last minute instructions. When she said nothing, he nodded Caylen forward, and they started into the woods.

They moved quickly at first, then slowed as they got closer to the enemy camp. Before they had a chance to circle around, Caylen saw movement, and she and Connell simultaneously sank closer to the ground. The intruders were on the move, heading toward the nomad camp. They were well armed, clearly going on the offensive...but they were sticking to the path. They were clinging to the sides, trying to find cover in the trees, but they weren't going into the forest, weren't spreading out.

And one of them, apparently the leader, was riding the messenger's horse, right down the middle of the path.

Caylen glanced at Connell to see if he was as confused as she was by the lack of stealth, but he was watching the enemy. The two waited as the men worked their way past, and then silently fell in behind, close enough to be in range, but far enough that they wouldn't be heard or easily seen. There hadn't been a lot of time for Jonah to move his men away, especially carrying the injured soldier—*Logan*, she remembered. But there had been more than enough time for the nomads to set up an ambush. Connell and Caylen might be able to help drive the enemy forward into the trap. And hopefully that would be enough to weaken the intruders and persuade them to find other prey. Of course, the intruders' level of determination would depend on their reasons for coming after the soldiers in the first place, and Caylen still hadn't heard any sort of an explanation for that. So it was hard to know how challenging it would be to dissuade them. Caylen wasn't happy about going into a situation with so little knowledge; the only thing that made her feel better was knowing that if it frustrated her, it must be absolutely enraging for Nora.

She and Connell trailed along at a safe distance. When the first shot was fired, Caylen recognized the distinctive crack of Nora's pistol. It was followed immediately by several more gunshots, and Caylen saw arrows finding their marks as well. By the time the intruders realized what was happening, there were five bodies on the ground, two of them not moving. The intruders were dodging for cover, then peering frantically into the forest, trying to find the source of the attacks. Caylen knew the routine; she was sure that the nomads were already falling back, shifting along the path, setting up the next ambush position. She looked to Connell for instructions.

He held his hand flat, parallel to the ground, and lowered it. *Keep cover.* She knew that his order made sense—there was no point in exposing their positions unnecessarily. But it wasn't very exciting. She obeyed, but she kept her eyes busy, scanning for any movement, any hint of a reason to get involved.

The intruders didn't seem inclined to give her one. They were still in the same place, firing wildly into the forest, wasting bullets and filling the air with a deafening blur of sound. They would have no idea what was going on around them, because they wouldn't be able to hear a thing.

Finally, the man riding the horse got everyone under enough control that he was able to order them to start moving backward. He was injured, one arm hanging limply at his side, and his other busy trying to control the horse. His voice was loud, though, and finally his repeated orders began to take effect. There was no organization to their retreat, none of the careful 'run, chose a spot, cover your buddy' that the nomads practiced. The false nomads were just running, although at least a few of them were disciplined enough to have grabbed their wounded comrades. Two bodies were left behind, already dead.

Caylen watched the intruders sprint past, and her bow itched in her hands, but her discipline held. When they were well clear, Connell stretched himself out from his cramped hiding spot. "We'll just wait and see if they're coming back," he said quietly.

Another sensible, boring order. She tried not to make a face as she stretched her own limbs. It was a surprise for both of them when they heard a whistle coming from the direction of the battlegrounds. It was the distinctive note that called Connell; coming right after a battle, it usually meant that he was needed to treat the injured. Caylen frowned. "What, did somebody sprain their ankle?"

Connell was already moving. "You stay put, and be sensible. Stay under cover unless there's a real reason to expose your position."

"I know..."

"Yeah, well, what you know and what you do aren't always the same thing, Cay." And with that, he was gone, moving quickly through the forest.

Caylen settled down with her back against a tree trunk. Once again, she was left alone in the forest while everything interesting happened somewhere else.

CHAPTER 7

Caylen hadn't been alone long before she saw Taryn coming through the forest toward her. Caylen raised the end of her bow to signal her position, and Taryn adjusted her direction and joined Caylen.

"You're wanted," Taryn said. She wasn't generally a chatterbox, but that was unusually terse, and Caylen waited for more. Taryn didn't oblige. She seemed preoccupied with the string on her bow. "You'd better go. They're about fifty paces back, then half-way up the hill. I'm supposed to stand guard here."

"What's going on?" This felt wrong.

"Nora said you should go back."

Apparently nobody wanted to tell Caylen *anything* anymore. "Okay, fine." She rose easily to her feet and started in the direction Taryn had indicated. She heard the nomads before she saw them, Connell's voice low, murmuring like he did when he was talking to a patient. So someone *was* hurt, then.

The nomads who weren't on guard were standing around, and Caylen saw that Jonah was with them. She spent a moment to wonder where the rest of the soldiers were, but then she moved forward far enough to see Connell kneeling on the ground, Nora standing over him, looking angry. They were both looking down at a nomad lying on the forest floor, and even though Connell's body was hiding his head from Caylen's view, she had no trouble identifying Darton from his hulking legs. The legs weren't moving, and she felt herself unconsciously straighten her back, bracing for what she might see as she moved forward. She forced herself to continue walking.

Darton didn't see her at first. He was staring up at Connell, his eyes wide but his features schooled into a stoic expression. When he noticed Caylen, a little of that discipline faded. "Little Cay," he whispered, and Caylen couldn't hear him through the blood rushing through her ears, could only tell what he said by reading his lips.

She fell to her knees on the side opposite Connell, trying to ignore the blood that was oozing out from under Connell's hands where they were holding a folded cloth to Darton's abdomen. "Hey, Dart. You got hit, huh?" She reached down and grasped one of his hands. It was cold, but she felt the fingers try to wrap around hers.

"Guess so," he sighed.

Caylen looked over at Connell, but he wasn't making eye contact with her, and she guessed that told her all she needed to know. She'd heard about treatments in the cities that would actually sew a patient's guts back together, but the nomads didn't have that kind of skill.

Connell finally spoke, but he was talking to Darton, not Caylen. "I think it hit your spine, Dart. And it definitely...it hit your intestine. It's going to get infected."

Darton understood, and he swallowed hard before he looked up toward Nora. "We can't be slowed down right now. Can't wait it out." His voice was still quiet, but it was steady.

Nora shook her head. "No, we can work around it. Don't worry about that." She stared fiercely down at the injured man as if daring him to say she was lying.

He just smiled, and even with bloodstained teeth, he looked sweet and gentle. "Well, maybe I should go on ahead anyway." He took a shaky breath. "Scout the path for you."

Caylen could feel her discipline breaking, but she fought to hang on. "No, Dart, stay with us. We need you here." She felt his fingers twitch as he tried to raise his hand, and she helped him, supported most of the weight as he lifted his huge arm up until he could pat the side of her face.

"No, Little Cay, you'll be fine." She was ashamed when she felt a huge tear escape from her eye, but Darton didn't seem worried by her weakness. Of all the nomads, he was the one who had always tried to shield her, to let her be soft when she needed to be. She sank down, his hand slipping around her head so that she was cradled between his arm and his barrel chest. "You'll be fine," he repeated, and she hid her face so no one could see her cry.

They stayed like that for a few minutes, and Caylen didn't even notice that Connell was gone until he returned, carrying a metal cup. He crouched at Darton's side. "It's poppy juice, Dart." He wasn't even bothering to try to hide his tears. "But if you want to, we can try. I can..." His voice trailed off. Caylen knew that there really wasn't much that any of them *could* do, but that didn't make it easier to do nothing.

Darton just reached for the cup, and Caylen forced herself to look away, tensed all her muscles to keep herself from knocking the vessel out of his hand. Connell helped steady the container, and shifted around so that he was supporting Darton's head, as well, lifting him enough that he could drink. Darton's whole body seized in agony from the movement, and Caylen pressed against him, trying to absorb the pain, or send her own strength to him, or to do anything to help, even though she knew she was helpless. When he was back in control of himself, he pulled the cup toward his lips and took a sip, making a face at the taste.

"Bitter," he complained.

Connell nodded. "It's mixed with syrup and water, but...the taste is going to come through. Sorry."
Darton took another sip. "It's fine—not your fault." Caylen saw Connell work to control himself, and even though he kept crying, his hand was steady on the cup. Darton's fingers twirled a little in Caylen's hair. "Remember when she was a baby?" he asked Connell. "No hair for so long. And now, so much...all grown..." He sipped again, then shifted his head a little, looking down

at Caylen. "I'm gonna go ahead, but I won't go too far. I'll find a good spot, though." Caylen nodded, and Darton continued. "Somewhere warm and safe. So you don't hurry, understand?" His voice was beginning to slur and fade. Caylen was pretty sure it was too fast for the poppy to be working, and wondered if Darton was just succumbing to blood loss. Somehow, that seemed better; it seemed less like giving up. Darton's fingers tightened in Caylen's hair, then loosened. "I'll wait. You take your time." Caylen nodded and pushed her face back into the space between his arm and his chest. She stayed like that as she felt his breathing get more shallow, more labored, until finally there was an exhalation that wasn't followed by a new breath.

She stayed where she was. She could hear the others moving around her, but she couldn't look at them yet, couldn't go on with business as usual in a world that was so suddenly, tragically empty. Nora was the one who dared to disturb her, but even she was gentle about it. "Caylen, we need to get going. We've found a nice spot to leave him."

"Who's gonna carry all his gear, though?" It was Pim's voice. "Damn, that's a lot of extra weight. Stupid bastard, getting hit in an ambush that clean..."

Caylen was up before she thought about it, launching herself full force across the few steps that separated her from Pim, and she hit him hard, her shoulder driving into his stomach. He was a nomad, so he knew how to fall, and he rolled her over and off him practically before they hit the ground. She wasn't done, though, and she landed a kick and several hard punches before she realized that Pim wasn't fighting back, just holding his arms up over his head and taking the hits. She paused, and she saw the tears streaking down his cheeks, saw the redness that hadn't been caused by her fists. "Stupid bastard," Pim repeated, but this time his voice cracked. Caylen pulled away and struggled to her feet, and she wished that Pim had fought back so that she would have a physical pain to distract her.

So Caylen had chosen the wrong target, but that didn't mean that her general idea was wrong. She saw her bow on the ground where she'd left it and tried to avoid looking at Darton's body as she swooped down and grabbed it.

"Caylen, no." Nora's voice wasn't loud, but it was firm. "There's too many of them for an attack." Caylen stared at her and didn't put her bow down. "We'll figure something out; we won't forget him."

Caylen shook her head. "They're sloppy. They never should have hit him—that was just bad luck. I can stay hidden, hit them from cover."

"If we had to, we could try it. But we don't have to." Nora was calm, as always. "We'll set up a plan, let them come to us. We need to fight *our* way, not theirs."

"No." Caylen knew that Nora was making sense, but she didn't care. "They killed Darton!"

"Don't you want to know why?" Jonah's voice cut into the conversation, and both Nora and Caylen swiveled to stare at him. He took a couple steps forward, looking at Nora as if for permission. "I believe Nora, when she says that they're not real nomads. I believe that they came from a city. Almost certainly from Yorkton."

Caylen's head was swimming. "Wait, aren't you from Yorkton?"

He nodded. "And I didn't recognize any faces, so maybe they weren't born there, maybe they don't even live there. But I'll bet that the gold that's paying them comes from there."

"I don't understand. Why would Yorkton hire someone to attack Yorkton soldiers?" Caylen knew that cities were confusing, but surely this was beyond reasonable, even for them.

Jonah took another step. "I'd like a chance to talk to you about that." He turned his head to include Nora in the conversation. "Both of you. I'd like your help in finding the people who are responsible for Darton's death, and for the deaths of my soldiers. The people who are *really* responsible, not just the goons they hired to do their dirty work." He took a step back. "I've got some theories. But my main priority right now is getting Logan to safety. Time for revenge later."

Caylen hesitated. She wanted revenge, but she also wanted to *do* something, something that would distract her from thinking about Darton. Connell stepped forward and put a rough hand on her shoulder. "Dart said he'd wait—he said not to hurry. He won't be impressed if you're right behind him." His voice changed, became more businesslike. "And we've got to set him right. I've got some good wool blankets we could wrap him in—you know how he loved being warm."

And just like that, Caylen's anger turned back to sorrow, and she could feel the tears running down her cheeks again. "He always slept so close to the fire..."

"Blankets burned more than once," Connell agreed. "So let's do that for him. There's a clearing back over there, and we could rig up a platform in the middle, so the sun would get to him."

Caylen nodded. "He'd like that."

"That's better, then." Connell turned to Nora. "Okay if we take a little time?"

She nodded reluctantly. "Not a lot, though. Get him set right, but..." She glanced at the sky. "We've got a few more hours before dark, and I want to get some distance before we camp."

"We're running away?" Caylen was outraged.

"We're not fighting their fight, Caylen." Nora's voice was steel. "We decide when to deal with them. We don't let them set the rules."

"But—we could decide to deal with them now! If we don't, we might lose track of them!"

Nora raised an eyebrow. "The way they plow through the forest? We'll be able to find them. We took a job, and we need to do it." She nodded at Jonah. "Your men are still moving, hopefully...We'll finish up here, then catch up to you by dark."

"But where are they moving *to*?" Caylen was frustrated. "Are they just running away, too?"

Connell stepped in. "Have you ever known Nora to not have a plan, Caylen? They're heading for Rock Ferry. They'll be safe there, and they can take a boat down the river back to Yorkton. It's not the most direct route, but..."

"It's safer than the forest," Jonah agreed. "Logan should have gone that way in the first place. He knew the risks."

"He should have stayed in his damn town where he belonged," Caylen snarled. All of this had happened because they'd found the stupid kid. Because he hadn't had the sense to die when he should have, after the first attack. If Caylen had never found him, Darton would still be alive.

Jonah gave her a quiet, assessing look, but nobody else acknowledged her statement. It was too obvious to comment on, she supposed. Connell went and found the wool blankets, and he and Caylen worked together to bundle their fallen comrade in his funeral shroud. By the time he was ready the other nomads had already built a rough platform in the middle of the clearing they had found. Connell, Caylen, Pim and Nora held the corners of two blankets as a stretcher to carry the body, and all the nomads except for those on guard accompanied them to the clearing. It was an old farm yard, Caylen saw, the stone foundation of the barn still poking up through the weeds. She remembered playing with Darton in a similar ruin, when she'd still been a child. She'd gone poking around in the rubble looking for treasures from the Time Before, bringing him every piece of metal or shard of plastic that she found. There had been a rusted-out vehicle, sheltered under one corner of the collapsed metal roof, and Darton had shown her the huge wheels and told her that it was a tractor, something that the people used to work their fields instead of horses or oxen. Back when there was fuel to run their machines. Darton had liked thinking about the Old People; it would be good for him to spend some time in one of their ruins.

There wasn't time for much of a ceremony, and the nomads didn't have elaborate funeral rites anyway. They just laid Darton on the platform, all of his possessions spread out around him. Then the nomads came forward in turn, each taking one of his belongings and replacing it with something of their own. It was harder than usual, because Darton was so much larger than the rest of the band that most of his belongings were far too big for them. He had a mighty bow, one that Connell had ordered made just for him, but only Connell would even have been able to string it, and none of them could have shot it properly. It would have been a great way to remember him, but nomads couldn't afford to carry things for sentiment, not if they weren't also useful.

Caylen exchanged her dagger. Darton had never used his as more than a pocket knife—he was too slow to be an effective bladesman, and had generally relied on strength and reach in any close combat. So his knife wasn't oversized, and Caylen was sure she could sharpen it into a useful weapon. And Dart would be able to remember her every time he needed to cut something, in his new place.

Caylen stepped back from the body and looked at the other nomads. Some had gone to relieve those on watch, so that everyone would have a chance to say goodbye. It wasn't the first time someone from Nora's band had died, but Dart had been a general favorite, and he'd been around forever. He was going to be missed.

And he was going to be remembered, Caylen vowed, looking down at the blade in her hand. Jonah was right, maybe—there was no point in hunting down the false nomads, no point in making them pay for a lucky shot, not when at least two of their own had died in the same skirmish. But according to Jonah, there was someone behind all this, someone who had set everything in motion, bringing this disaster to the nomads' forest. And whoever that was...Caylen stayed silent, but her lips curled into a snarl. Whoever that was, Caylen had a dagger for him.

CHAPTER 8

The nomads moved on immediately after saying goodbye to Darton, and they caught up to Jonah's soldiers well before dark. Caylen hadn't spent much time in the camp since the soldiers had joined their party, and she was waiting to be annoyed by them, by inappropriately loud voices or huge, smoky fires or just...anything, really. They were alive and Darton was dead, and the whole thing was their fault. They were surprisingly inoffensive, though, just quietly going about their business. So Caylen would have to look elsewhere for a distraction.

Her eyes fell on the stretcher where the injured boy was lying. Even from a distance Caylen could tell that he was getting better. His head was propped up on a bundle of blankets, and he was watching everything going on around him with bright eyes. When Connell went over with his bottle of medicine and some clean bandages, he was greeted with a smile. And he'd somehow gotten the fancy gun back from Nora; Caylen could see the handle of it sticking out of the covers. The kid obviously hadn't done anything to earn it. Probably some rich relative had given it to him in the first place, and then Jonah must have bought it back from the nomads. The whole thing was disgusting.

Nora was conferencing with Jonah, and Caylen waited at a respectful distance until she was acknowledged. When Nora waved her forward, she said, "Should I take a watch? Or go back and set up an ambush post, in case they're following?"

Nora frowned. "If I want you to do something, I'll let you know."

Caylen had her mouth open to argue, but her mind caught painfully. Darton's packs had already been redistributed to the nomads; that punishment, like the man himself, was gone forever. She never thought she'd be sorry about it.

"Logan could use some company, if you're looking for something to do," Jonah suggested.

Caylen didn't even bother trying to keep the scorn from her voice. "I'm not a nursemaid."

"I was thinking more of being a friend." His voice was gentle. He glanced at Nora before continuing. "Or family, really...you have the same great-grandfather, you know."

"Great-grandfather?" Caylen turned to Nora. "That's the big secret? Some guy hundreds of years ago?"

"Hardly hundreds of years," Jonah corrected. "He's still alive—he's the man who raised me."

"My great-grandfather raised you?" Caylen tried to sort it out in her head. "My...father's grandfather?"

Jonah nodded. "Lord Wiltern of Yorkton. He raised your father, as well—we grew up together."

Caylen could sense Nora's growing unease with this line of conversation. It was very satisfying. Maybe the next time Caylen wanted to go out on watch, Nora wouldn't argue. "My father, really? What was his name?"

Jonah looked startled by her ignorance. "His name?" He frowned at Nora, then turned his shoulder to her and focused on Caylen. "Your father's name was Willem. We just called him Will, though. He was my best friend—my brother, really."

Caylen had never heard any of this, and had never really been curious. She'd always had more parenting than she wanted, from all the members of the band; it had never occurred to her to look for anything else. But now that she was starting to her about it, she wanted to hear more. And not just to make Nora anxious. "You're saying 'was'. He's dead, then?" She tried not to think of the more recent death.

"Yes." Jonah was watching her closely, and Caylen realized that he expected her to be upset. "He died before you were born. And then Nora left town before any of us knew you were on your way. That's why I was surprised to see you, earlier."

"He was murdered." Nora sounded angry. "Don't say 'he died', like he fell off a horse. They slit his throat." She stared at Jonah, as if daring him to contradict her. "He wasn't armed, he wasn't fighting. He was just...murdered."

"Why?" As long as Nora was talking, Caylen wanted to keep her going.

Nora pointed her chin at Jonah. "Since you've decided to bring all this up, why don't you tell her 'why?'"

Jonah took a deep breath, and his face was earnest when he looked at Caylen. "The city...it's not like out here. There's...politics. People who want power." He sighed. "Your father was next in line to be Chancellor, after his grandfather died. He had enemies." Jonah turned to Nora. "We tried to find them, Nora. Tried to figure out who'd done it. There were just..."

"Too many possibilities?" she said icily. "And you wonder that I chose to keep her from you all, that I chose to keep her safe?"

"Safe?" Jonah sounded incredulous. "How can you say she was safe, living out here?"

"Because she's still alive." Nora's tone was firm, and Caylen had to admit that it was a pretty persuasive argument. Jonah didn't seem satisfied, though.

"For how long?" he asked quietly. There was no threat in his voice. He sounded concerned, and a little sad. "On top of all the usual risks—she looks so much like him, Nora. You must have been doing a good job, keeping her hidden, but it's a lot easier to hide a little kid than a full grown woman. And there were already rumors, like I told you. I ignored them, because— because I couldn't believe you wouldn't have told me." He sighed. "I couldn't believe you wouldn't have let me help."

"I didn't need your help. Obviously." Nora nodded at Caylen, proof of her competence.

"What happened to her face? That must have been a close call."

Caylen really wished he hadn't asked that. She braced herself for the explosion, but it didn't come. Instead, Nora's triumph was quiet.

"*That* happened in town. *That's* what they do to nomad children who are accused of stealing."

"What town? Not Yorkton!" Jonah seemed aghast at the thought.

"No. They mark nomad faces in Linden." Nora looked like she wanted to spit. "In Yorkton, they kill people."

Jonah took the hit, but didn't surrender. "People die out here, too, Nora. I lost eleven men this week, and it's only luck and Connell's good medicine that's keeping that number from being twelve."

"They were killed by people from the city!" Caylen jumped in. "And so was Darton—if you all would just stay where you belong, none of that would have happened." She lifted her fingers to her face and traced the scar. "And if I'd stayed where I belonged, this wouldn't have happened."

Nora reached over and pulled Caylen's hand away from her face. It was surprisingly gentle. "I should have kept you closer to me." Then she dropped the hand. "And it's not like it's some big tragedy anyway. You were too pretty before—it was going to get us into trouble. They did us a favor, really, even if they didn't know it."

Caylen had heard that argument before. She'd been so little when she'd been scarred, still running around weaponless and innocent, and once the pain had gone away, the mark hadn't given her any more trouble than self-consciousness when meeting new people. So Nora was right, it wasn't a big tragedy. It was hard to think of it as a favor, though.

Connell came to join them, then, and he and Nora started discussing strategy for the evening. Caylen stayed and listened quietly, as did Jonah. She caught him watching her a couple times, but ignored it. She didn't have much interest in some old friend of a father she'd never known, and she didn't feel like humoring his interest in her.

Connell and Nora decided that the nomads would work in shifts to set up another ambush, while the soldiers would take care of establishing a perimeter around the camp. Connell nodded toward Caylen. "She's been out quite a bit. Let's leave her in tonight, let her get some sleep."

Nora nodded absently, her mind already working on the next set of challenges. "Fine. And we'll put her on point tomorrow, since she'll be fresh."

There was a brief flurry of activity as the camp's inhabitants ate dinner, a strange stew of jerky, leaks and roots that Romy had come up with, and then slipped out into the darkening forest. The nomads who'd been on watch came back to eat and then joined Nora at the ambush site. Each of them would have a partner, and as long as one of them was awake to watch for trouble, the other could sleep. Caylen had spent many nights in that manner, and wasn't quite sure why she was deemed too fragile to be in the forest this time. She wasn't impressed about being treated like a child, stuck in camp with the invalid. She remembered her dissatisfaction the night before, when she'd *wanted* to be in camp, but... that was different. Somehow.

The soldiers had bundled their injured charge in blankets and placed him by the fire, and he seemed to be asleep, so Caylen let her curiosity direct her for a moment and eased a little closer to him. His face looked fuller now, not as drawn as when she had first seen him, and the stubble was longer than it had been, dark against skin too pale for any nomad. There was a faint sheen of sweat on his skin, and she wasn't sure if that was a sign of fever or just of his caretakers having wrapped him in too many blankets. It didn't look comfortable, but it wasn't her problem, so she pulled her own blankets out of her pack and moved toward the edge of the clearing. She didn't care how many allies there were in the forest around her, she knew she wouldn't be comfortable sleeping all alone in the middle of a big, open space like that. Maybe the city boy was sweating because he was nervous. But she doubted he had enough sense to realize how vulnerable he truly was.

She took some time to sharpen her new knife, making sure that it was ready for whatever work it found. Then she found a comfortable hollow in amongst the exposed roots of an old cedar tree, spread her groundsheet and lay down, wrapping her blankets around her. She hadn't known how tired she was, but as soon as she was horizontal it hit her, and she knew she'd be asleep in no time.

She awoke some time later, and wasn't sure why. Then she saw the movement in the clearing. The fire had died down to coals, and there wasn't much moonlight, but she could see the burly shape easing toward the center of the clearing, and she could hear it, too, the soft rustle of hard clothing brushing against itself. Not a nomad, then. The shape paused, peering around the camp, and Caylen realized that he was looking for her. She thought about saying something, calling his attention, but she still wasn't sure who it was or what he could want, so she stayed perfectly still.

Apparently he gave up on finding her, then, and he moved quickly to the sleeping boy's side. This didn't feel right, not at all, but Caylen wasn't sure what was happening, and didn't want to interfere. She saw the blankets move at the same time that the shape did, and then it was clear that there was a struggle. She heard the grunt of effort the injured boy was making, and then she saw the blade in the hands of the other man, saw the boy fighting with all his strength to keep it away from his throat.

Caylen didn't even stand up. Her bow was beside her, as always, and a single fluid movement had an arrow in hand and nocked to the bow. Her draw and release was almost instant, and she knew her accuracy and power wouldn't be as good from the angle she was shooting from, but she didn't have time to move, and the target was close anyhow.

Her arrow flew true, hitting the man in the shoulder. He let out a startled cry and fell backward. Caylen was already moving, Darton's dagger in her hand. She had to close the distance fast, before the attacker collected himself, and she made it barely in time, her knife slicing into the uninjured arm that had grabbed Logan's gun from his blankets. Another yell, and then Caylen had the attacker shoved over backward, her knife to his throat while her knees pinned his biceps. With her free hand, she wrenched the gun from his injury-loosened grip and sent it scuffling across the forest floor.

The noise had been noticed by others, finally, and Jonah crashed in from the forest, followed by several soldiers. The nomads had probably sent someone to check on things, too, but whoever it was wouldn't make enough noise to be noticed over the racket of the soldiers.

"Quiet them!" Caylen hissed at Jonah. "There could be more."

Logan was staring at the man she had pinned. "Sealy?" he said, and Caylen thought she could hear hurt in his voice. She looked down and noticed for the first time that the man's face wasn't unfamiliar. He was one of the soldiers that had come with Jonah.

She pursed her lips and gave the whistle that would call Nora. If Jonah's soldiers were disloyal, it was a new situation, a new threat, and Caylen didn't want to deal with it on her own.

CHAPTER 9

"You've got him?" Jonah asked. "He's secure?"

Caylen shrugged. "You should tie his hands, to make sure." One of the other soldiers produced a length of rope and performed the task with Caylen watching carefully to be sure it was done right. She had no idea whether she could trust the intentions of these men, but she absolutely knew she didn't trust their competence.

In the meantime, Jonah had gone to Logan to check that he wasn't reinjured, and he'd obviously heard enough of the boy's story to confirm that Caylen had been defending him, not randomly attacking one of the soldiers.

By the time Nora arrived, things were much calmer. Jonah had sent his men back out to guard the perimeter, and Caylen had double-checked the knots holding the prisoner and then yanked her arrow out of his shoulder. The arrow head must have hit bone, because it was dulled and would have to be filed, but the shaft was still straight and strong, so it wasn't a total loss.

Nora took a quick look at the situation, then spoke to Jonah. "Do we need Connell?"

Jonah shook his head. "Logan's fine—I think he reopened the cut a little, but Connell said not to worry about that until we're sure the infection's gone." He sneered at the prisoner. "And I don't care if this son-of-a-bitch bleeds to death."

"He attacked the boy?"

"Yeah. Logan got enough of a grip to hold him off a little, and then your girl took care of the rest. By the time I got here, it was all under control."

Nora frowned at Caylen. "Why did you let him get so far? You couldn't stop him earlier?"

"I didn't know what he was doing!" Caylen protested. "I thought he was one of the soldiers, just checking on things."

Nora didn't look satisfied with that explanation, but she let it go.

Jonah was staring at the prisoner with a mix of anger and disbelief. "So, Sealy? What's going on? What were you thinking?"

Sealy's face was white, and Caylen was pleased to see that having his arms tied was causing both of the injuries to stretch open. He wouldn't likely bleed to a dangerous level, but he would certainly be uncomfortable. He still wasn't talking, though.

Jonah bent over and stared into his eyes. "Somebody paid you, right?" He stood up. "That's the only thing that makes sense. But how could you expect to get away with it? If you'd succeeded? Did you think you'd just go back to Yorkton and we'd forget all about it?" He crouched down, and it seemed as if he was mostly talking to himself. "Even if you'd managed to slit his throat without getting covered in blood, which you'd have to know was unlikely, you'd know that we'd be watching everyone to see who had any new money to spend..."

"Who's 'we'?" Nora interjected. "If your boy dies, your power goes with him. There's no guarantee that the next in line would have any interest in finding out who killed him. Especially not if they're the ones who set it in motion."

Jonah frowned as if he was resisting the logic of that explanation. He clearly didn't want to admit that his city was that corrupt, at least not in front of Nora.

"Would he have to go back to Yorkton?" Caylen asked. "Couldn't he go to one of the other cities? If he had gold from doing this, it wouldn't be too hard to get set up somewhere new, would it?"

That suggestion seemed more acceptable to Jonah. He leaned down, trying to see the prisoner's face. "So, who paid you?" There was no answer. "You need to start talking, son. If we get back to town and there's still no answers, you'll be seeing the insides of the Dark House, and you know they'll make you talk there. If you tell me what's going on now, save us some time...I'll see what I can do for you."

There was a pained laugh, and the prisoner finally spoke. "You expect me to believe that? I tried to kill the heir...it's the Dark House for me, no matter what."

Jonah frowned, then nodded. "Yes, you're probably right. But what about your little girl? I met her last year, what was her name?" He thought. "Mahia, right? What about her? Seems like she's going to be growing up without a father, but don't think that the Dark House bastards won't drag her in if they think it'll be what breaks you. Don't think they won't do horrible things to her."

Caylen was aghast. The city people would do something like that, and then have the nerve to call nomads savages?

But the threat seemed to have been enough to break the prisoner's calm demeanor. "Good luck to them finding her," he spat. "I tried for two months before we left town, and I couldn't find a trace."

"What do you mean?" Jonah asked. "Where'd she go?"

"How would I know?" Sealy was almost yelling. "The bastards took her, right from the house. Knocked down my wife, stole my child, and told me they'd kill her if I didn't do what they said." His voice quieted as he slumped in defeat. "There was no money. I didn't get paid, and I knew I'd get caught. But they had my little girl. I didn't have a choice."

"Why didn't you tell me?" Jonah demanded. "And who are 'they'?"

Sealy stared back at Jonah. "I don't know who they are! That's why I couldn't tell you—for all I know, you're one of them."

There was a long pause while everyone digested the new information. Nora was the first to speak. "I'll call for Connell. We should get those injuries looked at."

Jonah didn't try to stop her. He looked old, for the first time since Caylen had met him. Old and tired. He watched Nora as she left the clearing, and then turned to Caylen. "Maybe she was right. To bring you out here. To keep you away from...from all this."

"I don't understand." Caylen didn't want to sound naive, but she wanted to figure this all out. "What's so important, that they're willing to do anything, to hurt little kids just to get it? Just...power? Like, telling other people what to do?"

Jonah looked like he was thinking about the answer, but it was Logan who spoke, his voice quiet but steady. "From the outside, it looks like it's about power, but from the inside—it's about trust. Trying to feel safe." He winced as he worked his way up so that he was propped on his elbows. "They don't trust me to not go after them, so they go after me first. But a lot of the time, it's not...I've never ordered anyone killed. I've never ordered anyone to do anything underhanded, really." He glanced over at Jonah, and looked almost ashamed. "But that doesn't mean that things haven't been done by people who are...who are on my side. Once they throw their support behind me, then all my enemies are after them, and if I go down, my supporters go down too. All it takes is for one person to do something dirty, and then everyone else has to sink to their level, or else they'll lose ground." He shook his head a little and slumped back down on the stretcher. Caylen could barely hear him when he said, "I hate it."

"So why do you do it?" She still wasn't happy that this boy had brought his trouble to her forest, and she didn't like him trying to pretend that he was some sort of a victim. "Why couldn't you just walk away?"

He nodded, and stared up at the stars. "I used to dream about doing that." He was speaking softly, like it was just to her, like the others couldn't even hear him. "But that's the trap. They wouldn't trust me to stay gone, and they'd come after me, and I wouldn't have my supporters for protection. Or they *would* believe that I was gone for good, and then my supporters would be vulnerable, and my enemies would take revenge against them, punishing them for things that they'd done in my name, things they'd done to try to help me..." His voice faded away entirely.

"That's a mess." Caylen wasn't sure she believed him, and if she did, she knew the words were inadequate, but they were all she had. She wasn't sorry when she saw Connell emerge from the forest and cross to where they were gathered.

Caylen went to find Connell's first aid pack while he examined the patient; when she returned she saw that the man's hands had been loosened, but not untied. Connell was poking at the arrow wound with his fingers

while Jonah looked on, frowning. As Caylen helped
Connell clean and bandage the wounds, Jonah and Nora
spoke softly with Logan.

When Sealy was as repaired as he could get,
Jonah returned to his side. "Are there any others? Any of
the other men—are any of them traitors?"

Sealy winced at the word. "I don't know. None that
I know of. But I might not know." That was honest,
Caylen decided. She knew she needed to keep herself
from getting involved in the affairs of these strangers, but
she really hoped there was some way to help Sealy. And
to keep him out of the Dark House, whatever that was.

Jonah was clearly worried about more immediate
concerns. He turned to Nora, obviously continuing their
conversation. "We need your band. We *need* them. If I
can't trust my men..." He shook his head. "They could all
be totally loyal. Or almost all of them could be, but if
there's even one more traitor..."

"He's not a traitor." Caylen was a little surprised
by how strongly she felt about this. "He was loyal to his
family—that's more important than being loyal to some
stupid city!"

"He tried to kill the heir." Jonah's voice was as
stony as his face. "It doesn't matter why, it just matters
that he did it."

"So you think he was wrong? You wouldn't have
done the same thing?" Caylen asked. "Do you have kids?
You wouldn't do whatever it took to protect them?"

Jonah looked her in the eye, and his voice was softer. "I would do whatever it took. Even something that would make me a traitor."

Caylen saw Logan stir a little on his stretcher, and she got the sense that there was more than she understood in that statement. As usual. But when Jonah continued, he was talking to Nora again, as if the interruption had never occurred. "If even one of them might be a traitor, I can't trust any of them. Your men...your band," he corrected himself, "haven't been in contact with anyone that could turn them. And Caylen's already risked her life once to save Logan."

Caylen wanted to say something snide about it not really being that much of a risk for her to have fought some puny city soldier, but she managed to choke the insult down. She waited quietly for Nora's decision.

Finally, Nora nodded. "Fine. We'll see you to Rock Ferry, and we'll take the boat to town with you. But we have two extra conditions. First...double the daily rate we set before. That was when we thought the only threat came from *outside* the camp." Jonah didn't look impressed, but he nodded, so Nora continued. "And second...you leave Sealy here. We can't afford the time to drag a prisoner along with us. And you leave him alive. Nobody's getting executed for trying to look after his family—not in my forest."

Caylen tried not to smile. There were times when she really did love her mother.

Jonah, on the other hand, was looking rebellious. He opened his mouth to argue, but snapped it shut when he heard a quieter voice coming from the direction of the stretcher.

"Agreed," Logan said calmly. He shifted around until he was looking straight at the prisoner. "And you have my word, Sealy—we'll look for her, when we get back. I can't guarantee anything, but...I won't forget about her. My people will do what they can." He lay back down, clearly exhausted by his efforts.

"Mahia," he said softly, and it sounded like he was talking to himself, trying to write her name on some internal roll. Caylen wasn't sure whether it was a list of people to save, or a list of people that had suffered because of his role in the struggle for power. She hoped for the first, but she looked at his sad, tired face, and she was afraid that it might be the second.

CHAPTER 10

Once Nora had agreed to the new arrangement, things happened quickly. Jonah went through Sealy's belongings and extracted anything that wasn't a personal possession, and Caylen frowned at him until he reluctantly pulled a bag of dried food out of his own pack and stuffed it into Sealy's. Connell added some medicine and clean bandages, with instructions for their use, and Nora gave rough directions for how to cut through the forest and end up not too far from Barth's Waypoint. From there Sealy could try his luck at joining up with a nomad band, or, Nora strongly suggested, find his way to another town and start fresh.

The man looked a little stunned, whether from the injuries or from the several recent turns to his fortune, but he gamely set off in the direction Nora had indicated. It wasn't a good idea for him to travel in the dark, especially with two fresh injuries, but it was almost dawn, and both Nora and Jonah wanted him well away before the other soldiers returned to camp. Jonah went with him until he was beyond the range of the sentries, just to be sure.

Once they were gone, Nora got the camp organized. The nomads would go ahead with Logan and Jonah, while Nora would stay with the soldiers and set them up as a rear guard against attacks from the false nomads. There was still no certainty about the reasons for their attacks, but it seemed like everyone was assuming that they were after Logan. Caylen cast a dubious look in his direction; she'd liked the way he'd handled Sealy, but other than that, he hadn't done much to make her think he was worth all this trouble. City people—who could hope to understand them?

By the time Jonah returned, the nomads had gathered from their watch posts and were ready to move out. Caylen was on point, while the others took turns guarding and carrying Logan. Connell was coming with their group, which was a relief, because Caylen didn't want to have to stand up to Jonah if he started thinking he was in charge. Connell would take care of all that.

They headed off through the forest, and after consulting with Connell, Caylen kept them off the path. The alternate route slowed them down, and she heard occasional curses when those behind her encountered some particularly tricky terrain, but it was safer. The forests were vast, and under-populated. Travelling on the paths was easier, but in times of danger, not always smart. And Caylen had been blessed with an unerring sense of direction, so she didn't need to worry about getting lost. She hoped that anyone looking for them wouldn't be so lucky.

They didn't break for lunch, just munched on some dried food as they walked. The nomads were used to this sort of work, and if Jonah couldn't keep up, that was his problem.

Midafternoon, they stopped to fill their canteens at a swift-flowing creek, and Connell took the opportunity to dash back and check in with Nora. Caylen had the urge to strip her boots off and wade, to feel the cool water and the smooth rocks on her skin, and she had a flash of doing just that when she had been little, playing in the shallows with a large leg beside her to lean on for balance. The little girl looked up at her protector and saw Darton's gentle face, and Caylen felt the pain of his loss wash over her again. She crouched down quickly and splashed water on her face, trying to cool down, and to wash away any tears that dared to escape.

She thought she'd been subtle, but when she glanced around she saw the city boy watching her, his face as sad as hers. It made her angry. The whole thing was his fault, and now he was trying to make her think he felt bad about it? Not likely. She gave her face one more quick splash and then straightened up. "Connell will be able to catch up with us—let's get started."

There was some grumbling from the nomads, but Jonah heaved himself to his feet immediately. He was obviously tired, but still game, and Caylen respected that. She wondered if he was innately tough, or if he was being driven by desperation, trying to get his charge back to safety. Either way, he was ready to go, and the group kept walking right through until the sun started to set. They had been following a stream for a while, one that Caylen was reasonably sure was going to drain into the river that gave Rock Ferry its reason for existing, and when she found a fairly level clearing on the banks, she waited for the others to catch up.

Connell gave the site a quick once over, then nodded. "Okay, good. Pim, Taryn—perimeter scout. Caylen—your turn to cook."

She tried to ignore the groans from the other nomads, but finally they got to her and she grinned. "Hey, anybody who doesn't like my cooking is welcome to take over."

Logan was propped up on his elbows on the stretcher, and he looked intrigued. "What, a weakness? A wilderness skill at which you don't excel?"

That didn't sound right. "Well, cooking isn't exactly a wilderness skill," Caylen started, but she didn't want to be the sort of person who'd wiggle out of a challenge. "Connell, can I borrow your line?" She nodded toward the stream, and Connell smiled and gestured toward his pack.

Caylen pulled the fishing line out of the canvas bag and carefully unwound it. It was one long stretch of light rope, with several shorter strings of wire hanging down from it, each with a hardened metal hook at the end. Caylen quickly baited the hooks with scraps of jerky, and then tied one end of the rope to a tree near the side of the stream. She pulled her boots off and waded across to tie the other end to a tree on the far side, and then adjusted the lines so they all fell into the water.

She'd seen trout in the stream, earlier, so she was fairly confident that this would work. It had better; she would have rather not tried at all than tried and failed in front of the city boy.

Her next step was starting the fire. She made it a bit bigger than she normally would have, and braced herself to be scolded if it was still so obvious when Nora arrived, but she needed coals, and it was nice to having something to take the chill off the spring air.

"Connell? Can you watch the fire and the line? I just need to go get a few things..."

Connell looked amused and nodded, and Caylen set out in a hurry. She'd seen a stand of old elm trees not far away, and at this time of year...she smiled in triumph when she saw the wrinkled fungi growing beneath the trees. Morels. And a quick look around found a patch of wild leeks. She harvested her bounty as quickly as she could, and made it back to camp just as Nora and the soldiers arrived.

The soldiers looked exhausted, and more than a little annoyed, as did Nora. Caylen tried to imagine the day, Nora frustrated by the soldiers' lack of skill, the soldiers angry at not being part of the trusted group, and having their leader replaced by some bitter nomad with unrealistic expectations. Caylen was glad she'd been well away from them all, and now that they were reassembled, she kept herself busy to avoid Nora's attention. Thankfully, Connell had let the fire die down to a more reasonable size.

Logan looked like he was just as uncomfortable as Caylen was trying not to be, and she decided that he probably needed something to do. He was sitting near the stream, propped up against a fallen log, and she dropped her pack of morels and leeks at his side. "These need to be washed," she said. "And peel the outside leaves off the leeks, until they're fresh looking—we want green and white, no brown." He seemed confused, but she had no idea why. She'd taken into account that he was from the city, and made her instructions extra-clear. "You can use a knife to trim off the roots." He still didn't move. "And wash them in water...from the stream..." Why was she still getting a blank look?

Jonah was watching, and looked amused. "Rethinking your idea of having your own wilderness adventure, Logan? Just because you've been asked to do a little work?"

One of the soldiers had heard Caylen's request, and jumped into the conversation indignantly. "*Woman's* work." He turned to Jonah. "Sir, it's bad enough that you're making *us* listen to that harpy, but Logan is the heir of Yorkton! He shouldn't be doing woman's work, and he shouldn't be taking orders from—"

"Ellis." Logan's voice was quiet, but the man stopped speaking immediately. "I'm capable of deciding for myself what's appropriate for me. And for speaking up for myself, when necessary. And if you have a concern about my treatment, you should address it to me, not to Jonah. Thank you." The dismissal was clear, and the man backed away reluctantly. Caylen was left wondering how the boy could be so good at talking, and so apparently useless at everything else. But then he was shifting around and pulling his knife out, reaching for the bag of foraged food. "Green and white is good...brown is bad," he echoed, and grinned at Caylen.

"Except for the morels...brown is good, for them."

He shook his head. "Now, don't go making it so complicated. I'll never catch on."

"Fine, start with the green and white—I need those first. I can come back and give you a refresher when you get to the brown." Maybe he wasn't so bad after all.

Caylen went to check on the fishing line, and found six fat trout already on the shore waiting for her; the lines had been replaced in the stream. Connell wandered over. "Need help cleaning them? I think a good feed might go a long way to calming a few people down."

"Even if their precious little heir is one of the ones helping with the cooking?" She kept her voice low.

Connell just smiled and pulled his knife out. "You find any clay, or are we rock-cooking them?"

"No, there's clay up..." Caylen glanced down the darkened stream. "Damn, it would have been better to do that before it was full night. But I'm pretty sure I remember where, and it's not like I can't find clay by feel. Who's on watch by the river?"

"Pim on this side...and Nora's sending a couple soldiers over to the other side."

"I'm gonna slip out before they get there. Make sure they know I'm out there, okay?" Being shot by accident would hurt just as much as being shot on purpose, *plus* it would be humiliating.

Connell nodded, and Caylen found the band's shovel and headed out. The clay bank wasn't far, but when she got there it was pretty tough digging, and then the clay was hard to carry, slippery and slimy all over her tunic. She had paused to get a better grip when she heard the voices.

"No, he's got to have a plan. He's setting her up, for something." Caylen didn't recognize the voice, and none of the nomads would ever have spoken so loudly when they were on watch, so it had to be one of the soldiers.

"For what? What could some wild-girl nomad have that he'd want? Besides the obvious." Another unfamiliar voice.

"I don't know...but you know what he's like—he's always got a plan, always thinking ahead. And he doesn't let himself get distracted by a pretty face. Or half a pretty face."

"Good body, though. And I bet she'd be wild. The kid's gotta cut lose sometime, doesn't he?"

"Not that I've ever seen. I'm telling you, he's got a plan."

Caylen got a better grip on the clay and slipped away along the river bank. When she got closer to camp, she heard Pim's voice challenge her. "Who's there?"

"It's me, Pim. And I just walked right by the soldiers, so make sure you're doing a good job, because they sure aren't."

Pim leaned down a little from the perch he'd found in an old oak tree. "You're just too good, Caylen. They didn't have a chance." The man had a gift for making compliments sound insincere.

"Yeah, okay." Caylen eased by him and continued back toward camp.

"Save me a good fish," Pim whispered urgently, but she ignored him. She tried not to think about the soldiers' conversation, but it was hard to ignore. It wasn't that she cared about the boy's opinion, any more than she cared about the soldiers'. It was just the idea that Logan was playing some sort of a game with her that was annoying. It didn't seem likely; as far as she'd seen, he'd barely noticed her, and surely he'd agreed to help with the cooking because he was bored, not because he wanted her to owe him a favor. No, it didn't make sense. But if he *was* playing a game...Caylen frowned. If he was playing a game, she needed to figure out what it was, and then she needed to get good at it herself. Good enough to make sure she was the one who won.

CHAPTER 11

When Caylen got back to camp, she found that Logan had finished up with the leeks and morels, and had somehow made his way over to the creek side, where Connell was teaching him how to clean the fish. Logan was being at least as friendly with Connell as he'd been with her, she decided, and Connell wasn't stupid or naive. Obviously whatever she'd overheard had been wrong.

She busied herself with picking the worst of the grit and muck out of the clay, and then pulled it apart and found a flat rock to use as a work surface. She pounded the clay out flat, then selected the first fish from the pile Logan and Connell had cleaned. She could tell that Logan was watching her, and she tried to look as if she had done this before, rather than just seeing others do it. She inserted a couple leeks into the cavity of the trout and wrapped clay around the whole thing, being careful that there were no holes in the seal. She set the bundle aside and moved on to the next, and then the next. Connell finished cleaning fish and rinsed his hands before gathering the clay bundles and taking them over to the fire. He nestled them in to the hot ashes and covered them over, and then returned for another load.

"Like a bunch of little ovens."

Caylen couldn't tell if Logan was being patronizing or if he actually liked the idea. "They'll taste good," she said. "And if we don't eat them all, we can carry them like that for lunch tomorrow."

"How do you get the clay off?"

"Once it's dry, it breaks off easily. Takes the fish skin with it. You'll see." She leaned over and rinsed her hands in the river.

"So, I have to retract my statement? You're an expert wilderness chef, after all?"

"You should wait and taste them, first." She wasn't sure if she trusted this boy or not, but it was hard not to like him. "I've never actually made them before. But Connell would have said if I'd done something really wrong."

"Well, I've never washed vegetables or cleaned fish before, so if they don't taste good, I'll be at least as much to blame."

She snuck a look at him, then, and frowned. "You look like you're going to pass out. Are you supposed to be moving around this much?"

"Shhh." Logan cast a furtive look toward the fire, where Connell and Jonah were deep in conversation. "They'll make me lie back down. I'm sick of lying down."

Caylen took a critical look at his face. It was hard to see with only the moonlight and the glow from the fire, but she was pretty sure he looked paler than he had when she'd first returned to camp. "Go lie down. If *they* aren't making you, I am."

"You know, I may have defended you earlier, about the vegetable washing, but I really don't think it's your place to order me around." He seemed to be serious, and she couldn't help laughing.

"You don't think so?" She shook her head. "This isn't the city...nobody out here cares who your great-grandfather is. All we care about is what you can do, and all I've seen you do so far is get shot, get stabbed, and get rescued. Not too impressive."

He looked like he was ready to argue, but Caylen stared him down. She wasn't sure she'd be able to do that if he was at full strength, but he was obviously far from that. He reluctantly started to work his way to his feet, and when he paused while still crouched on one knee, Caylen realized that it was because he couldn't make it any farther. She moved quickly, easing her shoulder under his and giving him a boost as unobtrusively as possible. He might be a little arrogant and argumentative, but she could absolutely sympathize with his desire to keep his weakness quiet.

They made it over to his stretcher without any serious problems, and Caylen helped him work his way down until he was lying flat. She rested a hand on his shoulder. "Take a break for a bit. Dinner won't be ready for a good while."

He shook his head in frustration. "I won't get better if I don't work at it."

"Have you never been injured before? You need to push, but you need to look after yourself, too. Maybe you don't remember, but I saw how much blood you lost. You're probably still half empty."

Caylen wasn't sure if he agreed with her or just gave up, but he relaxed onto the stretcher and she returned to her cooking. She made sure the fish bundles were all evenly covered in coals and ash, and then burrowed through the pack of cooking supplies until she found the band's frying pan and the little tin of oil. She held the oil up to Connell. "I'll just use a little, okay?"

He nodded. "And a little salt, too."

Oil was heavy to carry and salt was expensive, so the nomads were stingy with both, but Connell had apparently decided that they all deserved a treat. Caylen wasn't going to argue.

She heated the oil and added the morels, sprinkling a little salt as they cooked. By the time they were done, the clay covering the smallest of the fish was hard and scorched, and Caylen used a stick to drag a few of them out of the coals. Connell wandered over, looking hungry, and Caylen realized that her little project had drawn the attention of most of the camp. The fish didn't smell like much, yet, but the morels had a wonderful aroma. Caylen dug a tin plate out of the cook-pack and dished some morels into it, then pulled her sleeve down over her hand and used it as a mitt to allow her to pick up one of the hot fish bundles. She carried the meal over to Nora, who was re-lacing the leather ties on her boots. It was a bit awkward, because Caylen wasn't sure the fish was done, but Caylen wasn't going to show disrespect to Nora in front of the strangers, and that meant Nora had to be served first.

Nora accepted the offering absentmindedly, setting them both on the ground beside her as she focused on her work. Caylen tried not to let it sting that Nora didn't even seem to have noticed her efforts. And everyone else was very appreciative, especially after they cracked open the clay bundles and saw the succulent white flesh inside.

With half the camp on watch, there were enough small fish for everyone to eat at once, and by the time people came back for more, the larger fish were ready. Caylen sat back and surveyed the scene with satisfaction. She glanced over and saw that Logan was sitting up and eating easily, apparently recovered from his earlier weakness. He noticed her looking and raised one of the shards of his broken clay bundle as if toasting her achievement, and she grinned and raised a shard in return. After all, he had helped.

As soon as the first round of eating was done, the nomads in the camp went out to take over the watch duties from the nomads who'd been in the forest, and Jonah organized his men into a similar swap. The new arrivals ate happily, and Caylen was relieved to see that there was going to be enough food, although there probably wouldn't be much left over for the next day. Everything seemed to be going smoothly, until Nora started setting up the night's watches. Caylen was scrubbing the frying pan in the grit of the creek, so she didn't hear how it started, but when she heard a soldier's raised voice and looked over to see him standing chest to chest with an unflinching Nora, Caylen set the frying pan down, fast.

Her knife was with her, as always, but her bow was several strides away. She shouldn't have been so careless, but she'd felt safe, and she'd let herself be distracted. A quick glance took in the rest of the camp, also watching the conflict, and she was relieved to see that the other nomads were closer to their weapons. Connell looked like he was a breath away from raising his shotgun and taking the soldier out without further discussion, but then Jonah stood up and wedged himself in front of Nora, and he laid his hands on the soldier's chest and pushed him backward.

"Stand down, Ellis," Jonah ordered. The soldier hesitated, and it seemed like he wasn't going to obey. Caylen took advantage of the distraction to shift herself closer to the action. She'd been tempted to go for her bow, but it was too far, and her knife was quick and sharp. If she was close enough, it was all she'd need.

But then Ellis took a grudging half-step back, and the tension diffused a little. Jonah moved with him, pushing for another step, and then another, before he spoke again. "She's working for me, and I've put her in charge. Her orders are my orders." There was no hint of compromise in his tone.

The soldier seemed to be fighting for control. "She..." He took a deep breath. "She's stationing us all on the far perimeter. None of us in the camp."

"I know." Jonah's voice was quiet.

Ellis straightened up and lifted his chin proudly. "I have served in the Yorkton army all my life. My father was a lifetime soldier, and so was his father before him. My great-grandfather died defending Yorkton in the war with the Easterners." He stared right at his commander. "And you don't trust me with the life of the heir? You'd rather see him guarded by a band of savages?"

Jonah answered without hesitation. "You have good reason to be proud of your family's tradition, Ellis. Your family are soldiers—they're disciplined. They follow orders, even when they don't understand them." He waited a few moments for his words to sink in. "You've been given your orders. Follow them."

Nora stepped forward then, but she didn't speak to the soldier. Instead, she ignored him, and turned to Caylen. "Scout back a ways...about an hour. See if there's any sign of the others tracking us. If there is, report back. If there isn't, sleep out there, near our trail, and keep an eye out for them. We'll leave you on rear guard tomorrow." She turned, still ignoring Ellis. Caylen could see what she was doing, just assuming that the soldier would obey, and giving him a chance to save face. Caylen didn't think Nora would ever have been that easy on one of her own who challenged her authority, but it probably made sense in this situation. A full-scale battle between the nomads and the soldiers wouldn't help anybody. "Connell, you sleep in camp, near the kid. You'll be on point tomorrow."

Nora gave a few more orders, and Caylen paid enough attention so that she would know who was where, but her mind was already racing ahead, retracing their path through the forest, thinking of the best place to camp for the night. She loved being in the forest alone, especially when she'd already gotten a full, hot meal into her belly.

She stayed in the camp, though, until she was sure that things had calmed down. When the soldiers headed out to set up their perimeter watch posts, she went with them, and if her presence kept their complaints muted, she wasn't sorry. She was happy to leave them behind, though, to move beyond their stomping and brushing and grunting and muttering and get back to the peace of her home. Without the racket of the soldiers, she could hear the forest, and it was good. She retraced their path, just as Nora had ordered, but there was no trace of pursuit. Caylen knew that Nora had been on rear guard the day before, and could see a few spots where she had worked to hide the evidence of their passing, but if the followers had a good scout, they would be able to trace the path of the soldiers, if not that of the nomads. So, since there was no sign of followers, they either didn't have a tracker or had given up. Either way, it was good news, and Caylen found a cozy spot to curl up and slept peacefully.

She awoke at dawn, and ate a few bites of jerky before scouting back a little further down the path. There were still no signs of pursuit, so she made her way back to camp. The group was already moving, with Logan walking on his own, although Caylen noticed that the stretcher hadn't been put away yet, and that Jonah was keeping a close eye on the boy. Caylen made her report to Nora, and then headed back out to be the rear guard, watching for signs of pursuit and trying to obscure any traces of their passing. A fine drizzle of rain began to fall around lunch time, and it helped wash away the most obvious clues, although if it kept up long enough to create mud, it would actually make their path more obvious.

That didn't turn out to be a problem, though. By mid-afternoon, the stream they were following joined a larger river, and the band turned to follow the river downstream. Shortly after, the forest faded away into pastures and then fields, and finally the houses and outbuildings of Rock Ferry.

The nomads had gotten Logan out of the forest, but he still wasn't home. And the challenges of civilization were less familiar, and therefore more dangerous. The best they could hope for was a quick trip to the city and then a return to their forest routine. Caylen was a little surprised to realize that she might miss the disruption, once it was gone.

CHAPTER 12

Rock Ferry wasn't much of a town. There were about fifteen houses, all spread out along a single road, and there was an inn and tavern to serve the ferry customers. The ferry dock itself was a good size, long rather than wide, stretching out from the stony, rough shore into the deeper part of the river.

Even such a small town was uncomfortable for the nomads, and Caylen knew she wasn't the only one wishing there was more cover. She wasn't the only one who wanted to sneak along the back of the buildings rather than march down the middle of the street. She overcame the instinct, though, and caught up to the band as they proceeded into town.

They got more than a few strange looks from the townspeople. Nomads weren't that rare, and neither were soldiers, but they weren't usually seen together. And Logan had gotten tired at some point during the day and was now back to being carried on the stretcher, which added another mysterious element to their procession.

The band made their way down to the dock and waited on the shore, the nomads still in a loose circle around Logan, the soldiers sullenly kept to the outside. Jonah and Nora walked together to meet the Dockmaster. There was some discussion and negotiation before the two returned.

"We're staying tonight, leaving tomorrow morning," Jonah announced. Nora was frowning behind him, and Caylen knew that the attention of all the nomads was on her. There was a ferry waiting at the dock, half-loaded with sacks of what looked like grain and obviously ready to leave shortly. It didn't make sense that they wouldn't be on it.

Logan had risen as soon as the band had come to a stop, and now he clapped his hands together loudly. "Well, then, let's see about accommodations. I wonder how many of us the inn will hold?" He seemed a little over-enthusiastic, to Caylen's ear, but the soldiers didn't object, especially when he added, "And we'll have to see how much of the innkeep's beer *we* can hold!" He started off toward the inn with the soldiers falling in behind him, joking and pushing and generally showing their relief at being out of the forest and back into more-or-less familiar surroundings.

Caylen waited for orders. Nora still looked displeased as she stormed over and grabbed Caylen by the shoulder of her tunic. "You will stay with him. All night. I don't care where he goes or what he gets up to, you don't leave him alone." She looked at the other nomads. "The rest of you stay on guard and be ready to help out," and she turned back to Caylen, "but he's your responsibility." She shook her head at Jonah as if expressing her disgust at the plan, then released her hold on Caylen and stalked off after the soldiers.

Caylen looked at Connell in confusion. "Why's he *my* problem? What's wrong with all of you?"

Connell grinned and slung an arm around her shoulders before pulling her toward him, her neck locked inside his elbow. "'Cause he'll put up with you, maybe. You can use your feminine wiles."

"My what? Come on, Connell..." They started walking toward the inn. "And why aren't we on the damn ferry tonight? Why are we waiting around?"

Jonah was on her other side, and he answered this question. "Logan's idea. He wants the chance to re-establish his bond with the soldiers before they get back to town and tell everyone about not being trusted."

"But...but they still *can't* be trusted, can they?" This whole situation was annoying to Caylen. She much preferred that things be straightforward.

Jonah made a face. "No, they can't, really. That's why Nora wants you near him. Logan thinks that if they're drunk, they'll be harmless. And if one of them doesn't drink, well, that'll be the one we need to watch most closely." He seemed to pick up on their reactions, and shrugged. "I'm not saying it's a foolproof plan. But Logan's right, he needs the soldiers on his side. There's no point in getting him back to town safely if he ends up facing a mutiny as soon as he gets there."

"So he's going to keep them loyal by getting them drunk?" It didn't sound like a good plan to Caylen, but she saw the grin that Connell and Jonah exchanged; apparently they thought it would work.

The soldiers were already sitting at one of the two long tables when the nomads arrived at the inn. Logan had men on both sides of him, close, too close for people he couldn't trust, people who could have daggers or guns ready to use. She caught herself. If there was no need for secrecy, if the assassin wasn't going to at least try to escape, Logan could have been killed at many points in the last few days. So an attack in this situation, in plain sight, was unlikely.

Of course, possibly the traitor, if he even existed, would be more desperate now, more willing to take a risk as the return to the city came closer. Caylen tried to put herself in the assassin's shoes, assuming that someone else had been reached the same way Sealy had. She would be determined to kill Logan, even if it cost her own life, if she knew that it was the only way to save someone she loved. But she wouldn't be desperate yet, she didn't think. She'd wait, especially since it seemed like Logan was trusting the soldiers again. She'd hold out for a better opportunity, a chance to get him alone. There was no way to be sure the soldiers would think like she did, but they seemed fairly calm, generally, not overly inclined to panic, so she'd try to trust in that.

Logan was sitting on a long bench with his back to the wall, but there was enough of a space that Caylen could work her way in if she needed to, could stand behind him and keep an eye on things. But that would make her scrutiny obvious, make it clear that he was being guarded, and she wasn't sure that was a good idea. It might be better to lay low, set a trap. And if he was trying to impress his men with how much he trusted them, he might not appreciate having a nomad guarding him quite so obviously. In theory, he should be safer like this, surrounded by his own men, than he would be anywhere else in the world. Caylen wondered how it felt, for him to have been betrayed like he had been. She wondered what she would feel like if she suddenly became unable to trust the forest to shelter her.

A woman bustled by with a tray of glasses, followed by a boy carrying two large jugs of beer, and the soldiers cheered in appreciation. Logan smiled easily at the woman. "Keep them coming, please." Then his gaze shifted to find Caylen, standing there watching it all. She realized that the other nomads had found seats, had left her standing alone and awkward. She felt like a fool, and it didn't help when Logan smirked at her. "Looking for a seat, sweetheart?" He was playing it up for his men, nodding suggestively at the narrow space on the bench beside him. She hated to give any of them the satisfaction of a response, but, damn it, she had her orders.

She thought of Connell's suggestion to use her feminine wiles, but she couldn't quite bring herself to smile at the arrogant boy. "Yeah, I am," she managed, and she walked determinedly around the table to his side. The soldiers were hooting, and she could feel her face heating. She didn't blush often, but she knew that when she did, it made her scar stand out even more, pale pink against the reddish brown of her cheek, and that made the whole situation even more absurd, that she was playing the flirt when she looked like that. She wouldn't quit once she'd started, though, wouldn't abandon a plan just because she'd lost her nerve, so she braced a hand on Logan's shoulder and eased one leg over the bench.

"Shove down a bit," Logan instructed the man next to her, and he did, reluctantly, giving her room to sit. It was still a tight fit, and when Logan slung his arm around her shoulders it did actually make for a little more room. That didn't make it okay for him to lean in toward her, though, actually brushing his lips against her cheek as he brought his mouth to her ear. "So you're my bodyguard, are you?" he murmured, and she could feel his lips curve as he smiled. "Just how far are you willing to take this? Do I have your 'services' for the whole night?"

Caylen was glad that she had been there when Logan's wounds were first dressed. She worked her arm around his waist and gripped him, hard, where one of the bullet-grazes was. His muffled gasp was very satisfying, and now she had no problem smiling at him.

"I really don't think you'll need anything but a nursemaid tonight. I'd be happy to call Connell over if you want."

His smile was tighter than it had been, and that was victory enough. She took a careful sip from the glass of beer one of the men had put in front of her. She needed to be on her game, but refusing to drink at all would blow her cover. She looked over to the nomads' table and saw them all joking and laughing, and she had a sudden flash of pain, remembering Darton, seeing how empty the table looked without his hulking presence. Her hand moved to her dagger, his dagger, and she let her fingers play over the hilt.

Logan seemed oblivious to her changed mood. He seemed oblivious to her entirely, really, now that the initial greeting was over. The innkeeper and his staff brought food out, thick slabs of ham with mashed potatoes and fresh spring asparagus, and everyone ate with appetite. Jonah was jumping back and forth between the two tables, apparently trying to broker some sort of peace, and one of the soldiers was talking intently to Taryn, clearly trying to make an impression. Caylen wondered if the soldier knew that Taryn generally sought out the company of other women when the nomads ventured into town; she wasn't really sure if he'd care.

Logan needed both hands to eat, but as soon as the meal was over his arm was back around her shoulders, even though he was still ignoring her, just talking and joking with his men. The lack of attention gave Caylen a chance to observe them. They were all older than Logan, but none of them was past his prime. They were well-armed, and, while they hadn't been much use in the forest, Caylen had seen enough to suspect that they were well-trained, at least for their limited set of skills. And they all seemed genuinely fond of Logan, from what she could tell. Could one of these men really have sinister intent, or was Jonah being paranoid? And what if it was more than one? Was Logan strong enough yet to be of any use in his own defense, or would it all be up to her? Just how much was Nora expecting of her?

Caylen was a little startled when Logan leaned over to speak into her ear again. "You know, I'd be a lot more comfortable with this entire situation if I didn't think you were planning to stab me yourself." He looked down pointedly to Caylen's hip, where her fingers were again wrapped around the hilt of Darton's dagger. She quickly released her grip, flexing her hand and trying to make it relax. Logan frowned. "You okay?" He wasn't whispering now, just talking quietly, far enough away that she could see his face, and he could see hers.

"I'm fine." He didn't look convinced. "I just don't like crowds. You know...all these people, and I don't really know them."

He looked surprised. "Crowds? This?" He blew out a breath in disbelief. "If you don't like this, you're going to have a hell of a time when you get to the city. This is...it's a little family dinner, compared to the city."

"What are you talking about? We're not going to the city. I mean, we're going there, but we're just going to drop you off—we won't need to go inside." He looked confused, so she clarified. "Nora doesn't like Yorkton. We never go there."

"From what I hear, she used to like it pretty well—used to live there."

"Well—I don't know about that." What more could she say?

He nodded, accepting the truth of her statement. "According to Jonah, she stayed away from Yorkton because she was trying to keep you hidden, not because she doesn't like the place." He looked her straight in the eye. "You really do look like him, you know. Your father. I've seen paintings, and even a photograph."

Caylen wasn't sure if she wanted to hear more about this or not. "Where've you seen them?"

"There's a painting on the wall of the Great Hall, and another at our family home. And the photograph...my great-aunt—your grandmother, I guess—she had it in her sitting room."

"His mother? Is she still alive?" Somehow, the idea of a new set of relatives was becoming more interesting.

"No. Sorry. She died a couple years ago. Natural causes."

Caylen nodded thoughtfully. "So, who *is* still alive?"

"Of his relatives?" Logan took a thoughtful pull of beer. "He was an only child. Well, there are half-siblings, because his mother re-married, but they don't count, because it's his father that was the heir." He shot her a quick look. "You really don't know any of this? Nora never told you a thing?"

"Nora told me lots of things. Just not about this."

Logan smiled as if amused by her defensiveness. "Well, I can fill you in, if you want, but it's a bit noisy here. Do you want to find somewhere quieter to talk?" Caylen frowned at him, and he grinned back at her, perfectly aware of how it would look if they left the room together. His smile widened as he said, "Actually, I'm betting I don't even have to get you to agree. You have orders, don't you? You wouldn't have come over to sit here all on your own, not unless you were told to. If you're guarding me, and I get up and leave...you have to come with me. Don't you?"

Apparently her silence told him all he needed to know. He stood up and beckoned to the innkeeper, who was hovering anxiously in the background. Caylen wasn't sure if the man was worried about providing the best service possible or just about keeping the rambunctious crowd from breaking his crockery, but he seemed happy to talk to Logan, and even happier to take the coins that Logan pulled out of his jacket pocket. Jonah had supplied his young charge with a fresh set of clothes and apparently a fresh purse, as well, and Logan showed no hesitation about spending.

He didn't return to the table when his business was complete, though. He took a few steps toward the wooden stairs at the back of the room and then glanced over his shoulder toward Caylen with a wicked grin on his face. He nodded toward the stairs, then looked back at her. To Caylen, it was an obvious challenge—he was going upstairs, and she was under orders to follow him. To everyone else, though, she knew it must look like an invitation.

Her face was burning again as she stood up, and the joyful, idiotic hooting of the soldiers didn't help. She refused to even look over at the nomads, couldn't stand the thought of them seeing her humiliation, or of having to see her mother unmoved by the entire situation, concerned only that the job was done to her exacting standards. Caylen forced herself to walk to the bottom of the stairs to join Logan, and when he slung an arm over her shoulders, she managed not to flinch away. He pulled her in close, pushing his greater weight down on her, and she didn't know what game he was playing but she just wanted it over with, and she charged up the stairs, practically dragging him behind her. Let the goons in the tavern think what they would about that.

By the time they reached the top of the stairs, Logan was in control again, guiding them down the hall to the third door on the left. He opened it to reveal a small private room, with a table and two chairs, a double bed, and a chest of drawers. A lamp burned on the table, with another on the bedside table. There was a window open to the spring breeze, and Caylen had to fight the urge to climb through it, out into the early evening air and then back to the forest, where she belonged.

Logan had let go of her as soon as they entered the room, stumbling over to collapse on the bed. She braced herself for another round of innuendo, and wondered just how much he'd been drinking—it hadn't seemed like much. A closer look cleared those ideas out of her head. The boy was pale again, weak-looking and almost fevered. He'd clearly been overexerting himself on his first day back to walking.

"You could have just said so." She knew she sounded testy, but she didn't care. He'd humiliated her just to hide his own shame. "If you needed a rest. We could have brought Connell up, and had him check you over."

"Can't." Logan's voice was weak. "Can't show weakness. We'll be back in town by tomorrow night—the men can't know I'm still recovering."

"You don't have to show them, but you could have told *me*!" She crossed over to the bed and started working his jacket off his shoulders. She needed to be sure he hadn't re-opened his wound, and that it wasn't showing any signs that the infection was taking hold. "It would be a lot easier to like you if you would just be a bit less stubborn about things. Less arrogant!"

She felt a tremor go through his body, and eased her hands away immediately, worried that she'd brushed somewhere painful. The spasm repeated itself, and she realized that he was laughing. At her. "*I* should be less stubborn? Less arrogant? *Me?*" He laughed again, and sat up enough that he was able to shed his jacket by himself. "*I* should be less stubborn, she says." He stopped laughing, and smiled at her instead. "Funny, though—for all your stubbornness and arrogance, I have no trouble liking you. I like you just fine."

Caylen refused to blush for the third time that evening, so she busied herself with checking his injury instead. It seemed to be healing well, which was a relief, because she didn't want to have to figure out a way to withdraw Connell from whatever was going on downstairs in order to get his help. Logan was almost asleep by the time she had his shirt re-buttoned, but he struggled to sit up. "I said I'd tell you about your family."

Caylen shook her head. "Sleep now. You can tell me later."

He looked like he was about to argue, but instead he relaxed back into the pillows. "There's room," he invited, gesturing feebly to the other side of the bed. Caylen thought about it. She wasn't tired beyond her ability to work, but she could use some sleep, and an attack seemed more likely later in the night, when things had quieted down below. She checked the latch on the door and then reluctantly closed the window. No one would get in without waking her up, and the bed did look comfortable.

She rolled the sleepy but tractable Logan over to the middle of the bed, then gathered the covers next to him and rolled him back so he was lying on the clean sheets. She pulled off his boots and then covered him with the blankets before extinguishing the lamp on the table and turning down the one by the bedside. Then she kicked off her own boots and circled around the bottom of the bed to climb in. She unfastened the sheathed dagger from her waistband and slid it under her pillow, one hand gripping it lightly. The sheets were smooth and cool against her cheek, and she nestled down into them. She liked sleeping in the forest, but there was no denying the appeal of the occasional night of bed rest. She glanced over at Logan, who seemed to already be fast asleep. A safe night's rest would be good for him, too. Maybe he'd be less annoying in the morning. And with that cheerful thought, she let herself drift off to sleep.

CHAPTER 13

When Caylen woke up, it was still full dark out, and something in the room was moving. She hadn't even had a chance to get alarmed before she realized that it was just Logan. "What are you doing?"

"I was trying to be quiet."

"Terrible job. What are you *doing*?"

He sighed tiredly. "I just need to find a toilet. Is that allowed?"

"End of the hall." She had noticed it when they came up the stairs. She swung her feet over the side of the bed and pulled her dagger out from under the pillow. "Stay here for a second, I'll check it out."

"Oh, come on..."

"I need to use it, too," she said. It wasn't a lie, although her need wasn't enough to have woken her up. "Isn't a gentleman required to let a lady go first?"

He shook his head in exasperation, but he stepped away from the door, making room for her to go through.

"Stay in here with the door latched—don't open it for anyone but me," she said.

"Oh, you're the jealous type, are you?"

She ignored him, easing the door open and taking a moment to listen to the hallway before slipping through the opening and pulling it closed behind her. The hall was empty, and there were no nooks or crannies for someone to hide, although of course any of the doors could open at any time. She squinted down toward the stairway and frowned. It was dark, but...

"It's me," Pim whispered. He was up in the rafters above the top of the stairs, looking down at the hallway. It was a good spot; Caylen had barely noticed him herself.

Caylen walked down the hall until she was standing directly beneath him. "Everything quiet?"

"Yup. Nothing but trips to the toilet. How's your boyfriend?"

That was almost enough to make Caylen stop being so quiet. "He's not my boyfriend! He's a job!"

"Caylen, there's a name for women who sleep with men as a job." She knew Pim was joking, but it didn't make him any less aggravating.

"Yeah, well, in my case, *sleep* is the key word. He`s still getting his strength back."

"Uh huh." Pim grinned. "Too bad for you."

"Shut up. I'm going to use the toilet, then he's coming out. Keep an eye on things for me, okay?"

Pim nodded, and Caylen proceeded to the toilet. It was one of the flush kind, the kind they had in the cities, although she wasn't quite sure of how they got the water pressure for it here—she'd seen no sign of electricity. Maybe they had a cistern, or there was a source of water uphill somewhere. There was a sink, too, with running water, and she rinsed off her face and hands. There were parts of civilization that she could get used to.

She checked the room for any hiding spots, and stuck her head out the narrow window. It wasn't large enough for a person to fit through, and there was nowhere outside that someone could use to shoot from.

She went back down the hall and tried the door to the room. It was latched, as she had ordered, and she knocked.

"What's the password?"

"Logan, stop being annoying!"

The door unlatched immediately. "Yup, that's it." He stepped jauntily into the hallway, and Caylen was forced to remind herself of the weaker, paler boy he'd been only hours before. The memory made her a little less inclined to trip him. "The way is clear?"

"It's fine." She stepped in front of him and led the way down the hall, keeping her eyes and ears open at each doorway that they passed. When they reached the door to the lavatory, she stepped aside and made what she hoped was a gallant wave of her arm. "Your throne room, sire."

It was his turn to frown and mutter as he went through the door and shut it firmly behind him. Caylen crouched down with her back to the wall and waited. She heard the toilet flush, the water run, and then the door opened and Logan appeared. "In Yorkton, we have hot running water, and public baths, and in my family's home there are rooms with showers, to rinse the water off and wash it right down the drain," he said conversationally.

"You must be very dirty people, to need all that," Caylen returned in an even tone, walking back toward the bedroom.

"Oh some of us are, Caylen. Some of us are very, very, dirty." She didn't appreciate the snickering sound she heard from the rafters by the stairs. Pim was supposed to be on her side.

She got to the door and waited for Logan to precede her inside before shutting it and hooking the latch. When she turned back around, Logan was sitting on the side of the bed, watching her. One hand was rubbing absently at his chest, where the bandage covered his stab wound.

"Leave that alone," she ordered.

"It itches." He sounded like a petulant child.

"Good. That means it's healing." She circled around to her side of the bed. "Or rotting, I suppose. So either way, it shouldn't bother you too much longer. You'll either be better or dead."

"You are really not a very nice nurse."

"I'm really not a nurse at all. But I can get Connell if you need someone to hold your hand."

Logan lay back on the bed. "Connell's no fun."

"Neither am I." She sat down and burrowed her feet in under the covers.

"Sure you are."

"No, I'm not. No fun at all." She wasn't really prepared for the playful poke in her ribs, and she squirmed away. "Stop that."

Another poke. "Stop what?"

"Are you a child? Keep your hands to yourself!"

There were a few moments of peace, and Caylen was just starting to relax into the pillows when Logan spoke again. "I can't sleep."

"Neither can I. Some dolt keeps bothering me."

She felt the bed shift as Logan rolled over onto his side, propping himself up on his elbow and staring at her. "Tell me a story."

"A story? I don't know any stories."

"Sure you do. Tell me... tell me about your scar. Jonah said you got it in Linden?"

"Yes. Linden."

He waited until it was clear that she wasn't going to continue. "Because you stole something?" She nodded, and apparently there was enough light in the room for him to see it. "What did you steal?"

She sighed. Maybe if she answered him, he'd go to sleep. "An apple. It had fallen off a cart, and I picked it up, and I started eating it, and then all hell broke loose."

"Are you serious? They did that to your face over an apple? How old were you?"

"I don't know. Little. Six or seven, maybe." She glanced over, and saw him staring at her. She shrugged. "It's not important. I barely remember it." That wasn't true. She could still almost taste the fear, panic that came not from the pain but rather from the confusion and loud noises and angry faces that had surrounded her. "They'd been having a problem with outlaws, I guess. Wanted to make an example."

"We don't do that in Yorkton." He sounded as if he really wanted her to believe him.

"No?" She rolled over on her side so she could see him more clearly. "So what's the Dark House?" There was no answer, but even in the dim light she could see his face tighten. "Jonah used it as a threat, against Sealy. Said he'd end up in the Dark House, and if he didn't talk, they'd get his daughter, too."

Finally, Logan nodded. "Yeah. That's—the Dark House, it's—well, I don't know, not for sure. I've never been inside. I think—I hope—it's just sort of a scare tactic, you know? An empty threat. If everyone believes that it's hell on Earth, then no one will ever put it to the test."

"Shouldn't you know what the truth is? I mean, if you're going to be in charge?"

Logan's laugh was short and bitter. "Well, maybe not. Maybe it's best that nobody knows, for sure. The people can believe that it's worse than it is, because that makes it more effective. And I can believe that it's not that bad, because that lets me sleep at night."

"That's really cowardly, Logan!" She was surprised to realize that she'd thought better of him. It didn't feel good to be disappointed.

He flopped over onto his back, looking at the ceiling instead of at her. "It's not that simple."

"Why not?" He didn't answer. "I mean it. If you're the heir, or whatever. Couldn't you just change it?"

"You don't understand. The city, it's not like out here. Even without being able to trust the soldiers, everything out here, it's—it's simple. Simpler, at least."

Caylen thought for a moment. "You're right. I don't understand."

He nodded, and ran a hand roughly over his face. "The last person who tried to change things—tried to make them better—he got his throat slit. Nobody knows who did it—could have been one of maybe a dozen different people. Not that any of them would have done it themselves. They wouldn't have gotten their hands dirty." He glanced at her. "Your father was a hero, Caylen. There's people in town, lots of them, who still remember him, for what he tried to do. But it didn't work. There's too many people, with too much power, who like things just the way they are."

"And you're one of them?"

"No! I'd like to see change! If they're doing horrible things in the Dark House, I'd like to be able to shut that down. I'd like to know that I could walk down the street without guards, or that I could have kids and raise them in safety. I'd like to know that the people who kiss me on the cheek and call me friend aren't plotting to kill me behind my back." He'd gradually pulled himself up to a sitting position as he spoke, but then he slumped back down. "I'd like to know that my followers aren't plotting to kill anybody else."

"If you died, what would happen?" She supposed it wasn't exactly tactful, but she wanted to understand.

"What, like, the afterlife?" She wasn't sure if he was deliberately misinterpreting her or if he was genuinely confused.

"No, like in town. Who'd be the heir, if you died?"

"Well, that question got a lot trickier a couple days ago." He glanced over at her. "Honestly? I'm not the heir anymore. You are. Your father was in the direct line, and it passes from him to you. I only got the job because nobody knew about you. And there's another cousin, from a different line, that's just as close as I am. Mara." He shook his head. "It's expected that I'll get the nod from the council, mostly because I'm male, I think, but also because...well, because of Jonah, probably. He knows everyone—everything. And he decided to be on my side."

"So, this Mara—she's okay with all this?"

Logan snorted. "She says so. I have no idea, though, not really."

"But you don't sound like you really want it. If Mara does, couldn't you give it to her?"

"What about you? You're not going to try to take it?" He didn't sound worried, just curious.

Caylen laughed. "I can't even keep track of what you're telling me here tonight. There's no way I'd be able to figure out everything in a system like that. All the secrets, and the lying—no thanks."

"There's a lot of money, too. And power. You'd never have to lift a finger again; you could just sit back and let servants take care of you."

"Is that how you live? When you're in the city?"

"Not as much as some, but..." He had the grace to look sheepish. "A little, yeah. It's what's expected."

"So what were you doing out in Nomads' Land, by yourself? Was that what was expected?"

"No." His voice was serious. "It was stupid. I was visiting one of the family estates, and I was supposed to go back by ferry, but I decided to go overland, instead. There should have been enough troops; it shouldn't have been a problem. But it wasn't the plan, and a lot of men died because of it. Because I wanted to go for a ride in the woods."

"Darton," Caylen said quietly.

"And my guards. And the nomads, or whoever they were. A lot of men."

"Jonah said he was going to try to find out who sent them. Try to get revenge."

"Revenge. That..." Logan paused, as if he wasn't sure how to continue. "That doesn't really sound like

Jonah." He rolled over to face her again, and face looked earnest. "Caylen, be a little careful of him. He's loyal to me, I think. I trust Jonah more than anyone else, really. But he's cold. He used to be different, maybe; he was your father's best friend, and he was involved in the reform attempt back then. But he's not that way anymore. Revenge takes passion. Anger. And he's too calculating for that. I like him, and sometimes he's a real friend. But for other people... if he said revenge, it might just be because that's what he thinks you'd want to hear."

"Why would he care about me? About what I want?"

"Because of your father. Because you're the true heir. He—I think he really loved your father. I believe that. It might be the last pure emotion he ever felt, for all I know. So I don't think he wants to hurt you. But—that doesn't mean that he wouldn't be willing to use you."

"Use me?" She wasn't used to the city intrigues, but it still didn't take long to figure that out. "To help you."

Logan shrugged. "I can't be sure. I just—tomorrow night, when we get to town. I don't think he's going to just let you fade back into the forest. I'm going to talk to him, make sure he knows that you're absolutely not to be harmed. Just—be alert. Be on guard."

Caylen's mind was racing. She didn't have anything to say, and she couldn't even organize her thoughts well enough to ask more questions. The whole situation was absurd, and too complicated, and the more she thought about it, the less sense it made.

Neither of them said anything more, and after a while Logan's breathing got shallow and even. Caylen lay awake until dawn, but when she finally slid her feet out of bed and stood up, she still hadn't resolved anything. She looked over at Logan, still peacefully sleeping, and she found herself really wanting to trust him. She just wasn't sure that she could.

CHAPTER 14

Connell knocked on their door early the next morning, and he assumed the guard duties under the guise of checking Logan's injuries. Caylen took advantage of her freedom, grabbing a change of clothes from her pack and giving herself a make-shift bath in the lavatory. By the time she returned to the bedroom, it was empty, so she headed down the stairs.

As soon as she appeared there was a stir from the soldiers, a murmur that turned into a buzz of smart comments directed at Logan. Obviously the soldiers hadn't lost their taste for gossip, and just as obviously Logan hadn't done anything to quell their interest. He turned toward her with an embarrassed grin that stopped short of being apologetic. The soldiers were staring at her now, waiting for a reaction, and she looked over and saw the nomads watching her too. It felt like they were judging her for giving the soldiers an excuse to talk. Her eyes found Taryn, the only one who seemed sympathetic, and when Taryn raised an eyebrow in question, Caylen knew the part she would play. She shrugged nonchalantly, and lifted her hand to wiggle it back and forth with the fingers splayed, the universal sign for mediocrity.

Taryn grinned. "Not too good, then?" she asked just loudly enough to be heard, without it being an obvious play for attention.

Caylen shrugged again. "Nice to sleep in a soft bed, for a change. That was the highlight, I'd say."

Taryn nodded in exaggerated understanding. "City boys—can't expect too much."

"Guess not." Caylen refused to let herself look at Logan or the soldiers, but she could feel the hum of approval from the nomads. The whole thing was childish, but satisfying. "How long 'til the boat?"

It turned out that the ferry was all ready; with so many passengers, it was worth the trip even without waiting for cargo. As soon as the travelers were on board, the ropes were untied and they were underway. They were going downstream, so the ferryman just had to steer them out to the deep part of the river and keep them there, letting the current do all the work. About mid-day they saw another ferry, this one fighting its way upstream, pulled by a team of horses on the shore.

Caylen spent most of the trip watching the scenery go by, and letting the ferryman teach her how to steer the boat. She wasn't exactly interested, but Nora had taught her that all knowledge was worth having, even if she couldn't foresee a situation in which she would need it. And it wasn't like she had a better way to spend her time. Jonah was acting nonchalant as he kept an informal guard over Logan, who was sitting in the bow reading a book he had pulled out of his pack. Caylen wasn't a strong reader and couldn't imagine doing it for pleasure. And with Jonah there, she wasn't needed for guard duty, so she was just as happy to stay in the stern. Logan's strange warning of the night before was still running through her mind, and she wasn't sure she wanted to be close to Jonah until she had a better idea of whether she trusted the man.

The nomads found an empty portion of deck and settled down to Pig Knuckle, a card game that involved betting in gradually increasing amounts, and it wasn't long before the soldiers got interested. Caylen knew the nomads would lose just enough to give the soldiers confidence and then start playing with their full skill; if the soldiers were stupid enough to bet money on an unfamiliar game, they deserved to be poor.

Night came earlier than expected as dark clouds rolled in from the west, blocking out the setting sun. Nora found her way to the stern of the boat to consult with the ferryman. She didn't even speak, just glanced at the clouds and then back at him.

He spat over the side of the boat. "We won't make it down tonight. I could have kept going if there was a moon, but with the clouds..."

Nora nodded as if that was what she'd expected. "I don't want us on shore. Can you anchor?"

The man peered along the river, then up at the gathering clouds. "It'll be a rougher night than you'd have on land. The river's going to rise, and if there's wind, the boat'll rock like—well, to me, it's like a cradle, puts me right out, bur for them that's not used to it, it'll be rough."

"Still, safer." Nora didn't seem inclined to change her mind, and the ferryman nodded. "Alright, then—we can string some tarps up? Over the bow, there, maybe?"

"Not 'til I've found us some moorage. I need to see. But there's room in the hold for some of you—the ladies, at least."

Nora squinted at the soldiers, then at Logan. "Maybe for the boy. He's just getting over an injury."

"And he's used to better," the ferryman supplied, winking at Caylen. She winced. The ferryman had been hinting all afternoon that he recognized Logan, but Caylen hadn't responded. But with the ferryman acting like he and Caylen were gossip-friends, Nora would surely assume that Caylen had let the secret slip. One more thing for Nora to add to her list of Caylen's failings.

Nora didn't respond to the ferryman, at least not directly. "The boy will sleep in the hold, with Connell and Jonah. Caylen, get the tarps ready to be strung once you're given the okay." With that she walked away. As so often happened, Caylen wasn't sure if Nora's allocation of labor was a punishment or not; it all depended on whether Nora thought spending time with Logan was a treat. Caylen wasn't sure how she felt about that herself, so it wasn't easy to guess Nora's view on the matter.

As soon as the ferryman found a secure mooring point, the nomads and soldiers worked together to string up canvas tarps over the front of the boat. The gunnels weren't high, and the prow didn't curve up much, so there was nowhere convenient to hang the high end of the tarps. They ended up improvising a center pole made from a long oar, braced on all sides by ropes to the gunnels, with the canvas laid over top of the ropes. It wasn't exactly luxurious, with only about six feet between the deck and the canvas at the highest point, sloping down to about three feet of clearance at the sides.

Still, cramped was better than wet, and the card-players were sitting down anyway. The work was no sooner done than they were back at the game. Caylen noticed that some of the soldiers looked like they were beginning to realize just how much they were losing; she hoped that things didn't explode while they were still all stuck on the same boat.

There was no place to make a fire to heat anything for dinner, so the travelers made do. Caylen followed Nora's orders and broke open one of their packs of nuts and dried fruit and shared it around, and everyone still had jerky. The storm broke just as the make-shift meal was finishing, and the ferryman was too afraid of fire to allow his lantern to be taken down under the tarps, so there was no light to continue the Pig Knuckle. Just as well, probably.

She found a spot near the hold door and bundled up in her blankets. Normally, she loved a good storm.

She felt like she could absorb the raw energy from the weather, making her just as wild and strong as the storm itself. But this time, stuck in a boat on the rising water, she felt vulnerable. She kept craning her neck to see over the edge of the boat, trying to catch glimpses of the land not that far distant. She didn't notice that Jonah was creeping over to her, bent almost double under the low tarp, until he was only a few feet away.

He looked at her as if for permission before settling down with his back against the gunnel, facing her. "I've been thinking, Caylen," he started. His voice was low and rumbling, and it sounded warm. It made her want to trust him. She raised an eyebrow to invite him to continue, and he obliged. "I've been trying to figure all this out. Why was Logan's original group attacked? Why was he left alive? Was that sloppy work, or was it on purpose? Why did the attacks continue?" He rubbed his hand over his silver and black beard, and shook his head. "Too many questions, and not enough answers. But I've come up with a few things I think you should know."

"Okay..." There couldn't be any harm in listening to him.

"The first thing is that I think this could mean trouble for nomads. All of them, not just your band."

"What? How are we involved?"

"Think it through, Caylen." He didn't sound impatient, like Nora usually did when Caylen took too long to catch on. This was more like Connell, walking her through a new medical procedure. And Jonah actually sat and waited for her to think about it, as if he was really interested in teaching her how to understand these things for herself.

She took a moment. "Because the attackers were dressed up as nomads? But that shouldn't matter! You can tell them—the city people, the—whoever it is—you can tell them that they weren't real nomads!"

He made a face. "I can tell them what I saw, and what I believe to be true. But I can't prove anything."

"But they can't prove anything either!"

"They don't have to. There's a significant group of people who have been trying to get support for some time now—trying to get the city to band together with other towns and tame the Wildlands. Set up safe travel corridors, at least. People want to be able to trade, without worrying about their caravans being attacked by bandits, or lost in the forest."

"So, those people...they're going to use this as an excuse?" Caylen didn't like the way this conversation was going.

"Maybe. Probably. They'll try, at least."

"And you can't stop them? Logan can't? I mean, he was the one who was attacked."

"He was the one who survived. We lost soldiers in that battle. People are going to want revenge."

Caylen thought of the bodies littering the floor of the forest, and nodded. "So, what, then? You're going to go back and tell them what happened, and they're going to ignore you when you tell them it wasn't nomads, and they're going to..." Her imagination failed her. The wilderness was vast; she'd lived in it all her life, and still rarely walked a path twice. "Who cares what they want? They can't do anything!"

But Jonah shook his head. "One town, maybe not. But all of them together? How do you make your living, now? You live off the forest, sure, but you buy things in towns, too. Where does the gold come from?"

"From...jobs. From things like this, helping you get back to town. Or from escorting caravans."

"If the cities start taking this seriously, they'll send soldiers out with the caravans. Soldiers who'll shoot any nomad on sight. So you lose your income, *and* you have to worry about being attacked in your own home territory." He leaned forward earnestly. "Not that it'll matter that you don't have gold, because you won't be able to get into any towns to spend it, anyway. Not if they say that being a nomad is illegal."

"They wouldn't. I mean...why would they? They want our trade. Our gold's as good as theirs."

"Is that how the merchants in Linden felt, when they marked your face?" He waited a moment for her to catch up to his thinking. "It's happened before, in pockets—towns have soured on nomads. Too many bandits, or just looking for someone to hate—all different reasons for it. But ask Nora. Ask her if there haven't been times when she couldn't go to a certain town. Ask her why the band doesn't go to Linden anymore. And then think about how it would be if you couldn't go to any towns at all."

Caylen considered the implications of this. The nomads could survive in the forest, but they would certainly miss the towns. No manufactured goods. No leather, even, unless they could find somewhere to stay still for long enough to tan their own hides. No ammunition for their guns. And if they were facing attacks from soldiers at the same time, they would need ammunition. She didn't believe that the Wildlands could ever be tamed, but even the attempt would hurt the nomads. "So what can you do? Can you stop them?"

His smile was sad. "Me? No."

"Logan? Can he do something?"

Jonah's smile faded, and he looked out over the edge of the gunnel toward the river raging past. When he spoke, he was quiet, and Caylen had to lean forward to hear. "I'm going to advise him to not get involved."

She thought she must have misheard. "What? Why? I mean, a war between the cities and the nomads—that wouldn't be good for the cities either, would it?"

"Good for the cities? Caylen, that's not what this is about. I don't care about the cities. They're not who I'm working for."

She frowned. "Okay—so, wouldn't it be bad for Logan too?"

Jonah shook his head. "Logan needs to solidify his power. He's the named heir, but he isn't Chancellor yet. He can't afford to take a stand against a popular idea—and, I'm sorry, Caylen, but there would be a lot of support for a war against the Nomads."

"Even if it wasn't really Nomads who attacked him?"

"Even if."

"So why are you telling me this? I mean, if there's nothing to be done? Should we not go into town, tomorrow? Do you think things will happen that fast? Have you told Nora?"

"Nora knows. She isn't stupid. She was part of this game before you were born."

"She hasn't said anything."

The statement sounded weak even to Caylen's ears, and Jonah laughed as he replied. "And she's usually so happy to share."

"So, you can't help and Logan won't—so we just let it happen?"

He leaned forward again. "That's up to you."

"Me? What do you mean? What can I do?"

"Nora's never told you anything at all about your father?" Caylen shook her head, and Jonah leaned back as if he was getting ready to tell a story. "Your father was golden. He was larger than life. Everybody loved him. I mean, there were jealousies, and power-struggles, but the people? The commonfolk? They couldn't get enough. There was almost a revolt when he was killed. If they'd known who was responsible, if there had been a target for their anger, they would have been uncontrollable. As it was, the city was on the edge of chaos for at least a year afterward. And people still remember him." Jonah paused and looked over to see if Caylen was getting his point.

She wasn't sure that she was. "You think...you think you can use that? Like—people might listen to me?" Jonah nodded slowly. "But—that's crazy! And why do you even want me in town? Logan said that I was the real heir, if you went by bloodlines. Wouldn't having me around be a threat to his claim?"

"That's what I thought when I first saw you. But...I've been watching you, Caylen. You're not interested in power, are you? You just want to be left alone, free to run around your forest in peace. I can't..." He paused as if searching for the right words. "I can't see you making a claim for the Chancellorship. And if you did try, I can't see you succeeding. You're too innocent." He gave her a quick look, and she realized that he was checking to make sure that she wasn't insulted. "Logan's been training for this his entire life, and I still have to fight to get him to do what needs to be done. No, Caylen. You're too naive to succeed on your own, and too pigheaded to let yourself be guided by someone who might be able to help you. You're not a threat to Logan, but you could be an incredibly valuable ally for him."

That was a lot to absorb, and Caylen took a moment to think. She looked over the gunnel, thinking wistfully of the forest, where she could find somewhere to hide until things made sense again. A flash of lightning illuminated the river, still raging with storm run-off, and the rocky shore. Caylen startled, and sat up to get a better look. The next flash of lightning confirmed what she'd seen, and she wheeled away from Jonah, looking for her mother.

"Nora!" A familiar head lifted itself from the deck. "There's men on shore. I don't know how many. Hiding in the rocks." Nora wasn't the only one to hear that, and there was a scramble of bodies moving toward the gunnel to get a better look.

"What now?" Nora muttered, but there was no time to answer her. As she spoke, a ripping sound came from the tarp over the bow and an arrow wobbled through, falling to the deck. It was black and dead, but Caylen could smell something acrid, and the next arrow confirmed her fear. It hit the back of the boat, where there wasn't a tarp, and it was on fire.

The ferryman scrambled to extinguish the flame, and there was a rattle of sound from the shore as guns were fired toward him. He made it to cover, and the rain put the fire out anyway. This time. But there were more arrows coming, falling fast now, all on fire, all threatening the wooden ferry. If an arrow made it through the tarp to the dry wood beneath, there would be trouble. The nomads could all swim, and probably the city people could too, but the river was flooding and wild, and even if they all made it to shore they'd be scattered— easy pickings for their attackers.

Nora seemed to have come to the same conclusion as Caylen. "Cast off!" she yelled to the ferryman.

He looked doubtful, but another flaming arrow landed near him and he saw the wisdom of her order.

"Return fire!" was Nora's next shouted order, and Caylen was happy to oblige. She felt the boat begin to move as she grabbed her bow and poked her head up over the gunnel. Most of the arrows from shore were being fired high, allowing them to rain down on the tarp, but not posing much of a threat to someone just peaking over the edge of the boat. She held her bow sideways, glad that Nora had insisted she train that way, and it allowed her to stay under cover while shooting. The lightning was almost constant now, but the men on the shore were moving, showing up in a different place each time the sky flashed. Caylen acted quickly, finding a target, aiming and firing all before the lightning faded. The wind took her shot, but she had another arrow already set and ready. She wouldn't miss again.

CHAPTER 15

Caylen felt a jolt as the boat started to move, but she kept her balance and waited for the next flash of lightning. When it came she found her target, then fired her arrow, taking the strength of the wind into consideration. It was dark again before the arrow hit, but she was confident that it had been a good shot.

The boat was moving faster now than it had during the day. The daytime current had moved them at barely more than a brisk walk; if it hadn't been for the rough terrain and the danger, they would have been better off on the shore. But now, with the river flooding, they were moving along much more quickly, and it wasn't long before the attackers were too far behind to bother shooting at any more. There were a few smoldering patches on the boat that were being attended to, but otherwise they seemed to have escaped cleanly.

"Girl! Girl, get back here!" The ferryman was standing at the back of the boat, fighting with the rudder, the storm whipping his coat around him like the dark shroud of a ghost. Caylen scampered back toward him. "You steer, I'll go up front and tell you where to go," he directed. Before he could move, though, there was a dull thudding sound, combined with a shudder that ran through the whole boat. "Damn it!" the ferryman yelled. "We hit something. You take the rudder. Keep us midstream."

Caylen obeyed, and as soon as her hands were firmly on the wooden bar the ferryman was gone, running toward the door to the hold. That afternoon, the rudder had been heavy but responsive, as long as Caylen took her time. With the storm, everything had changed, and the boat was fighting against her with quick jabs and long pulls. She had to throw all her weight into the wooden bar just to keep them relatively on course, and a few times she almost lost control. It seemed like the boat was getting heavier, less responsive, and she wasn't totally surprised when the ferryman reappeared with a grim face.

"Huge chunk of the hull's torn away—can't patch it." He peered anxiously into the darkness. "We need to find somewhere to land. I'm going up to the bow. Whatever I do with my arm, you do with the rudder."

And with that, he was off. Caylen thought briefly about the damage to the boat, and whether there was any chance that the city would compensate him for it. If not, he was just one more person whose life had been ruined by this whole mess. But she didn't have time to worry about it, not with the rudder dragging her half-way across the deck every time the foundering boat hit a new eddy or current.

Once the ferryman was in place, it wasn't too difficult to follow his directions, although the current had picked up to the point where the message from the rudder was more of a suggestion than an order. He had her steer to the inside of a bend and stay close to shore, and when they'd made their way around the corner, he jerked his arm hard toward the outside and Caylen mirrored the movement with the rudder. Within seconds there was a grinding sound and the boat slowed, leaning over precariously to the side. They'd hit a sandbar, right next to a gently sloping area on the shore.

"Let's go, move it!" the ferryman yelled, and no one was inclined to argue with him. Connell was the first to jump. The boat was slanted toward the middle of the river so the shore-side gunnel was high in the air, but Connell pulled himself over it and let himself drop into the water below. It was about waist deep where he landed, and he staggered a bit before beginning to fight his way out of the landing area. He had barely started off before others were jumping off the boat and splashing into the water. It wasn't organized, but it wasn't exactly a panic, either.

Nora was clinging to the gunnel, watching everyone as they jumped, and Jonah shepherded Logan up to the railing. Caylen realized that his injury had probably reduced the strength of his arms, so this was a bit tougher for him than for the others. Still, he made it over the edge. Caylen didn't have a job to do now that they were aground, so she headed for the edge and looked below to make sure she wasn't going to jump on top of anyone. Logan was still close to the boat, as was one of the soldiers. Logan was starting toward shore, but there was something strange about the soldier. He seemed to be focused more on Logan than on the situation in general. Caylen was ready to think that he was just being overprotective until she a flash of lightning glinted off the exposed blade in the soldier's hand. He took a big step toward Logan, his dagger pulled back ready to strike, and Caylen heaved herself over the edge of the boat and dropped.

She landed half on the soldier, half on Logan, and for a horrible moment she thought she might have driven the blade toward Logan instead of away, but then he was sputtering and swearing and dragging himself to his feet in an un-injured manner. The soldier took a little longer to get up, and Caylen was careful to keep herself between him and his intended target.

Nora was there almost instantly, as was Jonah, both of them dropping in unison into the water. The ferryman was the last off the boat, but he stayed well clear of the skirmish.

"He had a knife," Caylen said quickly. "He was attacking Logan."

The soldier's eyes widened and he stared at her, and then at Jonah. "What? That's crazy! I was just wading ashore." He sounded so surprised, so convincing, that Caylen had to replay the incident in her mind. Was there any chance that she'd seen something else? Had she made a mistake?

"I saw it." Ellis, the soldier who'd almost come to blows with Nora about being relegated to the outer circle of guard duty, was standing in the shallows. Caylen braced herself for an accusation, but then she noticed that Ellis was looking at the other soldier with a hurt, confused expression. "I saw the knife." Ellis stepped closer, frowning toward his colleague. "Why? He's the heir, we're sworn to protect him..."

"You're both crazy! I don't know what you saw, but it wasn't a knife." The soldier took a step backward, but he was jammed up against the hull of the boat and had nowhere left to go.

"Show us your belt knife, please." Logan sounded almost hopeful, but Caylen saw his eyes darken when the soldier didn't immediately respond.

"He must have dropped it when I hit him," Caylen said. The water was dark and muddy, and even in their sheltered spot the current was fairly strong. "It could be anywhere."

"It's not where it belongs, though," Nora said. "It should be in his belt. There was no need to have a knife drawn in order to jump off a boat." She turned to Jonah. "This is your problem. The most recent price involved a boat ride; if you want us to walk you down the shore, we'll have to renegotiate."

"Nora!" Jonah sounded shocked, and almost disappointed. "There are larger issues at stake here."

"They're your issues. Not mine, and not my band's." She nodded Caylen toward Logan. "You're back on guard duty, for now at least."

Jonah and Ellis were dealing with the attacking soldier, tying his hands and dragging him to shore. Logan just stood in the water and watched it happen. He didn't even seem to notice that he was shivering.

Caylen checked her pack; it was waxed canvas, not waterproof but close, and its exposure to the water didn't seem to have gotten it more than externally damp. Logan's pack was leather, and might have made it through a brief dunking, but he was holding it limply in his left hand, almost completely submerged.

"Let's get on land. We'll see if we can borrow something dry for you." If Logan heard her, he showed no sign, so she grabbed his pack and slung it over her own shoulder, then shoved him toward the shore. He stumbled, but caught himself and kept going.

Once they were on dry land, she ran her fingers firmly over his torso. "Did he get you? I thought he went to the side..."

Logan caught her hands. "I'm fine." He shook his head. "Sorry. Just..." He let his voice trail off, then took a deep breath, and seemed to control his shivering by power of will. "Right. Something dry." The leather pack over Caylen's shoulder was still shedding its load of water. Obviously its contents wouldn't be much help.

"I've got a tunic you can borrow—it fits really loose on me." Caylen dropped his pack and started working the drawstring open on hers. She found the tunic she was looking for, and handed it to Logan before she pulled out her other spare. It was ratty and in need of a cleaning, but it would be warmer than the one she had on. She found her extra pair of leggings, too. Her boots were soaked, of course, but they were her only pair, so she'd have to make do.

She re-bundled her pack and straightened up to find that Logan was still standing there, staring at the tunic in his hands. He was shivering again. "Logan! Let's go. If you're not injured, you need to pull it together!"

"My men are trying to kill me," he said quietly, and he sounded like a lost little boy. Caylen thought for a second about how she'd feel if her band of nomads ever turned on her, but she really couldn't imagine it. And she didn't think they had the luxury of allowing Logan to spend much more time with his thoughts. She made her voice brisk. "Seems like. A couple of them, at least." She reached over and shook the tunic in his hands. "Now, let's go. No servants to undress you out here—you'll have to be a big boy and do it yourself."

His frown of annoyance was reassuring, and she turned her back long enough to strip off her wet tunic and replace it with dry with at least a pretense of modesty. She glanced over to see him working his wet shirt over his head before she started on her leggings. By the time she was changed and had her boots back on, he seemed to have snapped out of whatever state he'd fallen into, and was rubbing his arms absentmindedly, trying to warm up.

Connell wandered over and supplied Logan with a spare pair of leggings, and then everyone just waited around for orders. Nora and Jonah were speaking intensely but at low volume near the shore, and when they finally came back to the group, they instantly had everyone's attention.

"We're going to make a run for it," Nora announced. "We'll move fast, get down to the shore opposite the city and ferry across." She was talking loudly enough that everyone could hear, but she was obviously addressing herself just to the nomads. "Get the boy back to his castle and be done with him."

Logan barely seemed to notice her dismissive tone, but Caylen wondered about it. Prior to this, Nora hadn't shown much interest in him, but she hadn't seemed hostile, either. There was no time for discussion, though. As soon as Nora had made her decision known, there was a scramble for packs and then Nora was deciding on the formation for travel.

"Caylen, you're on point—keep it moving, but don't get too far ahead."

"What about watching Logan?"

"Follow the orders you're given. I'll take care of him."

That didn't sound too promising, but Caylen knew better than to ask any more questions, and she trotted out along the shore. She'd seen the map at the Rock Ferry docks, and while she didn't know exactly where they were, she knew that the river flowed southeast in a fairly straight line—she'd stick to the shore when she could manage it, and go by her sense of direction when she couldn't.

They started off at a fast pace, slowed only slightly by the necessity of dragging the tied soldier along with them. Caylen mentally calculated the head start they had on their attackers, and was confident that they'd be able to stay ahead. Even if the followers managed to catch up, they'd be on the other side of the river, and it was still flowing too fast to allow a crossing. So they weren't much of a threat. Caylen let herself slip back into the spirit of the forest, alert for anything unnatural. They might have evaded the most recent attackers, but that didn't mean they were altogether out of danger. And judging by the stories Caylen was hearing about the treachery in the city, it seemed unlikely that they'd be any safer inside the city walls than they were outside.

The rain let up with the dawn, and the combination of less water and more light allowed the group to move even faster. Everyone was well-rested after the day on the boat, but Caylen still found herself worrying about Logan. He had seemed reluctant to admit to weakness in front of his men, the other night in the inn—she hoped he wasn't feeling pressured to overexert himself. She was tempted to slow down a little, to give him a chance to rest, but then thought better of it. The whole point of this mad rush was to get him to safety, after all.

By mid-morning they were into the rough pasture land, the area of cultivation that was allowed to exist at the greatest distance from the city. Raiders or invaders couldn't do much to hurt pasture, and the animals were easily moved into town in times of danger.

Once they were out of the forest the risk of ambush diminished greatly, and Caylen fell back to walk with the main group, following a rough track that was gradually turning into a bit of a road. They were all moving smoothly, easily, although the ferryman looked as if he was about to drop from exhaustion. It felt natural for Caylen to fall in next to Logan, and once she had given him a quick look to ensure that he didn't seem to be overworking, she let her natural curiosity take charge.

"Where are the goats?"

Logan looked surprised by the question, so she elaborated. "I've seen cows, and sheep, and horses, and I smelled pigs. But I don't see any goats."

"Uh, no. We don't raise goats."

"Why not? Most towns do; they're really good on scrubby land."

Logan watched her for a second and then smiled wryly. "Well, that's probably why we don't. Goats...in Yorkton, they're seen as something that poor people would eat. I guess we want to show how rich we are. Our land is all good enough that it can support the other animals."

"Really?" Caylen thought about. "Too bad. I like goats' milk better than cows'. And the meat's pretty good, too."

"Well, we'll have to see if we can't find you one, then." Logan's tone was casual, but Caylen didn't miss the way he was watching her for a reaction. She deliberately didn't give one, and after a few steps he started talking again. "We could get you a horse, too. Do you know how to ride?"

Okay, time to react. "Logan, what are you talking about? We're dropping you off on the shore. I don't think I need to start collecting a barn full of animals!"

"What if you didn't drop me off?" He was watching her closely now, and not paying much attention to where he was going. Caylen wished she could find a tree and try to get him to walk into the trunk. But there were no convenient obstacles, and Logan continued. "You could come into town with us, and stay for a while."

"Why would I do that? I already said I wasn't interested in your stupid Chancellorship, and if I was, why would you be trying to get me to go for it?"

"No, I know you're not interested. But...you've saved my life several times on this trip, you know. And I'll be safer in the city, but still not exactly secure. Not until the Chancellorship is actually declared, and that won't be for some time yet."

"For some time? What does that mean? Who declares it?" It was a bit of a deflection from the main topic, but Caylen was curious.

"Lord Wiltern. Our great-grandfather. He's the Chancellor now, but he's old, and looking to retire. The problem is, he won't declare an heir, not for certain, until things are calm. But things won't calm down as long as there's still all this fuss about who the heir is."

"Wait a second. I thought you already were the heir?"

Logan's face colored a little. "Yeah, uh...well, that's what my side says. If you ask Mara's side, they say *she's* the heir. Both sides just...you know, they talk as if it's a sure thing, but it really isn't."

"Huh." Caylen thought for a while. "But if you don't even know when he's going to declare it—you just want me to be your bodyguard forever? I mean, how long are we talking, here?"

"Well, you know." Logan looked awkward again. "I don't really need another bodyguard. I've got..." He frowned. "Well, I guess I need to look at the loyalty issues. But if I check on everyone's families, and make sure that I'm surrounded by supporters, I should be okay."

"Yeah, you've lost me. If you don't need a bodyguard, what would I be doing there?"

Logan's pace slowed. Caylen didn't want to fall behind the group, but she couldn't leave Logan alone, so she matched her stride to his. He shot her a quick look and then stared at his feet as he started talking. "Okay, well, Jonah's got one idea, but, you know, that's just him. I would...I mean, I see his point, and I can see how advantageous it would be, but I absolutely don't expect you to go along with it. Although if you were interested, it would be the best thing, really. And I promised him that I would at least raise the idea with you. Just...you know, just in case you would possibly be interested."

Caylen stopped walking altogether, and turned to her companion in exasperation. "Logan, what on Earth are you talking about?"

Logan's blush deepened, and he took a half-step toward her, glanced furtively at the group of travelers that was still walking away from them, and then back at Caylen. When he spoke, his voice was oddly formal. "Lady Caylen of the Nomads' Land—would you do me the honor of becoming my wife?"

CHAPTER 16

Caylen had never been proposed to before, and she wasn't sure of the proper rules for the situation. She was pretty sure they didn't involve quite as much laughing as she was doing. She'd started walking again as soon as Logan had managed to get the question out, and she was fine as long as she didn't look at him, but it was hard not to look, with his face such an interesting scarlet color, and every time she glanced over she started giggling again.

Finally, he got up enough nerve to object. "That's really rude, you know."

She nodded her head emphatically. "I know. It's shocking, really, how poorly raised I am. It'll be quite a trial to you when we're married!" And that set her off again, not just giggling, but full laughs.

"I'll have you know that I am considered the most eligible bachelor in Yorkton! In the entire region, even!"

"Oh, I'm sure you are. Really."

"I am."

"I *know* you are." If she'd had any reason to believe that he had real feelings for her, she might have felt bad about the teasing, but as it was, she was enjoying herself.

They walked in silence for a while, and the next time Caylen glanced over, Logan's face was back to its regular color.

He saw her look. "So, that's a 'no', then?"

Another little giggle escaped, but she managed to keep herself under control. "Of course it's a 'no', Logan. What were you thinking?"

"Okay, in my defense, I was thinking that you'd say 'no'. I didn't think you'd laugh quite that much, though." He seemed to be regaining his composure. "But, okay, not marriage. Still, it'd be useful if you came to town. If you seemed to be on my side."

"I don't understand how that would help."

"I told you, your father was well-loved. By the people, and by his grandfather. Lord Wiltern."

"So you think that having me on your side will make it more likely that you'll be named heir?"

"Absolutely. I mean, we'll have to be a bit careful. Try to clean you up a little, and, you know...probably not put you in too many situations where you need to talk."

"What's wrong with the way I talk?"

"There's nothing wrong with the *way* you talk. It's the things you say that could get us in trouble."

"Like what?"

"Like everything!"

"You're just mad because I won't marry you." That was going to be useful ammunition for quite a while, Caylen mused. Then she realized that if she didn't go along with at least some part of Logan's crazy plan, there wouldn't be many more opportunities to tease him. The thought affected her more than she would have expected.

She could see the walls of the city on the far side of the river, and see the boats ferrying across to the farmland on their side. It wouldn't be long before the nomads and the city dwellers would be separating.

"It could be useful for you, too, you know. I wouldn't have suggested it if I thought there was nothing in it for you." Logan seemed serious. But maybe not quite... not quite normal.

"What? How could it be good for me to marry you?"

"No, not the marriage. Forget that. I told Jonah I'd ask, so I asked. That's all." He sounded impatient. "I meant it could be good for you to come to town for a while."

"How do you figure?"

"Jonah said he told you about the attitudes toward nomads. About how people have just been looking for an excuse to start something?" Caylen nodded, and Logan continued. "So, you could come in and speak for your people. Some random nomad wouldn't get much attention, but Lord Willem's daughter? They'd hear you, for sure."

"I thought I wasn't trusted to speak. And if I *did* talk, what would I say?"

"We could help you with that. Coach you. But, you know, basically you'd just explain the situation. You'd be a character witness, sort of. And a diplomat." And Caylen realized why Logan sounded unnatural to her. It sounded like his words were rehearsed. Or maybe like they'd been supplied by someone else. She looked around for Jonah, and found him walking with Connell, one on either side of the bound prisoner.

Caylen didn't want to start making accusations, so she tried to address the content of Logan's words. "Come on. I'm not good at that sort of stuff."

"You weren't a good cook, either, but you made a good meal the other night." He saw her look of surprise, and smiled. "You're smart, and you're stubborn. You rise to challenges. Seriously, Caylen—I think you'd be fine."

She almost felt bad about the giggling and suspicion, after that. Almost.

"And Jonah was serious about trying to find out who's behind the attacks. So if you still want to know who killed your friend, you might want to be involved."

Her hand fell to the dagger in her belt. She might not be confident in her aptitude for diplomacy, but she had no doubts about her ability to use the knife. If only she knew who to use it on. "So I'd go with you to the city, and I'd support your claim, and in return you'd help me calm people down about the nomads, and Jonah would help me find out who sent the people who killed Dart?"

Logan nodded. "Everybody wins."

Somehow, Caylen doubted that was true. "But what about the rest of the band? What would they do in town?"

Logan grimaced. "I can't stop them from coming, but I wouldn't recommend it. You could be there a while, and bored nomads in a town that already distrusts them...it's asking for trouble."

Caylen's thoughts ground to a halt. She had dreamed about separating from the band, sometimes, usually when she was so angry at Nora that she believed she'd have to leave in order to keep herself from committing matricide. But it had always been a quick, emotional impulse, never the calm, rational thing that Logan seemed to be suggesting. It made the idea seem much more real, and much more frightening. Who was she, if not a member of Nora's band?

Logan gave her a funny look. "It's really that much of a problem? I left my family when I was five years old."

"Well, *you*. They were probably glad to be rid of *you*." It was easier to pick on Logan than to confront her own feelings, so she didn't hold back. "*My* people would actually miss me if I was gone." He didn't bother to respond.

They were approaching the landing, now, walking through another cluster of rough buildings, and being stared at by the locals. Nobody seemed to recognize Logan, but that wasn't too surprising, Caylen decided. He was wearing rough, ill-fitting clothes, his stubble had grown into the beginnings of a beard, and neither his soldiers nor the nomads were treating him with much deference. The imprisoned soldier was drawing significantly more interest than the disguised heir. *Possible* heir, Caylen reminded herself.

Jonah fell back to walk next to his young charge, and Caylen covered his other side, but there was no real risk, as far as she could see. Just farmers and lumbermen and fishers, busily sending their goods across the river to the city.

The river was wide and slow here, and the boats were flat-bottomed, able to be pulled right up on shore for loading. There was a long loop of cable strung across the water, slipping through a huge pulley on the near side and then running back over to the city. Caylen couldn't see how it was driven, but it seemed to be moving in an endless cycle, with the boats clipping on to one strand and being pulled over to the city, then unclipping while they were unloaded at the dock before attaching themselves to the opposite strand and being pulled back for reloading. It looked efficient, but tedious.

When they reached the landing, Jonah moved forward to speak to the pilot of one of the barges. Nora was already organizing the nomads. Caylen had assumed that they would be seeing Logan all the way home, but apparently that wasn't the plan. That was strange—with all the scavenging they'd done, they were carrying more guns than they had ammunition for, so it only made sense to go into town to trade. And Nora usually liked to look for jobs in each town they got near—they didn't earn anything just wandering around, so where were they off to in such a hurry? But Nora wanted them ready to go as soon as Logan stepped foot on the boat. It didn't leave Caylen much time to make up her mind, and there was no opportunity to speak to Nora in private.

Caylen could tell that Logan was watching her as she stepped forward toward her mother. "Nora? Uh...I was thinking maybe I'd go into the city for a bit."

Nora barely looked at her, but Caylen could see a slight tightening around her mouth. "No, we're moving right on."

Caylen knew she shouldn't, but she pressed on. "Jonah and Logan—they were saying that there could be trouble. Because of the imitation nomads. They said that the cities might end up looking for revenge."

Nora still wouldn't look at her. "The cities are none of our business."

"And Darton," Caylen continued. "Someone from the city probably sent those men. Jonah said he'd find out who." She knew that Connell was listening now, and some of the others. There was no way Nora would back down in front of an audience, but Caylen had a pretty strong feeling that there was no way she would have backed down anyway.

Nora was angry, now. "'Jonah says' and 'Logan says'...well, here's what *Nora* says: we're leaving as soon as the boat's in the water. And since you have so much extra energy for arguing, why don't you help Connell out? Carry his pack."

Somehow, it was the old punishment that made the difference. It was supposed to be Darton's pack that Caylen carried, but it couldn't be, because he was dead, and Nora didn't even care about trying to find his killers. The word was out of Caylen's mouth before she even thought it through. "No."

Nora froze, and so did all the other nomads. Caylen had never said that to her mother before; she'd never heard anyone else in the band say it, either. There was a moment of brittle silence, and then Nora's voice was clear and strong. "Nomads, get ready to move. Connell, you're on point. Pim, bring up the rear, make sure nobody's following us." She took one deep breath, and then she spoke with less volume but even more intensity. "Caylen, get your pack on and get moving."

Caylen's mind was racing in random circles, but she couldn't stick to a clear thought. All she knew was that she had a good point, and Nora wasn't even listening to her. "No, wait. We need to figure this out. If we can get revenge for Dart, *and* keep the cities from causing trouble for nomads..."

"Caylen, *now*. No more talk."

Her hands ached to reach for her pack, conditioned by too many years of obedience, but she kept herself strong, and stood straight. "No."

Finally, Nora looked at her, and Caylen wished that she hadn't. It was easier to think of her mother as being angry, being stubborn or even cruel. It was harder to realize that the expression in Nora's eyes was hurt. Caylen tried once more. "We could just camp nearby, or even go into town, and we could talk about it, try to figure out what to do. Logan and Jonah..."

Nora turned away abruptly. "Nomads, move out."

Connell's mouth was open, as if he wanted to intercede but had no idea what to say. "Nora..." he started, but Nora ignored him and strode forward to take the point position herself.

Connell turned to Caylen. "Caylen, come with us. We'll wait 'til she calms down, and we'll figure something out."

"But as soon as the soldiers get to town, they're going to start talking about the attacks—people will get angry, and whoever killed Dart will have time to cover his tracks." Connell took a reluctant few steps backward, his eyes still locked on Caylen even as he moved away from her. This was all happening much too fast, and Caylen felt unbalanced and lost. But she clung to one idea. "Connell, I have to try..."

He looked torn, casting a look over his shoulder toward Nora, who was resolutely marching away. The other nomads were following her in stunned silence, although they were casting long looks over their shoulders as if hoping that Caylen would suddenly decide to rejoin them. Connell dug frantically into his pack and pulled out his bag of coins, and stepped forward to press it into Caylen's hands. "Okay. Yeah. You take care of it. Then you find us. She'll be glad to have you back."

Caylen wasn't so sure about that, and she wasn't sure about taking Connell's gold. "This is yours, Connell..."

"Yeah, it is, and I'm giving it to you. I'll leave messages for you at the inns—you know the ones." He was walking backward again. "And we'll check in if we're in the area." There was a catch in his voice, and then a stir behind him. Caylen looked over his shoulder to see Nora striding back toward them, looking fierce. Connell stepped aside, and Nora filled the space. Caylen braced for a blow, but it didn't come.

Instead, Nora grabbed her shoulders. "You're a nomad. Don't forget that." Caylen tried to speak, to explain that this wasn't about her trying not to be a nomad, but Nora didn't give her the chance. "You're not strong like they are. If you go toe-to-toe with them, you'll lose." That stung. Caylen had hoped that her mother had a bit more faith in her. But Nora continued. "So you don't fight their way—you fight yours. You're quick, so you dodge. You're unknown, so you use the element of surprise. And you're tough, so you outlast." Nora took a deep breath, with just a little jag in it. "They can't hit you because by the time they know where you are, you're somewhere else. They can't catch up, because they can't predict your actions. And they can't wear you down, because you never quit. Let them see your weakness, and they won't expect your strength." Caylen nodded, trying to keep the tears in her eyes from spilling over. Nora gave her a hard look, and then stepped back. "You're a nomad," she repeated quietly. "Don't forget that."

"I won't," Caylen promised, and maybe she was crying a little, but Nora's eyes weren't quite dry either.

Nora nodded, and then abruptly turned away. She strode away again, and this time, she didn't turn back.

END OF PART ONE

DARK HOUSES PART TWO

CHAPTER 17

Nobody talked to Caylen as they were ferried across the river. Logan stood beside her, and that was nice, she supposed, but he was Logan, not Connell. In the forest, she'd begun to think of him almost as a friend, but now that he was in his own environment, he seemed like a stranger again.

They drew close to the dock on the far side of the river, and Caylen could hear the sound of whatever machinery powered the tow cables. It was a low thrum, strangely menacing, and it made her wish for the cheerful, lighter sounds of her familiar forest.

She had refused to look behind her while there was a chance that the nomads would still be in sight; she'd been afraid that if she saw them, she'd run after them, dive into the river and *swim* after them if she had to. But she turned now, and she felt more alone, there in a crowd of people, than she ever had on any of her solitary trips through the forest. She felt her chest start to tighten and she looked away quickly, back toward the city. She would absolutely not cry in front of these strangers. She needed to get her mind back on business.

"So, I guess I need to find an inn, right?" Nora had generally tried to keep Caylen out of the towns they had visited, so she wasn't sure of the rules, but she was pretty sure she wouldn't be allowed to camp out, not in the city.

Logan shook his head. "It would be better for you to stay in the guest apartments, near the Great Hall. Better security, and more—appropriate."

"Are they expensive? I have some coin, but not a lot." Caylen was beginning to think this whole adventure had been poorly thought out. Who was she, to be living alone in a city? It made no sense.

"You'll be a guest of Yorkton," Jonah said, his voice firm. "There will be no cost."

Caylen didn't know how to feel about that. Nora had always said that only the forest gave things for free; what was it that Jonah, or Yorkton, would expect from her in exchange for accepting their hospitality?

The boat was tied to the dock now, and Logan sprung agilely to the wooden walkway. He extended a hand to help Caylen, but she had watched how he'd managed the trip and duplicated his effort almost as smoothly.

He shook his head. "It wouldn't kill you to take a courtesy from me, now that we're in town. People will be watching, and we want them to think you like me."

"What's liking you got to do with getting out of boat? I like you fine—doesn't mean I need your help."

He seemed genuinely surprised for a moment but recovered quickly. "You like me fine? Since when?"

"Well, maybe that was a bit of an exaggeration." She looked up the dock toward the city. They were outside the wall, still, at the foot of a road so steep it had to wind back and forth along the hillside in order to be passable. There were wagons making the trip, pulled by teams of great draft horses, and a few smaller carts pulled by lighter horses or mules. The animals were working hard, their heads low and spiritless, and Caylen wondered if they did the same thing all day every day, up and down the same hill, endlessly. Maybe that's what life in the city was like: safer, but not easier. Freedom given up in exchange for security.

Logan seemed to understand that she needed some time to absorb her new environment, and he didn't press her to continue their conversation. Instead, he walked beside her, offering a quiet commentary as they proceeded up the hill.

"This is the River Gate. Most of the city's food passes through here. There are two other gates, the Forest Gate and the Hill Gate. Not the most original names, I know." She could feel him glancing over, checking on her, but she didn't really have a response. "The walls are interesting, maybe—most of them are from the Time Before, although we've repaired them extensively, and added in parts. One of Yorkton's great strengths is its defenses. And we have food stores for over a year inside the walls, so we've withstood many sieges."

That caught Caylen's interest. "When? Who's attacked you?"

"Uh...well, it's been a while, actually." Logan sounded like he was realizing the truth of his words even as he spoke. "The last real attack was before I was born. But there have been raids on the farmlands, outside the walls. And one of the biggest reasons that no one attacks the city is because they know they wouldn't succeed."

Caylen nodded. She knew that conflicts weren't uncommon between the smaller cities, although from what she'd seen, even those tended to be based around raids and small skirmishes rather than full-scale warfare. Everyone seemed a little too safe and happy behind their walls to want to venture out into the Wildlands and march against one of their neighbors. She briefly toyed with that as an argument in favor of leaving the Wildlands alone—were the nomads a sort of buffer against the aggressions of the neighboring towns? She'd have to remember that, and think about it more later. Maybe she should mention it to Jonah, and see what he thought.

They reached the top of the hill, where the wall stretched out in both directions, and guards armed with pikes and swords stood on either side of the heavy wooden gates. There were slots in the wall above the gateway, and Caylen thought she could make out movement behind the openings. Archers, she supposed, or even gunmen. Apparently Yorkton was prepared for trouble, even if it rarely came.

The carts were being waved through the gates with only a cursory review by the guards, but individual travelers were being questioned more closely. As soon as Jonah and the soldiers arrived, there was a buzz of interest; apparently the party was finally being recognized.

"Lord Jonah," one of the guards said. "Welcome home." His eyes ran quickly over the company until they came to rest on Logan's battered, lightly-bearded face. "Lord Logan." The guard still had a trace of doubt in his voice, but he seemed satisfied when Logan moved forward. "Welcome home, sir. We've been hoping you would make it back safely."

"Unfortunately, not all of your colleagues shared your hopes," Jonah said, and he nodded toward the imprisoned soldier. "Have someone take him to the Magistrate in the Great Hall. I'll be down shortly to make a statement."

The guard's eyes widened slightly, but there was no other sign of surprise as he gestured two of his men toward the prisoner. Jonah continued talking to the guard. "This is Lord Logan's guest, Lady Caylen, daughter of the late Lord Willem, great-grandaughter of the Lord Chancellor."

Caylen wasn't sure why she was being introduced to the guard, but was happy to have something to distract her from the sight of the prisoner as he was bustled away. She was the one who'd stopped him; in a way, she was the one who had caught him. Did that mean that she was responsible for what happened to him now? She thought about the Dark House, and what Logan had hinted at about the place. She didn't want to be any part of sending someone there. "What if he's like the first one—like Sealy? Maybe he was forced to do it..."

Jonah frowned at her, then started walking, forcing her to move in order to keep up. "He tried to kill the heir. His motives are important, because then maybe we can try to figure out who's behind all this. But in terms of his punishment—it shouldn't matter. We've got to make it clear that anyone who attempts to harm Logan will be dealt with harshly." He paused as if thinking. "I shouldn't have let Sealy go. It was a mistake."

Caylen didn't have a response to that, but she shook her head emphatically. She couldn't put her objection into words, but that didn't mean she agreed. Jonah seemed to be done with the conversation, though, ordering his remaining men into a formation surrounding Logan. Caylen was a little surprised to find herself on the inside of the protective lines, walking beside Logan as if she were something special. The streets were crowded, and it was nice to have some protection from the jostling, she supposed. Men in work clothes, women in long, colorful skirts and blouses, and children scampering around amongst them—they all stepped aside and made space for the soldiers. Caylen didn't really enjoy the sensation, especially as she was shorter than most of the soldiers and had to strain in order to peer past them. She didn't care how good their intentions might be, she still thought she'd be safer and happier if she was able to see what was happening and look after herself.

She didn't make a fuss, though, and Logan resumed his commentary on the city as they walked. "That's the market square, over there—full markets once a week, and a few shops set up around the edges that are open every day. And those are the traders' inns, along that side—they're busy on market days, but pretty empty the rest of the time." Caylen nodded and followed his gestures with her eyes. She might not like her new setting, but she should learn about it, she supposed. Nora had always taught her that all information was potentially valuable. She caught herself before she thought any more about her mother and the rest of the nomads.

"Down that way are most of the craftsmiths—tools, weapons, that sort of thing. You can buy little stuff from them in the market or some of the shops, but if you want something special, you should go straight to the source." That sounded right to Caylen—the nomads were in town so rarely that they didn't often hit market days, but even if they had, Caylen was pretty sure Nora preferred to deal directly with the person who'd made whatever she was buying. Liked to see the shop, and the tools that had been used. "We're going right into the heart of the city—there's another big square up here, just outside the Great Hall, and that's where the guest apartments are. It's one of the two parts of town that have electricity wired into the buildings." Logan sounded proud. Caylen had seen electricity work a few times, and she had to admit that it was impressive, but she didn't really see how it would be safe to have it sent into buildings. She'd have to wait and see, she supposed.

They were approaching another set of gates, perpendicular to the road they were on. There was no free-standing wall to go with them, but they were attached to the buildings on either side of the street, making a barrier almost as effective as the larger gates on the outside of the city. And there were guards here, too, armed with pikes and pistols, staring forbiddingly at the   townsfolk   walking   by.

Jonah marched the soldiers right up to the gates before ordering them to halt, and the front two soldiers stepped to the side to open a space for Logan and Caylen to move forward through. Logan walked casually toward the guard who was wearing a slightly more ornate uniform than the others, and nodded. "Captain."

The captain gave a sharp salute. "Lord Logan. Welcome home."

"Thank you." Logan nodded toward Caylen. "This is Lady Caylen, daughter of the late Lord Willem, great-granddaughter of the Lord Chancellor. She'll be a guest of the city for the foreseeable future, and will be welcome at all times at my family estate. Please extend her every courtesy."

Caylen tried to appear calm as the captain swiveled his head to look at her. The surprise at her identity was obvious in his face, although he still seemed respectful. "Of course, my lord. And welcome home to you too, my lady. Your journey has been even longer than Lord Logan's, it seems."

Caylen wasn't sure how to react to that—it seemed laughable that anyone would think of this place as being her home, but she doubted that was the response the captain was looking for. "Thank you," she managed.

The captain's smile was kind, as if he recognized her bashfulness for what it was. And maybe Logan was looking out for her, too, or at least didn't want her to embarrass him with any blunders. He half turned away from her and spoke to the Captain again. "We'll cut through The Estates. These soldiers have been marching hard through the night; I'd like to send them to their well-earned beds. Can you arrange for an escort to meet us at the far gates?" Caylen noticed that Logan had spoken his praise of the soldiers loud enough for them to hear, and she approved. The loyalty of a few might be questionable, but that didn't mean that they were *all* corrupt, and they'd worked hard to keep him safe.

"Of course, Lord Logan." The Captain turned to the soldiers as if to dismiss them, but then Jonah spoke up.

"Actually, I think we may need to delay their rest a little longer." He glanced over toward Logan as if looking for approval; Caylen could honestly not tell if it was a pre-arranged charade or not. "I'm sorry, Lord Logan, but with your permission—we need to address some of what took place in the Wildlands. These men need to be questioned." He looked toward the soldiers and his expression softened. "It's not a question of us doubting the loyalty of any among you. But we need to get accurate accounts of what happened, and that will go most smoothly if we debrief you now, while things are still fresh in your minds." He turned back to Logan. "With your permission and with the cooperation of the City Guards—I'd like to have the men sequestered until we can speak to each of them individually."

The Captain looked as if he didn't fully understand, but he didn't object, either. "Lord Logan? Is this your wish?"

Logan looked toward his soldiers, and sighed. "I'm sorry, men. I know you're tired. We'll have you put up somewhere comfortable, and you can rest while you're waiting. And we'll have food sent in—and drink, if we keep you that long. Captain, you can arrange this?" The Captain nodded, and the men looked resigned rather than rebellious. Logan spoke in quieter tones to Jonah. "If you can, please accompany Lady Caylen and me to the apartments; you and I can visit the Chancellor together, once she's settled."

Jonah nodded. "Of course, Lord Logan." There was no hint of the casual affection that Caylen had seen between the two men in the forest; apparently in town, at least in public, they were more formal with each other. She didn't think she liked it.

The Captain gave a few curt orders, and then the soldiers were on the move. Caylen stood for a moment, watching them march away. They hadn't exactly been friends, but at least they'd been familiar faces, and she felt even more alone now that they were gone. She hadn't realized how close Logan was standing until he nudged her shoulder with his. "You okay?"

She forced herself to nod. "Yeah, of course. Tired, I guess. So, what's next?"

"We get you somewhere you can rest." He smiled gently, as if he knew that it wasn't just fatigue that was draining her usual energy.

And then Logan was leading her through the gates, with Jonah falling in on her other side. Caylen turned her head to look back at the guards.

"No soldiers allowed inside the walls of the Estates," Jonah explained.

Logan shook his head in amused disgust. "It's supposed to be symbolic of how much the Families all trust each other. But really it's just so we have one less weapon to try to kill each other with."

Jonah didn't disagree. "The Families have never seemed to have trouble making do with the remaining options."

"The Families?" Caylen looked around her at the large stone buildings set back from the road behind huge fences and expanses of closely cropped lawn. Surely the buildings were too large to be homes—they were bigger than most inns Caylen had seen. And more walls—how many walls did these people need to hide behind before they could feel safe?

"The Families," Logan said. "Technically there are eight Founding Families, descendants of the people who first set up a settlement here, after the Dark Times. Or maybe they stayed here right through the Dark Times—nobody seems too sure about that. But they made Yorkton what it is, one way or the other." He sounded like he was reciting a lesson he'd heard too often. "They've all intermarried so much that there's not really any point in talking about separate lines anymore, so they're just 'The Families.'"

"'They'? Aren't you one of them?" Caylen asked.

"Well, okay, 'we'. And that means you, too, not just me." Logan glanced over at the man walking on her far side. "Not Jonah, though. He's a commoner, I'm afraid." There was a teasing affection in his voice, and Caylen wondered, not for the first time, about the relationship between the two men. Jonah's loyalty to Logan seemed firm, as did Logan's trust in Jonah. It was one of the few things that made Caylen think she might actually like Jonah. Or fear him.

"But you said you were raised with my father? You were living with them?"

Jonah nodded, and there was a hint of the same gentle teasing in his voice as he explained—the content was for Caylen, but the tone was clearly for Logan. "The Families like to pretend that they're the only citizens with any power or any history, but my family's been around almost as long. And while the Families were busy in the foreground, fighting each other and trying to gain power, my family was working away behind them. Watching and listening, and making money. So now we know everything about everybody, and we own half the town. One of the things that gave Lord Wiltern the edge in his own quest for the Chancellorship was his relationship with my family, and his access to our gold." Jonah seemed more relaxed, here behind the walls, and he reached over and grasped the back of Logan's neck, giving the younger man a gentle shake. "And don't you forget it, young Logan. My people aren't kings, but we're kingmakers."

Logan didn't argue. "Kingbreakers, too," he said quietly.

Jonah looked startled, then a little sad. "Sometimes," he admitted.

Most of the conversation dealt with things beyond Caylen's knowledge, hinting at history that she wasn't sure she even wanted to know. When Logan and Jonah paused in front of one of the great houses, she stopped as well. There were two huge oak trees on either side of the walkway, and she had to fight the urge to scramble up the trunk of the nearest one, looking for a safe nest. Instead, she stood silently as Logan looked toward the house, and then over at Jonah.

"The gate runners must have been here by now," he said quietly. Caylen had seen several boys sprinting away from the main gate as the party had entered the city; apparently they'd had a job to do. "They'll be wondering about me."

Caylen assumed this was Logan's house; she wasn't sure who 'they' were, but she didn't think she really needed to know. "If you just give me directions, I'm sure I can find my way. I don't need a guide."

Logan looked like he wasn't sure whether to be amused or annoyed. "Really? So you'll just march in and demand accommodations? Looking like you do? Knowing nobody?" He shook his head. "You were in charge when we were in the forest; now it's the city, and it's time to follow *my* lead."

Caylen didn't like the sound of that. "Your *lead*? You're standing in the street, trying to decide I-don't-know-what. I really wouldn't call that *leading*."

For a split second, Caylen saw what looked like genuine hurt on Logan's face, and she was just starting to regret her words when his arrogant, annoying smile returned. "My apologies, Lady Caylen. It was not my intention to keep you from your well-earned rest. Please, allow me." He made a gallant half-bow and extended his arm in the direction that they'd been taking earlier.

Caylen didn't like being made fun of, but she had no idea what to do about it. In the forest, she would have ignored him, and done things her way, but in the city— she had to admit, she needed his guidance. She was tempted to quit. She could make her way back to the gate without any problems, and if she hurried, she could have Nora's band tracked and caught up with before night fall.

At which point she'd have to admit that Nora had been right, and beg for her forgiveness. There was no way Caylen was ready to do that; she'd rather stay in the city and tolerate Logan's mockery. She refused to look at him, refused to see the smugness that she was sure he was oozing. Instead, she started walking, doing her best to seem calm and determined.

Jonah and Logan fell in on either side of her, but they didn't try to restart their conversation, and Caylen was happy to be silent. In only a few minutes they crested a small hill and saw another set of gates in front of them. Just like the others, these were set into the walls of the buildings on either side of the road, and Caylen could see soldiers on guard just past the iron bars.

Logan greeted the four soldiers that presented themselves as he came through the gate. "You're our guards? Excellent. It shouldn't be a long trip, just over to the guest apartments. And then I guess I'll need you to walk me back here." Logan didn't seem too impressed with the situation, and Caylen remembered what he'd said about having to have body guards with him in the city. She wondered if it was really safer than being alone, considering the loyalty problems that had plagued him in the forest. But these men seemed to have been sent at random, so maybe there hadn't been time for his enemies to reach them. Still, it seemed like an unnecessary risk.

"Logan, honestly—if you need to go see to your family, that's fine. If Jonah can't take me, maybe you could just send a message with the guards."

Caylen saw Jonah's subtle head shake, but Logan hadn't needed it, and was already speaking. "You saw me through the forest, Caylen; the least I can do is walk you to your quarters."

But she didn't think she wanted to play that game, not with Logan. "And if a lot of people see you with me, that's not exactly a problem, I guess. I mean, you were careful to announce who I was, at both gates—now you need to make it clear that I'm on your side, right?"

Logan did her the courtesy of only looking a little surprised. "Welcome to the city, Caylen," he said softly, and he made another gracious bow and guided her down the crowded street.

CHAPTER 18

The rooms Caylen was shown to were grander than anything she'd ever seen, at least up close. When Logan had apologized for their modest dimensions, she'd thought he was making fun of her again, but he'd seemed sincere, for once. He'd hurried to show her the electric lamps, and the hot running water in the bathroom, as if it was important to him that she approve, and she was pretty sure she'd managed to hide how overwhelmed she was by it all. By the time he got around to explaining how she could use the knob on the tubes by the wall to adjust the room's heating, she was more or less back to herself.

She nodded to the gracious stone fireplace that took up most of one wall in the sitting area. "Does that not work, then?"

Logan frowned. "Well, I'm sure it works. We can have wood brought up for it, if you like. But using the radiator is easier. The water's all heated at a central location, and then piped all over the city. It's very efficient."

"*All* over the city?" Caylen was genuinely curious; she'd noticed that Logan seemed to be fairly ready to allow himself to see the pleasant aspects of the town and ignore the unpleasant.

And it looked like she'd caught him again. He said, "Well, not *all* over, I guess. It goes to the Town Hall, and here, and to the Chancellor's Residence, and..."

"To the Families, right? So the hot water's piped to all the *important* parts of the city." She didn't bother putting any sarcasm into her voice; she knew he'd pick up on it without her help.

He frowned. "Fine. It goes to all the important parts. Because I don't think anyone but me or mine is important. I get it."

Caylen was gearing up for her reply when Jonah stepped between them. "Maybe we could all use a rest. Caylen, are you fine if we leave you here? There are runners downstairs that you can send to find either of us, if you need us, and they can also bring any meals to you, or anything else you might need. It's best if you don't venture out on your own, right now—it might not be safe."

"You want me to stay inside? For how long?" Caylen asked. She didn't want to be a nuisance, but she had come to town for a reason. And just the thought of being trapped in the apartment made her skin crawl. It made her think that Logan had been right, when he'd said how small the space was. "You said that people were going to start talking about attacking nomads as soon as the news got out. And the longer we wait, the more time the people who killed Darton will have to hide their tracks."

"I'll make sure that things are set in motion before I go home," Jonah reassured. "The Chancellor's office is just across the square, so Logan and I can stop in there on our way. And the soldiers that were with us in the forest are isolated, at least for now. That will buy us a little time."

"So I didn't have to come at all? I could have..." Caylen stopped. She didn't want to say what she could have done, didn't want to think about being in the forest with the nomads, safe and secure and at home.

"No, we do need you," Logan protested. "You just need to be well-rested, and prepared. And we need to have a plan. Think of us as scouting ahead, while you hang back and reserve your strength." He sounded sincere and smiled reassuringly, their squabbling forgotten.

Caylen nodded reluctantly. "So I'll stay here. I'll sleep, maybe. And you'll come back and get me? When?"

Jonah and Logan exchanged a look; she got the feeling that they hadn't planned quite this far in advance. Finally, Jonah said, "It's already mid-afternoon. By the time we meet with the Chancellor, and Logan sees his mother, it'll be time for dinner. And it's important that Logan be seen out and about, and healthy. Ideally you'd accompany him, but you haven't got the clothes for anything like that, not yet." He gave her a quick look from head to toe, then shook his head. "We'll have to do something about that."

Then he turned back to Logan. "And we need to get you seen by a city doctor." He raised a hand to wave off Caylen's objection. "Just to confirm the excellent care that he received in the forest." He paused for thought, and Caylen realized just how tired he looked. She might have felt at home and safe in the forest, but it must have been a strain for him, especially with the added worries he'd had heaped upon him. And now that he was home, and trying to get things organized, he had to find a way to deal with the petulant nomad he'd agreed to help.

"Okay. I won't go out alone. You'll come back for me in the morning, though?"

"Absolutely." Jonah's smile was warm, and seemed sincere.

"We'll ask the steward to send up dinner for you, if you like. And you understand the way the water works in the bath room, right?" Logan sounded solicitous, rather than patronizing; it was a nice change.

"Yes, I understand. Are you telling me that I should get cleaned up?"

Logan grinned. "It wouldn't hurt. I'll ask them to send up a robe, or something—we'll need to get you measured for most of your wardrobe, but I'm sure they can find something that's *about* your size. And they can take away your nomad clothes." He saw the look on her face and hurried to add, "Just for cleaning! They'll bring them back."

"I'm not going to start wearing skirts all the time, not like the women I saw in the streets. I'm not going to do that, Logan."

Logan didn't have time to respond before Jonah jumped in. "Let's save that fight for tomorrow, shall we?" He reached out and gripped Logan's shoulder, turning the younger man gently toward the door. "For now, we have work to do, and you need to get some rest before you go out tonight. You're starting to look grey."

"I'll be fine, Jonah," Logan said, but he didn't fight his mentor's guidance, and spoke over his shoulder to Caylen. "We'll see you tomorrow morning, then. Sleep well."

And then they were gone, the door shut behind them, and Caylen was alone in the apartment. It felt cold, but she didn't think it was something that would be helped by her turning the knob on the water tubes. She hugged her arms around herself and looked through the open doorway into the bedroom. The bed was huge, with white pillows and a crisp white blanket. She bet the sheets were white, too. There was no way she was going to lie on that, not in her current state. But she was reluctant to bathe. It was stupid, but she didn't like the idea of washing away all traces of her old life. Her fingers found her scar, and it was comforting, at least; no amount of water would ever erase that reminder.

She took one last look at the bed, and then unlashed her blankets from her pack. Logan wasn't coming back until the next morning, so he wouldn't be able to laugh at her. She laid the blankets out on the cold stone floor in front of the fireplace, then lay down on them and let her tired body fall into a light sleep.

CHAPTER 19

The sharp knock on the door startled Caylen awake. She could tell by the sun that was still streaming in through the tall, narrow windows that she hadn't been asleep for long. Maybe someone was bringing her the dinner or the robe that Logan had promised, she decided, and she rose easily to her feet. She kicked the blankets over toward her pack on her way to the door.

She hadn't bothered with any of the locks earlier, so she just turned the door knob and pulled. As soon as she did, she was pretty sure that her visitor wasn't bringing her food. The woman standing in front of her was young, maybe no older than Caylen herself, but she was dressed finely, a fitted blue jacket over a dress a few shades lighter, with a floor-sweeping skirt covered in tiny, dark blue embroidery. Her hair was coiled elegantly up, the ends nesting in a tiny scrap of a hat that was the same blue suede as the jacket. And her face was beautiful, angular and delicate, with a smile that didn't falter as she took in Caylen's ragged appearance. It took Caylen a moment to even notice the three women that stood behind the first. They were dressed more plainly, and were carrying cloth-wrapped bundles. And beyond them, two young men in uniforms stood waiting.

"Lady Caylen?" the woman asked, her voice light and controlled. "I'm Lady Mara—I hope you don't mind me dropping by without an invitation, but I've been told that we're family, and I was very eager to meet you." She waited, and Caylen scrambled to regain her composure.

"Oh! Hi! I mean, hello." That wasn't a great start, but she fought through it. "I—Logan mentioned you, yes. I'm still not totally clear on all the family stuff, but I guess if you're his cousin, and he's my cousin—second cousin, I guess—I guess that means we're related?" Caylen wasn't sure that was exactly true, but she was pretty sure that Logan had said that all three of them had the same great-grandfather.

"I believe so, yes." Mara's smile was still in place, and still pleasant. "Do you have time to visit now? Or..." She turned to gesture to the women behind her. "I've brought my seamstresses, if you're interested. I thought you might like a few new outfits, for your time in the city. Although now that I see you..." she looked critically at Caylen, who tried not to shy away. "I think you may fit into my clothes. You're a little more petite, but it's less trouble for them to turn up a hem than to create a whole new dress." Mara stepped back. "But I'm being presumptuous, and family or not, I should be more polite. Would it be better if I came back at another time?"

Caylen was bewildered. This elegant creature wanted to spend time with her? Was acting as if it would be a privilege? "Oh, no, now's good. It's fine." She had no idea how to proceed. "You can—would you like to come in?"

"Thank you." Caylen stepped aside and Mara glided through the doorway, her seamstresses following in her wake. Mara spoke quietly to one of them, and she obediently turned and headed back out the door, which Caylen still hadn't closed. "I've sent her to get some of my clothes. You can try them on, and see if they suit you."

Caylen thought of the bag of coins that Connell had given her. It had seemed like a small fortune at the time, but she had a sinking feeling that it wouldn't be enough to pay for even one dress as finely made as the one Mara was wearing. "I couldn't—I'm watching what I spend..."

For the first time, Mara looked surprised. "Oh, sweetie, no, of course I wouldn't *sell* them to you. I just— we're family. I hoped you'd accept them as a gift. Well, they're hand-me-downs, so I wouldn't want you to think of *them* as a gift—the *new* outfits would be my gift. The clothes I've sent for—they're just a loan, until you're set up properly." She smiled. "Besides, if you're really Lord Willem's daughter..." she caught herself. "Which, of course, you are... then you're entitled to money from his family. I'm not really sure how it's been distributed, but I'm sure there's still *some* that hasn't been spent."

She stopped talking for a moment, and gave Caylen a chance to absorb at least a little of the information. But she started again before Caylen was quite re-balanced. "I know it's presumptuous, but apparently that's my way, this afternoon... You don't have any servants here with you, and I'm sure you're in need of some pampering. Would you let me draw you a bath? You can soak, and relax, and then when my girl gets back, we can try the clothes on and maybe you'll let me play with your hair? And a little make-up? Then we could go out and I could show you around. You must not like being cooped up inside like this, not after all the freedom out in the forest."

Caylen wasn't sure about the first part of the plan, but she absolutely liked the sound of the second part. She'd told Logan and Jonah that she wouldn't go out *alone*, but she hadn't even thought about the possibility of going out with someone else, and apparently they hadn't either.

If a bath and some fussing was what it took to get her outside, it was a small price to pay. "That sounds good. Thanks." Another wave of shyness swept over her. "If you have the time, I mean."

"Of course I have the time. It'll be fun!" Mara started toward the bathroom decisively. "Come! It won't take me long to get the bath ready."

Caylen followed obediently. She wasn't sure just what was expected of her; she knew that people in some of the towns were very modest about nudity, but that didn't seem to be the case here. Was she expected to just strip down and hop in the tub? She didn't really care, for herself; the nomads lived so communally that she had never really developed any shyness about her body. She just wanted to do what was proper.

Mara didn't seem to even notice Caylen's hesitation, but she dealt with it anyhow. "I'll just get the water ready for you," she explained, "and then you can have some privacy. I'm sure you could do it all without me, but there's just something so decadent about being waited on, isn't there? And it makes me feel good, too, to be able to feel like I'm helping out." Her smile was bright and innocent. "Here, I'll make it quite hot—is that to your liking? You can adjust the temperature with these knobs—this gives you more hot, this more cold. And we have this lovely oil." She pulled a glass bottle out of one of the baskets carried by her servants, and Caylen had to fight back a painful memory of Connell's medicine jar. Mara's bottle was more delicate, but it was almost the same color of glass.

"Hot is fine." Caylen had no idea if that was true, but at least it was something to say. "Thank you."

Mara waved her fingers under the running water and then straightened, apparently satisfied with the temperature. She poured a generous portion of the oil into the tub, and soon the steam that filled the bathroom was scented with something sweet and delicate. It suited Mara, but Caylen couldn't imagine herself being perfumed that way.

"So, you have a lovely soak." Mara moved toward the door. "Take as long as you like; we can entertain ourselves."

The whole thing seemed surreal, but once Mara left, Caylen stripped down and stepped into the tub. It was scalding for someone used to bathing in lakes and rivers, but she forced herself to stay in it, and scrubbed away at her skin with the cloth that she'd found hanging on the wall. She only hoped that she was putting it to its intended purpose. A few hours earlier, she'd been walking through the countryside, free and independent; now, she was sitting in a too-hot bath, washing away all traces of her former life while some sort of city princess waited for her in the other room. Her life was changing too quickly for her to keep up.

Once her body was clean, Caylen emptied the tub and wrapped herself in one of the large towels Mara had pointed out to her. She had the tub partially refilled when there was a knock on the door. "Come in," she called, and dumped her dirty clothes into the tub.

Mara entered, and stared. "We --" She collected herself, and smiled. "You don't need to do that yourself. We can send the clothes out for cleaning."

"Logan mentioned that." Caylen couldn't explain it, but she didn't want her nomad clothes to go too far. They were one of the few links to her old life, and she didn't want to lose track of them. "But this is fine. They can just soak for a while."

Mara looked dubious, but didn't press the issue. "If you prefer." She brightened. "Come out to the main room, and I'll do your hair, if you like."

Caylen wasn't at all sure that she did like, but she followed anyway. It was sort of soothing, to have Mara fussing around her and making all the decisions. It made Caylen feel like a child, she supposed, but at least she was a child with a solicitous, gentle parent. So she let herself relax, and listened with half her attention to the quiet chatter of the women while they combed through the knots in her tightly curled hair, smeared creams and potions on her face, and finally laced her into the elaborate dress that one of the servants had quickly hemmed to Caylen's length. "We chose one with split skirts," Mara explained. "We thought you might be more comfortable with it, to start with. Women here wear split skirts or trousers to ride, but otherwise we generally wear skirts—you'll get used to them in no time, I'm sure. And you're feet are smaller than mine, so I couldn't loan you any shoes, but try this pair, for now. They're not perfect, but they'll mostly be hidden."

It was hard to bend over with the tight jacket, but Caylen managed, and pushed her feet into the supplied shoes. The leather was soft and flexible, and they would have been the most comfortable footwear Caylen had ever worn, if it wasn't for their heels. She could see that they weren't as high as the shoes worn by Mara, or even by her servants, but it was still more than she was used to.

"Maybe I could wear my own boots?" she suggested, but even as she spoke she knew what the response would be.

"Oh, no, these shoes are lovely! And they go so nicely with the skirt. Besides, you're so athletic and balanced—I'm sure you'll have no trouble with the heels." Mara smiled encouragingly, and then tugged on Caylen's arm. "Come look at yourself in the glass—you'll be amazed, I'm sure."

And Caylen was. The girl looking back at her was almost completely unfamiliar. Her golden-brown skin was the same, she supposed, but even that... she leaned forward and brought her hand to her face.

Mara saw her gesture and smiled. "It wasn't hard to cover it up. There was barely any texture to it—just a little discoloration, really. Your skin's dark—lovely and dark, so exotic—so it was hard to find a cream that matched, but my girl is excellent, isn't she? I'll leave the jar here for you, and you can use it whenever you like. We all have a few scars and blemishes—unfortunate that yours is so prominent, but..." she waved her hands grandiosely and laughed. "No match for my skills, apparently!"

Caylen felt unbalanced, as if her scar wasn't just hidden, but gone, and as if the loss of its weight was throwing her off. But then she saw Mara moving toward the door, and the promise of getting outside distracted her from her thoughts. She was tempted to take her bow with her, but knew that Mara wouldn't approve. At least she had Dart's dagger, although she'd had to tie it around her ankle in a way that would make it hard to access quickly.

"We have some time before dark," Mara said. "I thought maybe I could take you on a quick tour of the city, and then we could go to the Gallery, and have something to eat there." The tour sounded excellent, and so did the idea of food, so Caylen didn't worry too much about what 'the Gallery' might be.

They headed downstairs, Caylen walking more slowly than usual in her new shoes, and found six city guards waiting for them. Mara swept past them as if they were invisible, and they fell in easily around her. The front doors of the building were wide enough that the party could exit without really changing position, and Mara linked her arm through Caylen's. "I was told that you've just arrived, so I assume you haven't seen too much, yet? How unfortunate of Logan, to have left you without a guide. I suppose his adventures in the wilderness must have worn his manners right away." A quick squeeze of Caylen's arm, and then Mara continued. "But I'm happy to help. That's the Great Hall, over there. I suppose you may be spending some time there..." She frowned as if just realizing that she wasn't fully informed. "Or maybe you won't be. I'm sorry, Caylen, but I don't think I know—are you planning to take part in public life, here in the city, or are you more inclined to remain a private citizen?"

"I don't really know what that means. I just—I want to make sure that people leave the nomads alone, and I want to find out who was responsible for—I want to know who was attacking Logan in the forest." Her goals sounded childishly simple, here in the great city. She might as well have said that she wanted to find a new doll. But Mara was nodding in understanding.

"Of course. You're a sort of ambassador, really." She frowned. "It's a bit awkward, though—with your links to the Families, you're one of us, but you're representing someone else's interests. I'm not really sure how that will be seen." She smiled and nodded at a well-dressed man they were passing, then returned to her conversation. "We'll have to think about that, a little." She waved one elegant hand at the building they were in front of. "This is the library. We have thousands of books there; some are antiques, from the Time Before. Of course, the originals of those are behind glass, but we've had many of them typeset and re-printed. We'll need to register you so you can borrow items."

"And that building?" Caylen pointed across the street. The black iron gates were closed, and the stone walls were high, but Caylen could see a tidy gravel courtyard and an imposing, windowless building, made of the same cold stone as the walls.

"That's the Office of Intelligence Services," Mara said. "They do important work there, but it can be— unpleasant. People don't often discuss it in polite company."

"The Office of...I thought you were going to say that it was the Dark House."

Mara's delicate features creased, and for the first time, she looked displeased with Caylen. "People who call it that are being disrespectful. It's easy to criticize things when they aren't fully understood." She waited only a moment before allowing her easy smile to return. "But that's not a pleasant topic. Come, down this street— there are some beautiful shops."

And so the tour continued. Most of the city was marvelous. Mara was a skilled guide, steering them carefully through busy streets, finding just the right angles from which to view the monuments, and even allowing Caylen a moment to peek inside the city museum, where the treasures from the Time Before immediately had her thinking of Darton. He would have loved to spend time there. Caylen was able to get her bearings fairly quickly, and took note of a few areas that she'd like to return to on her own. By the time they came to a stop in front of yet another large stone building, Caylen's feet were sore from the heels and the poorly fitted shoes, but she felt much more comfortable in her new, temporary home.

"This is the Gallery," Maya explained. "It's for the Families, although a few of the wealthier private citizens have bought access for themselves, as well. It's somewhere we can go to meet casually, away from prying eyes, and without the pressures of entertaining in our homes. Logan really should have at least brought you here, but no matter—I'm happy to make the introductions. They always have the best food in the city, and they're very good about sending monthly bills, instead of insisting on payment at the end of the meal, as some of the inns do." She led the way up the broad stairs. At the top, there were several clusters of guards, obviously waiting for people inside. Mara's own escort opened the door for her and then moved to join their colleagues as Mara and Caylen went inside. "We consider the Gallery to be an extension of the Estates," Mara explained, "so no guards are allowed in. Not that they'd be needed, of course." She smiled reassuringly, as if she thought that Caylen might be nervous without protection.

Caylen followed Mara down an opulent hallway lit by electric lights, and then through a set of double doors that were opened for them by uniformed footmen. There was a quiet buzz of genteel conversation, but that stopped abruptly as soon as Mara and Caylen appeared. Mara didn't seem surprised as all eyes in the room turned toward them. "Good evening, everyone." Her voice didn't seem strained, but it was loud enough to carry to all corners of the room. "It's lovely to see you all here. Please, allow me to present a new addition to our happy families—" She stepped slightly to the side, directing the attention of the room toward Caylen. "Lady Caylen, apparent daughter of Lord Willem, Great-grandaughter of our beloved Chancellor, Lord Wiltern," and she paused again, just long enough to wrap her arm around Caylen's shoulders, "My long-lost second cousin! I know everyone will make her welcome."

The conversations started again, louder this time, and Mara smiled warmly. "We'll get you something to eat—making them wait a while will just make it all the sweeter when I *do* let them talk to you."

"When *you* do?" Caylen asked. She didn't want to be ungrateful, but maybe she needed to get a few things straight, here. "I appreciate the time you've taken, showing me around. And the clothes are—well, they're not altogether comfortable, but they're beautiful, really. But, Mara, I can decide for myself who to talk to."

Mara looked crestfallen. "Of course you can. I just thought I could help. Because you don't know anybody, yet. I'm sorry—I guess I got a little carried away."

The guilt came quickly. "No, it was kind of you to offer. I just—well, you know. I'm a nomad. I'm independent."

"Well, you're not really a nomad," Mara said, and before Caylen could correct her, the wave of interested citizens reached them, and Caylen was dragged under. Everyone seemed friendly enough, but they were somehow—hard. Sharp. They made Caylen feel as if she were being assessed, evaluated and found wanting. Their conversation was quick and clever, filled with references that she couldn't begin to understand, and she knew that she was coming across as slow. She was a country bumpkin, an ignorant nomad, and the only reason they were taking any interest in her was because of some accident of her ancestry, some blood tie that meant nothing in Caylen's world, and apparently meant everything here.

She tried to focus on the people she was meeting, tried to remember faces, names—anything. But it wasn't long before they all blurred together, and she began to wish she'd taken advantage of Mara's offer of protection and guidance. There were too many people, too much noise, everyone staring at her and talking to her and wanting her attention. She didn't notice the gentle tug on her arm, at first, but then Mara leaned in closer and brought her hand from Caylen arm to her shoulder. "Shall I steal you away, now?" she asked quietly, her mouth close to Caylen's ear. "There are private rooms where we can dine, and then if you'd like to come back out, you can."

Caylen nodded gratefully, and Mara smiled at her, then at the others in the room. She didn't seem to raise her voice, but as soon as she spoke, everyone paid attention. "Caylen and I still haven't had our dinner; I'm afraid we're going to have to leave you all, for a while. It's only her first day in Yorkton—I know you'll understand if I sneak her away after our meal, to give her a little well-earned rest."

Another charming smile from Mara and the audience drifted away, obedient if reluctant. Caylen took her first deep breath in far too long.

Her sense of relief didn't last, though. As Mara turned and began to guide them toward a side hallway, Caylen's eye was caught by two new arrivals. It was wonderful to spot familiar faces, but neither Logan nor Jonah seemed happy to see her. They didn't seem happy at all.

CHAPTER 20

Caylen spent that night sleeping on the floor. She had drifted off with the memory of Logan's face, tight and disappointed, staring at her, and she woke to a similar thought. She was torn between resentment and guilt. It wasn't as if she owed him anything. After all, she'd saved his life, multiple times; just because the nomads had been paid for their services didn't mean that he shouldn't be grateful to her. And she'd come to the city for her own reasons, not to help him with his power-grab, so he shouldn't have expected her to act like his obedient servant, waiting all locked-up in her room until it suited him to use her. And she hadn't done anything wrong; she'd just looked around the city and met a few people. He was out of his mind if he thought she owed him anything, including loyalty. So why couldn't she control the tight churning in her stomach, the near-nausea as she remembered the way he'd stared and then turned away for a moment before turning back with a careful, friendly smile on his face. A mask on his face, with her, just like the ones he had to wear with everybody else.

She pushed herself up from her bedding with a disgusted grunt. It wasn't like her, to worry about stupid things like this. She just had too much free time on her hands. She needed to find a way to get busy, and distract herself from worrying about actions that she couldn't take back. Not that she was sure she *wanted* to take them back, but...

No. No more of that. She padded to the bathroom and used the flush toilet almost as a matter of routine; amazing how quickly she was adjusting. Still, she clung to some of her old ways, and washed her face with cold water, even though she easily could have added warm from the tap. Then she spent a little time scrubbing the clothes that she'd left soaking the night before, and found a way to hang them up on the open windows to let them dry. And that was it. She had nothing else to do. The day stretched out before her, seemingly endless.

There had been talk, the day before, of Johan and Logan coming to get her for breakfast. But that had been before... before the incident that she wasn't thinking about. Mara had said that they should go to the library, which hadn't really excited Caylen, but at least it would be something to do.

But it wasn't what she *should* be doing, she reminded herself. She was in town for a reason, and it didn't involve sightseeing. And if Logan and Jonah weren't going to help her, then she'd just have to do it herself.

She pulled her spare tunic and leggings out of her pack and dressed quickly, then slid her feet into her comfortable, worn boots. She thought about the guards who always seemed to be waiting in the foyer, and poked her head out the open window and peered below her. She was on the third floor—too far to jump, but the stone walls were rough, and there was an assortment of shrubs below, so her fall would be broken if she slipped...

It was worth the risk. The guards were friendly enough, but she wanted to be alone. She slung her bow over her shoulder, checked her dagger, and eased her way out the window. She worked her way down the wall, slowly and smoothly. Pim was the climber in the nomad group, and he'd taught her well.

She reached the ground without any problems; if it came down to it, she was pretty sure she could travel back up the wall by the same route. Of course, that meant that others might be able to make *their* way up, too; she'd have to remember to stay on her guard, and not fall into the trap that these city people seemed to be stuck in, believing that their walls somehow made them safe.

It was still early, and the streets weren't crowded. Even at that, she saw more people in the first five minutes than she'd usually see in a week, but at least there was room to move. She followed her nose to an inn, the smells of food making her mouth water. She hadn't eaten much the night before, not with Logan sitting there beside Mara, the two of them working so hard to each be nicer to Caylen than the other, even though neither of them would have given her more than a disinterested glance if her father had been someone different. It had been enough to kill her normally enthusiastic appetite.

It took a moment for Caylen's eyes to adjust from the bright morning sunlight to the gloom inside the inn; apparently electric lights hadn't made it to this part of town. Once she could see, she decided that the place looked a bit worn, but clean enough, and her nose was still sending messages of approval, so she found a seat at the end of a long central table, nodding politely to the three burly men sitting in the middle, obviously grabbing a meal before heading off to work for the day.

"Breakfast?" a woman called across the room, and Caylen nodded enthusiastically.

"Yes, please."

The woman squinted at her and took a couple steps closer. "You have coin, right?" She jerked her head in the direction of a straggly looking blonde girl wiping down an empty table. "Because I've already got one 'customer' working off a meal she couldn't pay for—I don't need another."

"No, I have coin." Caylen tried to make her smile convincing, but when that didn't work, she pulled Connell's bag of coins out and fished around until she found a small one. She had no idea what a meal would cost; on the rare occasions that the nomads ate at inns, Nora paid, and it was always for a whole group, not just one person. But surely it couldn't be *that* expensive, and the woman seemed satisfied with what she saw.

"Just checking," she said.

"Like you wouldn't have fed her anyway, Taz." It was one of the burly workmen, his rough face creased into a kind smile as he looked at the woman, and then at Caylen. "She's the biggest softy in the district."

Taz had quickly filled a tray with food and bustled over to set it in front of Caylen. "Well, she could have had *this*," she said, as she placed a huge bowl of oatmeal on the table, "but she wouldn't have gotten my bacon. And no syrup for the oatmeal..." She raised a small jug above Caylen's bowl, her eyebrow raised in a question, and Caylen smiled. She wasn't sure what the syrup was, but if she was paying for it, she wanted as much of it as she was allowed.

Taz poured and then trotted back over to her work area, where she kept an eye and ear on the patrons while she cooked. Caylen kept herself busy with her food initially, but when she finally looked up, she saw the kindly workman watching her.

He smiled again. "You're new to town?"

She nodded and swallowed her mouthful of oatmeal. "Just got in yesterday. It's a pretty big place."

"The biggest city I've ever seen," he agreed. "'Course, I was born and raised here, so I haven't seen much of anywhere. You have the look of a traveler, though..."

The question was clear, even if it sounded like a comment, and Caylen had no intention of hiding herself. "I'm a nomad. Just here for some business."

The man nodded, slow and thoughtful. "You want some advice?" he asked in a way that made it seem like it would be just fine if Caylen declined. When she shrugged agreement, instead, he said, "You might want to be quiet about that. There's some people who are a bit heated up, lately, and they might be looking for trouble. They might think that a nomad, all alone—and a pretty girl, at that—they might see you as a target." He took a thoughtful sip of whatever was in his mug, and watched to see her reaction. "There's no point in looking for trouble, is there?"

"Well—I don't know." She hadn't gotten any concrete suggestions from Logan or Jonah, and Mara hadn't been any better. Maybe this man could help her out. "That's actually one of the reasons I'm here. I was told that there might be trouble, and I thought maybe I could do something to head it off." It sounded impossibly arrogant, to think that she had any chance of making a difference. "I—I couldn't just do nothing."

"Probably safest to keep your head down, sweetie." It was Taz, who had been drawn away from her stove by their conversation. "It's bad times. The whole city's tense, just waiting for an excuse."

"Because the chancellor hasn't named an heir?" It was a shot in the dark, but she wanted to keep the conversation going, and get as much information as she could.

There was a snort from a small table along the side of the room, and Caylen turned to see the old man who'd been eating his breakfast there looking straight at her. "An heir? Who cares about that? How does it matter to us who sits on the big chair? This Chancellor seemed good enough for a while, but now he's the one sitting there while the Dark House swallows our children, chases whole families into hiding! One heir or another," he said, his voice warbling with disgust. "They're all the same."

Caylen wasn't prepared for the almost violent reaction from the other occupants of the room. The burly man jerked his head back to look over his shoulder, and Taz took a threatening step toward the old man. "You be quiet, Pa! You know better!"

He sneered at her. "What are they going to do to me, at my age? How many years do I have left? If they kill me, it's no big loss. I've been quiet too long, watching all this. Maybe it's time for the old to speak up, since we have nothing to be afraid of."

"You don't fear death, maybe," the workman said, "but that's not the worst they can do to you, and you know it."

"The Dark House," Taz said quietly, and her rosy face was somber. "They'd have you *praying* for death, if they got you in there." She took another threatening step in his direction. "And don't you forget, they don't just take those that caused the problem! They'll take family too, and anyone who happens to be nearby. How many houses are going to be dark tonight, with no one left inside to light the lamps?" She looked over at Caylen. "We follow the rules in this Inn. We aren't looking for trouble."

Caylen looked over at the old man, but he was quiet now, looking down at his bowl. All the fight seemed to have drained out of him.

"You all finished, here?" Taz asked Caylen, and the message was clear. It was time to pay up and go. She handed her coin over, and Taz looked at it critically and then reached into a jar behind the counter. She pulled out two carved wooden tokens and handed them to Caylen. "It's three meals for a copper coin. You can bring these back with you and trade them in for lunch or dinner, if you want. And if you're looking for somewhere to stay, you can trade in one of them for a bed in the common room." Apparently the sight of the coin had made her a bit more hospitable toward her nomad customer. She gave Caylen a quick look from head to toe. "If you're looking for clothes—something more suitable for the city—there's a stall down in the market square that's open even when the market isn't, and they've got good, sturdy dresses for not much coin." She shook her head. "Because if you're looking for work while you're here—you need to understand that nobody is going to hire you looking like that."

"Thank you." Caylen wasn't sure she was going to follow any of the advice, but she appreciated the thought behind it. She turned to the workman. "And thank you, as well." His smile was a little sad, as if he could see that she didn't like what she'd been hearing. She tried to catch the old man's eye, but he was staring deep into his bowl and wouldn't allow himself to be disturbed.

The street was much busier than it had been when she'd gone to the inn, and she found herself slinking along the walls, as if she was trying to fade off the path and into the shelter of the forest. But there was no shelter, here, just hard stones and harder eyes. For the first time, she felt self-conscious about her clothes, and the way that her practical leggings marked her as an outsider. She didn't want to wear a skirt, but she didn't want to be stared at, either. She took the turn that would lead her to the market square—it wouldn't hurt to *look* at the clothes.

She found the stall without much trouble, and after her experience in the inn she wasn't too surprised when the proprietor approached her immediately. "If you don't have coin, don't go pawing through my goods," he said.

"I have coin," she replied, and she managed to keep most of the resentment out of her voice.

"Enough coin for a whole new wardrobe? 'Cause from the looks of things, that's what you need." The man didn't seem like he was trying to be cruel; she was pretty sure he'd say he was just being honest.

"I don't know—how much would that be? And what would I get for it?" She still wasn't sure she wanted to do this, but as usual, she liked to gather information.

The stall-keeper looked her up and down. "I'll set you up with two skirts, two blouses, and a jacket for five coppers. I'll throw in underclothes, stockings, and boots for a silver coin." He smiled as if he was sure he already knew the answer, but was willing to humor her. "Do you have a silver coin, little girl?"

Of course she did. She had Connell's savings for what must have been most of the last year. She wondered what he'd think of her spending his coin on skirts and blouses. Probably he'd approve; he'd been the one who had taught her the most about camouflage, and blending into her surroundings. "Could I take them with me now? Or would they have to be fitted, and hemmed?" She tried to remember what else Mara's seamstresses had spoken about when they'd wanted to outfit her.

He leaned back as if to get a better view, as if trying to decide whether she was a serious customer or just wasting his time. "I've got stuff that'll fit you, close enough. The skirts have drawstrings, so you can just tie them tighter, and if they're too long, you can roll them up at the waistband."

"Well, let me see the boots," she said, and it wasn't too long before she was heading back to the apartments with a string-wrapped bundle of new clothes dangling from one hand. She'd even let the stall-keeper talk her into getting blouses that weren't her usual colors of moss green or bark brown. She'd turned down the bright yellow one, but there was a fairly muted blue that she'd liked, and a deep, rich red. As she walked, she looked at the other women on the street, and tried to keep track of the way they were dressed, the way they wore their hair, even the way they moved. She wasn't giving in to pressure, she told herself; she was just trying to blend in.

And she wasn't quite ready to go back to the opulence of the apartments, she decided. Her bundle was bulky, but not heavy, and she was used to carrying much worse. She chased her mind away from that thought, and focused on the streets around her. She'd been here before, on her tour with Mara. But they'd stuck to the main streets, the public face of the city. Caylen took the first side street that she could find.

She wandered for a while, the streets getting narrower and the paving rougher as she went. There wasn't too much activity; a few children playing or running errands, a few adults busy with their own affairs, but not the bustle of the main streets. When she saw a small crowd up ahead, it was unusual enough for her to take notice.

The crowd was watching a harried, almost panicked-looking woman trying to herd four small children along the street. "Come on, keep moving," she said, and three of the children complied, but the fourth was distracted, trying to hold onto a cloth-wrapped bundle that seemed intent on escaping his grasp. His mother noticed his plight. "Antin, what have you got? It had better not be that dog, Antin! I told you to leave him behind!" She strode over and grabbed the bundle roughly, and sure enough, a non-descript canine head popped out and looked at her cheerfully.

"He doesn't eat much!" the boy protested. "And he'll be good. We can't just leave him behind, Ma—he'll starve."

Caylen was close enough that she could hear the woman as she hissed, "You can leave him behind to starve, or you can drown him at the next well, but we *cannot* take him with us." The boy began to cry, then, and the mother looked like she wanted to hit him. Then her own face crumpled. "Antin, we *can't*. We have to move quickly. You know what's happened—we can't stay here. It's not safe. We don't have time or money for a pet, and if it comes down to losing an animal or losing one of you all—the animal goes."

Caylen didn't really understand what was going on, and she had no real plan, but she was used to following her instincts. "Excuse me," she said, stepping forward. "That dog—he's not for sale, is he?"

The woman and the boy both looked startled. "*This* dog?" the woman said. "For sale?" She glanced down at her son, then back at Caylen. "If you promise to feed him, you can have him for free."

The boy looked confused, then nodded his vigorous agreement and stepped forward to thrust the dog toward Caylen. "He'll eat anything. And he's really smart. And he only chews a little, but that's just because he's still a pup."

Caylen set her bundle down and accepted the dog into her arms. He squirmed and tried to lick her face. "I couldn't take him for free. He's..." She struggled to find some possible explanation for wanting to take the dog; she didn't want the woman to think that it was just charity. "He looks just like the dog I had growing up. Such an excellent dog—I've missed him so much. I'd really like to buy this pup, if I could." She wasn't sure where the lies were coming from, but she hoped the source didn't dry up before she was done. "I'd give him a good life—running loose through the fields and the forest, free and wild." That part was maybe a little much; the woman was looking at her doubtingly, but the boy seemed enthralled. "I'd really like to have the dog. I'd be happy to pay you for him."

The boy looked up at his mother, and when she grudgingly nodded, he held out his hand. Caylen burrowed around in Connell's purse. How much could she give, without making it suspicious? She settled on a silver coin, and handed it to the boy with her hand covering it so the mother wouldn't see how much it was.

Then she grabbed her bundle and the squirming puppy and hurried down the street. "Thank you so much," she called over her shoulder.

She had no idea what the family had been running from. And she certainly had no idea what she was going to do with a puppy. Well, she had one idea, she realized as the creature squirmed up closer to her face. "You need a bath, you little stinker," she said, and that was enough to make her decide that it was time to go back and see what was happening at the apartments.

CHAPTER 21

The guards downstairs at the apartment gave Caylen strange looks when she arrived back, obviously wondering how she'd left the building. But they said nothing to her; maybe there were some advantages to being considered nobility, after all. Her optimism disappeared when she opened the door of her own apartment and saw Logan standing by her open window, while Jonah sat on one of the plush chairs, both looking impatient and frustrated.

They turned toward the opening door at the same time, and Caylen had to steel herself to walk into the room. They didn't have any authority over her, she reminded herself. If they weren't friends, they were nothing, and she had no reason to be afraid of either her friends or of nothing. "Hi." She tried to imagine how Mara would handle a situation like this. "I hope you weren't waiting too long—I didn't know to expect you."

"We said we'd be by in the morning," Jonah said, and his voice was dangerously quiet. Caylen wished he didn't have a good point.

Still, she did the best she could. "Well, it's still morning. I was hungry, so I went out for breakfast." She held out the bundle of fabric. "And, look, I bought some skirts. I don't know if I'll actually *wear* them, but buying them's a good first step, right?"

Jonah looked amazed. "Those?" He took a step closer and looked down at the clothing. "What, from a stall in the market? You can't wear skirts like *that*, Caylen. You're not a peasant."

"No, I'm a nomad!" she fired back. "We don't wear skirts at *all*." She tossed the bundle into the corner. She had been stupid to even try to fit into this strange city, with its strange rules.

"It looks like you found a new friend." Logan spoke for the first time, and he sounded much calmer than Jonah.

Caylen looked down at the puppy, who had fallen asleep sometime on the way home and was happily snuggled in under her chin. "He stinks," she said.

"I can help you bathe him, if you want." Logan walked over and peered down at the little animal, then noticed Caylen's suspicious look. "I'm not trying to curry favor! I just like dogs." The finger that he reached out found just the right spot along the puppy's jaw, and as Logan scratched, the puppy, still half-asleep, arched his back and pushed his head into Logan's caress. "What's his name?"

"I don't know. They didn't tell me."

"Well, he's still young—you can just make up a name you like, and he'll learn it fast enough." Logan's smile was easy and relaxed, and here, without the crowds watching and judging, it felt like the old Logan, the boy Caylen had gotten to know in the forest. She liked him *much* better than the smooth politician she had dealt with the night before.

"Did you climb out the damned window?" Jonah didn't seem interested in any more talk about puppies.

"I didn't want to deal with all of the guards. I wanted to explore."

"You could have broken your neck!"

"I could have fallen down the stairs and broken my neck, as well. But I didn't."

Jonah sighed heavily. "No, you didn't. So we still have to deal with you. You have an appointment with the Chancellor. Midmorning, which means—now, really." He looked her over. "But you can't go looking like that." He cast his eyes toward the bundle of clothes Caylen had thrown, and shook his head. "And those aren't much better." He shook his head. "Mara beat us on this one, Logan. We should have—well, I don't know. We should have gotten a woman on side faster, got some damn clothes made. But—Caylen, you've still got what you were wearing last night? That'll have to do."

Caylen wanted to protest; she wasn't sure she'd even be able to put the fancy clothes *on* by herself. But if Jonah had actually gotten her an interview with the Chancellor—that was an opportunity to do something, surely. She decided that she should take his advice, at least for the time being. "I can't do—whatever she did with my hair, and the creams on my face—I don't know how to do any of that."

"Just get changed, and—you can tie your hair back, right? That'll have to be enough."

Logan smiled encouragingly at her. "Here, I'll take the pup down and find someone to look after him while you're gone, okay?"

Caylen didn't like the sound of that; she'd just promised a little boy that the dog would be taken care of, and now she was going to hand off her responsibility at the first possible chance?

"I'll find someone good, I promise." Logan looked over at Jonah. "And I'll try to find someone to lend us a lady's maid for a while—or at least tell us who to talk to in order to get some damn dresses."

Caylen followed the instructions and made herself look as presentable as possible. The final result was nowhere near as good as the night before, she knew, but it would have to do. The Chancellor was old; maybe she'd be lucky, and find that he was a little short-sighted.

Logan and Jonah hurried her down the stairs and barely gave her time to check that the servant Logan had found for the puppy was acceptable, and then they were out on the street, the obligatory guards surrounding them, practically sprinting the short distance to the Great Hall. It wouldn't have been a problem if Caylen had been wearing her own clothes, but even with the split, the skirt was still much more fabric than she was used to around her legs, and the high heels made even walking a bit of a challenge. Jonah was impatient with her, but Logan seemed to find the whole thing amusing. A good night's sleep had done wonders for his mood.

There wasn't time for Caylen to do more than take a quick look around the magnificent foyer they crossed to get to the ornately carved doors of the Chancellor's office, and then they were inside and Jonah was announcing, "Lady Caylen, daughter of Lord Willem, to see the Chancellor." His voice was louder than usual, and quite grand, but it didn't seem to have much effect on the official taking notes outside the door.

"Thank you. I'll let you know when the Chancellor is able to see you," he said. "Please, have a seat." He nodded in the direction of several rows of chairs. They were almost empty, except for...

"Mara." Logan's voice was dry. "Of course."

She turned when she heard her name, and her smile was wide and warm. "Caylen! I heard you might be coming by. I just wanted to check in and say hello."

Even to Caylen, that sounded like an unlikely story, and she could tell that Logan wasn't convinced. Still, Caylen didn't want to be rude to the woman who'd taken so much time with her the day before. "It's good to see you, Mara."

And there wasn't time for any more, as the official returned from the inner office and nodded in Caylen's direction. "The Chancellor will see you now," he said, with no acknowledgement of the fact that he'd just told them to sit down as if he thought they were in for a long wait. He opened the large doors for them with a somewhat grandiose flourish, and Caylen, Logan, and Jonah entered; Caylen was only a little surprised to feel Mara's arm looping through her own and following along.

The man sitting behind the ornate wooden desk wasn't as old as Caylen had expected. His hair was grey and his skin was wrinkled, certainly, but his bright eyes didn't seem to be missing much that went on, and when he stood to greet her it was in a fluid, easy motion. "So you're the little nomad, are you?" Some people in the city used the word as if it were an obscenity, but from the Chancellor's mouth, 'nomad' sounded more like an endearment. "I remember your mother very fondly. I held her almost as dear as I held your father."

That sounded promising. Caylen really had no idea what Logan and Jonah thought the purpose of this meeting was, but her goal was clear, at least to herself. She had two missions to accomplish, and she wanted the most powerful man in the city to help her with both of them. "Thank you, sir. I never knew my father, but my mother is very—impressive." She probably could have been smoother if she'd made something up, but instinct told her that this man would be better at catching lies than she was at creating them.

"Come sit down, Caylen." The Chancellor looked over her shoulder. "I don't think we'll need chaperones," he said, and just that easily, Logan and Jonah and Mara were dismissed.

"I wish I could learn that trick," Caylen said once the others were gone. She immediately regretted it. Honesty was one thing, but total candor was probably inappropriate. And, really, her self-appointed guardians weren't that bad. "I mean—they've been very kind to me. I appreciate their efforts."

"Kindness, you say?" The Chancellor shook his head. "I'd have thought I'd gotten that trained out of them, by now. Although if they're clever enough to give the *impression* of kindness—well, that's a valuable skill." He gestured to two large chairs facing each other near an enormous window. "Sit, sit. I'm afraid I don't have much time for small talk." Caylen obeyed, and as soon as he was settled into his own chair, the Chancellor asked, "So—what brings you to the city? Interested in claiming your birthright?"

"My—my birthright? My birthright is the forest, sir. And, yes, I'm interested in protecting it. I was told that there might be problems for the nomads, coming from the cities, and from what I've seen since I arrived here, I think I was told right. So I'd like to do what I can to prevent the bad feelings from spilling beyond the city walls."

"So I've been told. And how do you plan to go about that, Caylen?"

And that was the big question, wasn't it? "I'm not sure, sir. I'm looking for advice, really. I mean—I hoped to be a witness, to explain that the people who attacked Logan weren't real nomads. I thought that if I figured out who had sent those men, I'd be able to..." She trailed off. She didn't think the Chancellor would appreciate hearing the details of her plan for whomever had sent the men who killed Darton. "Well, I'd be able to show that nomads aren't really a threat."

The Chancellor nodded slowly. "I see. And how do you plan to go about all this?"

"Well, as I said—I'm looking for advice on that."

"Advice. And the advisors you've found so far— Mara and Jonah, and Logan—what advice have they given you?"

"Not much, really. Not so far. It's mostly been about what to wear, and how to act. Other than that— Jonah and Logan seem to want me to stay in the apartment, and Mara seems to think that we should just walk around together all day."

The Chancellor nodded as if this was exactly what he'd expected. "Would you like my advice, young nomad? Caylen, daughter of Nora and Willem?"

"Yes, sir. Please."

He took a breath, then fixed his gaze on her with a burning intensity. "Run away, Caylen. Go back to your forest. If the cities attack, hide for a while, and when they get tired of chasing ghosts, go back to your life.

There's nothing for you here, and if you stay, you'll be destroyed." His voice was deep, almost unnaturally so, making his words sound more like a prophecy than a simple prediction.

Caylen wasn't normally superstitious, but this was chilling. "'Destroyed'? Do you mean—killed?" She'd been in life-threatening situations many times, after all. Was there really anything new here?

"There are fates worse than death, Caylen," the Chancellor said.

She remembered the words from the inn that morning. "Like the Dark House, you mean?"

He looked almost surprised. "That wasn't what I meant, no. And, as no one seems to be challenging the facts about your birth, the Office of Intelligence Services would not have any power over you. They only deal with commoners, not nobility."

"That's not fair!" Caylen tried to control herself. She sounded like a child, prattling on about 'fairness'. And it was a distraction from what she should be asking about, anyhow. "So, if not the Office of... the Dark House, what *did* you mean?"

The Chancellor looked as if he was picking his words carefully. "The city—the politics in the city—it has a way of changing people. It will change you, too. And the person you are now—the person you are now would hate the person you will become."

Caylen frowned. It didn't make sense. Then she remembered her mother's words. *You're unknown, so you use the element of surprise.* She wasn't sure she had much potential for an actual surprise, but at least she could stick to the first part. "You don't know me. You don't know 'the person I am now', so you can't predict the person I might become."

"I don't know you, little nomad?" The Chancellor sounded amused, but Caylen wasn't interested in being his entertainment.

"No. If you did, you'd know better than to suggest that I run away and hide." She wanted to stand up, to stride out of the room in indignation, but that wouldn't work. She still needed this man's help, or at least wanted it. "I appreciate the advice, but I'm afraid I'm not going to be able to go along with it. But if you have the time, I'd really appreciate hearing any ideas you might have about how I could figure out who sent the men to attack Logan, and…"

"And how to prevent an invasion of the Nomads' Land." He waved his hand vaguely through the air. "Yes, yes. All of that." He considered her for a long moment, as if deciding whether to humor her or dismiss her for her impertinence. Finally, he shook his head. "'The people is a beast of muddy brain'. I read that in one of the old books. And it's true. It's not the people you need to be worried about—they can complain all they want, but they'll never get organized. They can create trouble in the city, certainly; they must always be considered on domestic affairs. But a war? The people will never start a war. And they won't send out assassins, either." He shook his head. "There are a handful of commoners so rich that they might as well be nobles, and there are the nobles themselves. That's where you need to look, for the answers to *both* of your questions."

"But—okay, that makes sense. But *how* do I look there? What do I do?"

"My young nomad, you can't expect me to give you full instructions on how to uncover the very people that I'm in office to protect, now, can you?"

"It's your job to protect murderers?" She was pretty sure she was being dangerously disrespectful, but the Chancellor wasn't objecting, yet.

His smile was sad. "I told you, Caylen—the city changes people." He rose and walked to the window, and didn't turn around as he spoke again. "You're too busy asking 'who?' when you should be asking 'why?'" There was a pause, and then he said, "And, now I'm afraid I have business to attend to. It's been very nice visiting with you, and I certainly hope to see you again during your stay in our city. If I can be of any assistance to you, please speak to my secretary, and we'll see what can be done." He turned toward her and his face was calm and politely disinterested; she recognized the mask as one that Logan sometimes wore. The dismissal was clear.

She stood up. She would have liked to have fought to stay, would have liked to have insisted on the chance to ask more questions, but the truth was, she had no idea what to ask. The question shouldn't be 'who?' but 'why?'. She needed to think about that. "Thank you for your time," she said as she headed toward the door, but the Chancellor was already back at his desk, reading from the stack of papers in front of him, and if he heard her, there was no indication.

Jonah and Logan were waiting for her right outside the door, while Mara was back on the chairs. She stood and came over when she saw Caylen, though.

"So? How did it go?" Logan asked.

"It was fine, I think. I don't know. He seemed very pleasant, mostly."

"Well, did he *say* anything?" Mara was better than Logan at seeming casual, but she wasn't fooling Caylen this time.

"Not much. He mostly just welcomed me to the city." She decided that she needed to give a little more than that, if she wanted these people to help her. "And he said that it would be the nobles who would cause the war with the nomads, not the people. Does that make sense?" She was a little surprised, herself, that it was Logan that she was turning to for advice. Mara was fine, but Caylen had seen Logan in the forest, and he'd done well for himself, considering. Maybe it wasn't a good reason to trust somebody, but Caylen didn't have any better evidence to go on.

Logan nodded. "Did he give you the 'muddy brain' line? That's a favorite of his. And he's not wrong, I wouldn't say. I mean, people might grumble about nomads, but they aren't going to actually do anything about it without organization, and without money for weapons and supplies."

"Okay," Caylen said. "So—how do I convince the nobles that the nomads aren't a threat? How do I get them to just leave us alone?"

"It won't be easy," Logan said. He looked over at Jonah, then at Mara, as if deciding how much to say with an audience. Finally, he said, "We're out of space, close to the city. All the good farmland is taken. People want to spread out more, and they want to have safe passage to get to their more distant estates. They want safe trade routes, too. It's about coin, really. So every raid on a caravan, every theft from a wagon bringing goods to the city—that makes people want to tame the wild lands."

Caylen tried to put the ideas together in her mind. "The person who sent the attackers after you—that was meant to do two jobs at once, right? I mean, they wanted to kill you, but they also wanted to make nomads look bad. So whoever they were, they must have…"

Mara interrupted Caylen's thoughts. "Wait! I have a brilliant idea! The Council is going into session in only a few minutes. I'll have to go to sit in on it, and I assume Logan will do the same. But, Caylen—you have a right to be there. You have a right to participate. This could be your chance to speak to representatives from each of the Families, all in one place at the same time. You could tell them that the nomads aren't a threat. You could—I said yesterday, you could be a sort of ambassador. We could work together, and figure out a compromise, some sort of solution that would make everyone happy." She was practically clapping her hands she was so excited.

Neither Jonah nor Logan seemed to be as enthusiastic. "You're not ready for that, Caylen," Jonah said. "You'll want to speak to the Council eventually, maybe, but not until you've had a chance to prepare yourself better."

"What would you even say?" Logan added. "We haven't got a strategy yet, we're still figuring out a plan..."

"So I don't have to be here, after all? I could still be in the forest?" Caylen wasn't at all reluctant to let her bitterness show. "Yesterday, I *had* to come with you right away, because we had to control the story before it was spread all over town. Today, I'm just supposed to sit back and wait? Let me guess—you want me to go back to the damned apartment!"

"You're a noble; you have a right to speak to the Council." Mara was nodding slowly, as if she was running over the possible objections in her head, and overriding every one. "You have nothing planned, but that's fine; you can just tell them what you know. You aren't well dressed—did you forget how to put the cream on your scar?—but that shouldn't matter, because they know you're new to town, and they know where you've come from." She seemed convinced. "I don't want to argue with Logan or Jonah, and of course you should make your own decision on this, but I think it would be a great idea."

Jonah was staring at Mara, and opened his mouth as if to speak, then closed it again. He turned to Logan, instead, as if hoping his friend would speak for him. Caylen wasn't sure whether Jonah was being cautious about offending someone as potentially powerful as Mara or if he just couldn't think of the right words to say. Either way, it was nice to see him without an easy answer, for a change.

Logan seemed ready to keep trying, though. "Caylen, it's not..." And then it was his turn to look frustrated. "It's not that we want to keep you quiet. It's just not the right time. Not yet. I know you're impatient—we can try to get you some one-on-one meetings with people, starting as soon as possible. This afternoon, even."

Mara shook her head. "We don't have the time to waste on individual meetings, not with the anti-nomad sentiment as high as it is. Caylen, it's your decision."

And that was what did it. Caylen was tired of being pushed around, and of not being expected to look after herself. If Mara was the only one who realized that she had a right to make her own decisions, then Mara seemed to be the only one who understood how things really were. "Okay, I'll do it."

"Excellent." Mara's smile was warm, and Caylen found herself wanting to soak up the approval. She fought the impulse, and tried to focus on what Mara was saying. "We should go over now, probably. I can introduce you to anyone you haven't already met. And we'll need to get you recognized, at least conditionally, in order to establish your right to a seat. Logan—I assume you'll be willing to testify on Caylen's behalf?"

"Testify?" This wasn't sounding nearly as simple as it had just a few moments before. "What does that mean?"

Mara put a reassuring hand on Caylen's arm. "We just need to establish, to a reasonable probability, that you're Lord Willem's daughter. Logan's testimony about your mother, and the testimony of anyone who's ever seen a picture of Lord Willem—that'll almost certainly be enough for the initial recognition. After that, your status would be open to challenge for a set period, but there's nobody likely to do that, not with me introducing you and Logan backing you. Assuming he *will* back you—Logan?"

"Of course I'll back her. But, Caylen—maybe this would be enough, for today. You don't have to speak. We'll introduce you, have the vote, and that will be more than enough, really. There's no need to do more, right away."

"The decision's been made, Logan." Even Caylen could hear the slight trace of smugness in Mara's voice, but it wasn't something Caylen could blame her for. There was just something about Logan, with his arrogance, that made people want to beat him at any contest. "Caylen, let's go. We'll get to the chambers a little early, and you can collect your thoughts."

Caylen wasn't too dazzled to notice that as soon as Caylen had agreed to Mara's ideas, Mara had gone right back to making plans and assuming that Caylen would follow them. But she couldn't really object now, not right after making her decision, so she fell in beside Mara as she led the way deeper into the cold stone building.

CHAPTER 22

Caylen was pretty sure that the Council room was larger than any indoor space she'd ever been in. And it was certainly grander. It was set up in a semi-circle, the floor steeply terraced up from a low central stage, and there were carved wooden chairs with deep red cushions spread all over each of the wide steps. The walls were a pale, highly polished stone, and there was a glass dome at the top of the room, letting in light. Not that the light was needed, with all the electric lanterns shining from every wall. Caylen wanted a moment to just stare, but Mara took her by the arm and led her over to a middle-aged man standing on the stage.

"Father!" Mara called. "Father, please let me introduce Lady Caylen, daughter of Lord Wiltern—I suppose she's your cousin, once removed." She turned to Caylen. "This is my father, Lord Rolston. He's the Speaker of the Council—that means that he's in charge." She winked playfully. "So I'm hoping we won't have too much trouble convincing him that he should make time for you on the agenda."

Rolston stepped down off the stage and said, "Of course—I'm sure everyone would like to hear from the newest addition to our happy family."

"And maybe you could make time for a conversation about your work for the Office of Intelligence Services." Caylen hadn't even known that

Logan had followed them, but he was there now, standing between her and Rolston almost—well, almost protectively. But she didn't think he was trying to protect her from any *physical* threat. He looked over at her, and she tried to read the warning in his eyes as he said, "I remember you were interested in the Dark House, Caylen. Lord Rolston's in charge of that—organization."

This didn't sound like the cautious Logan that Caylen remembered from the forest. This sounded like a young man looking for a fight; she was intrigued.

Unfortunately, their conversation was interrupted by the deep, loud ringing of bells. Caylen looked around and couldn't see them, but their rich tones were obviously a signal to the people in the room, who finished their conversations quickly and headed for the wooden chairs.

"Caylen, you should stay with me," Mara said, without even glancing in Logan's direction. "We'll start with your introduction. If that meets with your approval, Father?" The question seemed to be a mere formality, and Caylen found herself wondering whether Rolston was really in charge of the Council, or whether he was merely a spokesman for his politically savvy daughter.

"Of course," he said, and his smile for Mara felt like the first genuine expression Caylen had seen from the man. He stepped back up to the stage and the room instantly hushed. "I call this session of the Yorkton City Council to order." His voice was rich and effortless. "We have an addition to the order of business—Lady Mara will introduce a candidate for inclusion in our body."

That seemed smooth and easy, almost rehearsed. Mara had sounded like this was a spontaneous idea, but her father didn't seem too surprised by any of it. Or maybe he was just that good.

Mara stepped onto the stage and gestured for Caylen to join her, then turned and faced the audience. There must have been well over a hundred people in the room, but Mara seemed as calm as if she were speaking to a small group of dear friends. She smiled, and then began. "We were all so worried when Lord Logan didn't return from his estate visit on time. We heard that he'd decided to go cross-country, rather than taking the river as originally planned." The words weren't much, but Mara's tone made it clear that, while she had affection for him, Logan was essentially a foolish child. "His little adventure could have been disastrous, but he was lucky enough not only to be rescued, but also to stumble across a young woman who turned out to be our long-lost second cousin!" She smiled at Caylen, who was too busy feeling bad for Logan to return the expression with any enthusiasm. "And since she's been in town, Caylen and I have spent time getting to know each other, and I can assure you: she may still be learning our city ways, but once she gets her bearings, I'm sure she'll be a wonderful addition to our social circles. Many of you met her last night at the Gallery. If she seemed a little overwhelmed and awkward, just put yourself in her shoes—imagine moving from the primitive Wild Lands to the most elevated social circles of one of the greatest cities in the world, overnight!"

Caylen felt cold. Mara was making her sound confused and useless. Her eyes searched the room and found Logan—he seemed completely uninterested in the speech, leaning back in his chair as if he were about to fall asleep. Was it another one of his masks, or was he really that indifferent?

Mara continued with her speech. "I present Caylen to you as a candidate for membership in this esteemed Council. I have no evidence of her ancestry other than her word and the strong resemblance to Lord Willem, the late grandson of our beloved Chancellor, but I believe Lord Logan has further evidence to present. Lord Logan?"

Logan stood, and spoke casually from his place. "We found Caylen in the company of a nomad woman who was identified by a citizen who knew her when she was partnered with Lord Willem. The timelines match up, the nomad woman claims that Caylen is Willem's son, and the family resemblance is strong." He sat down as if the entire proceedings were boring to him.

Mara raised an eyebrow. "Thank you, Lord Logan. How succinct." She turned toward Caylen, and the smile that had seemed friendly previously now seemed sharp. "Caylen, please come forward." Caylen did as she was told; she couldn't think of anything else to do. "Caylen, do you wish to present your claim as a candidate for membership in this body?"

Caylen certainly didn't, not right then, but it was clearly what was expected of her. She nodded.

Mara said, "And do you swear that you are the daughter of Lord Willem?"

Caylen frowned. She looked into the audience, but Logan was spending all of his attention picking at a seam on his jacket, and none of the other faces told her anything. "I—I can't swear to that. I mean—I wasn't there. At conception, I mean."

A ripple washed over the audience—was it amusement, or something else? Caylen tried again. "I can swear that my mother didn't want me to know who my father was, but she didn't argue when Willem was named. And I can swear that she didn't want me to come to the city, so she'd have no reason to let me believe something that wasn't true." She paused for thought. "And I can swear that she and Jonah seemed to agree that I look a lot like Willem. But I've never seen a picture."

Mara frowned at her. "We don't use the names of commoners in this chamber." She made it sound as if Caylen had spit on the floor.

"You don't—really? You don't use their names? That must be really confusing." This time, Caylen was sure that buzz from the audience was mostly amusement, although there were several faces frowning at her, as well.

"We manage," Mara said. "Do you have any other evidence to bring forward to support your claim?" She sounded disappointed, as if she had expected more, but that made no sense.

Caylen kept trying; she didn't care about the opinions of these people, but she'd be damned if she'd quit the fight. "The Chancellor seemed to believe it. When I spoke to him earlier—he said he held my mother almost as dear as he held my father. That sounds like he thinks I'm Willem's daughter, right?"

This time when she looked out onto the sea of faces, she saw quite a few of them looking surprised, and when her gaze reached Logan, he was finally looking at her, a hint of a smile on his face. Maybe she'd finally done something right.

Mara was smiling again, although Caylen didn't think she was imagining a certain tightness in the expression. "Very well," Mara said. "We have heard the evidence. Does anyone have anything to add, before we vote?"

"Isn't that the Speaker's job? Calling the vote?" It was Logan, still looking lazy and uninterested, except for his eyes, which were locked on Mara's. "Lord Rolston?" Logan didn't even look in the older man's direction. Caylen could feel currents of tension running through the room, but she couldn't begin to interpret them. "Isn't it *your* privilege to call the vote? Or is Mara running the Council completely, these days?"

"It's a privilege that I'll be happy to exercise, my young friend." The emphasis Rolston put on 'young' was unmistakable, and the tight way he said 'friend' was not much more subtle. He nodded at his daughter. "When Lady Mara has finished speaking." Caylen had expected the tensions between these two factions to be more understated than this. No one else in the room seemed too surprised by the exchange, though.

"Thank you for the reminder, though, Logan." Mara smiled patronizingly. "It's reassuring to see that you haven't forgotten *all* the rules of our society while you were out traipsing through the forest." She gestured slightly with her arm, enough to make it clear that everyone was included in the next address. "So, I present to you—Caylen. The evidence of her kinship is not as strong as we might like, but under the circumstances, I think it's as strong as it can reasonably be. We can't expect birth witnesses and sworn statements of paternity in the wilderness, can we?" She smiled benignly at those who were tittering at her little joke. Caylen tried to keep from sneering, and Mara continued. "So, despite my acknowledgement of the problems, I tentatively accept Caylen as my second cousin, and urge you all to do the same." She bowed graciously and stepped back to stand next to Caylen.

Lord Rolston stepped forward. "Does anyone else wish to speak to the matter?" There was no movement from the crowd, and after a moment, Rolston continued. "Very well. On the matter of Caylen's conditional membership in the Yorkton City Council—how do you vote? Raise your hand for Yea." To Caylen's surprise, most of the hands in the room were raised immediately. "And Nay?" Rolston asked, and Caylen sensed Mara tense beside her, looking out into the room as if eager to recognize those who would dare to defy her recommendation. No hands were raised.

Rolston turned to Caylen and nodded officiously. "Please accept my congratulations. You are now considered a member of the Council—this membership is conditional for the first year; if no objections are raised during that period, you may come to us and apply to have your membership made permanent."

"Thank you," Caylen said. The membership meant nothing to her, but Rolston obviously felt that he was giving her a great gift, so it seemed impolite to show her disinterest. "Does that mean that I can speak to them, now?"

Rolston raised an eyebrow and looked toward his daughter; Caylen could see her slight nod of agreement. He turned to face the audience and said, "And now, our newest member will be given a little time to address the Council." He made a slight bow to Caylen and stepped back just as Mara retreated on her other side, and

Caylen was left alone, staring at the huge group of rich, powerful city dwellers. She didn't think she'd ever spoken to more than a couple people at a time, before, and they'd always just been nomads. Still, she was here for a reason.

"I—I thank you for your time." She hoped that was a polite introduction, because it was about all she had. "I just—I was told that there were some bad feelings toward nomads. And I was told that, because the people who attacked Logan and his men were dressed as nomads, that bad feeling might turn into something more. I just wanted to come here and say—they weren't real nomads. The people who attacked Logan. He can tell you, and J--" She caught herself. "The citizen and soldiers who were with us can tell you, the people who attacked Logan were dressed to look like nomads, but they weren't. So..." Was that it? Was that all she had to say? She'd come to the city, and gone through this entire process, just to repeat some basic facts that would have been more compelling coming from Logan's mouth, rather than her own? She realized with a rush of mortification that Jonah and Logan had been right. She was in no way prepared for this address.

"Nomads aren't dangerous!" She blurted out.

"So my son wasn't killed by nomads last year?" The man who spoke was grey and stooped, but his voice was strong. Caylen was chilled by the hatred she heard in it. "Is that what you're here to tell me? He *wasn't* set upon by thieves and robbed and beaten to death? Less than a day's walk from the city walls? That didn't happen?"

Caylen froze. Her mind raced, but only around in circles, not taking her anywhere useful, or even coherent.

"And my estate wasn't razed to the ground?" It was another man, from the other side of the room. He seemed more bitterly amused than hateful, but he was staring at Caylen almost as intently as his colleague. "The buildings weren't burnt? The fruit trees weren't chopped down, and the livestock wasn't stolen or slaughtered? My peasants weren't forced to flee into the forest, where they barely managed to escape with their lives?"

Caylen frowned, and then stopped, because she was afraid that if she put any pressure on her eyes the tears of mortification might escape. "I don't...I don't know. That wasn't us. Not my band. It doesn't sound like any other band I know, either."

"But nomads are lawless. You recognize no authority, right?" The second man shook his head. "Do you even believe in private property? If you burned the buildings, would it be *my* buildings, or just *some* buildings?"

"We recognize authority," Caylen protested. She wished she could introduce this man to Nora and show him what authority really looked like. "Private property?

We don't live like that, but we don't have a problem with people who do..."

"You don't have a problem with us? How *generous* of you." Caylen still felt bad for the first man, but the second speaker's attitude was burning through her sympathy pretty quickly. He didn't seem concerned about her opinion, though turning toward Mara and then Logan as he said, "If the two of you want your little pet to sit in the Council, I won't object. But, please, keep her quiet until she has *some* idea what she's talking about."

Caylen really wanted to sprint up the steep stairs and launch her fist right into the bastard's smug face. But she also really wanted to run out of the room and keep going until the city walls were far behind her. The conflicting wishes apparently paralyzed her, and she stood motionless and stared at the crowd.

"She's a member of the Council, Lord Balter." Logan sounded calm and friendly, and he smiled easily. "She has the same right to speak that all the rest of us do. And the nomad question is certainly a pressing one. I think all perspectives are necessary in order for us to fully understand the issue. Caylen certainly has unique experiences to inform her opinions."

Rolston stepped forward and gave Caylen a patronizing smile. "And I think we've heard her primary message. So, for now—" He turned to speak to the Council. "We will move on to other business. Please consult your agendas—Item 2.1 is an address from Lord

Elgin about the drainage in the southeast region of the city."

And just like that, Caylen was dismissed. A man that she assumed was Lord Elgin had stood up and was lumbering down the stairs toward the stage, and Mara's hand slipped gently onto Caylen's arm. "If you'd like to stay and listen to the rest, you can sit with me," she began, but Caylen pulled away. She was done with accepting Mara's 'guidance'. She was tempted to rip off the borrowed clothes and shove those back at Mara, as well, but that seemed a little over-dramatic. Instead, she looked up and found Logan. He saw her and nodded his head toward the outer door, his eyebrow raised questioningly. She nodded, her agreement not nearly as subtle as his suggestion, and headed off. She knew the city ways well enough, now, knew that all eyes were on her as she rejected Mara's offer of friendship in favor of Logan's, and she knew that, if Logan and Jonah were right, there could be ramifications. But she didn't care. She wanted to stir things up and make things happen, and she wasn't going to get too far by trying to be sneaky.

CHAPTER 23

"She set me up, right?" Caylen was walking quickly, forcing Logan to lengthen his stride just to keep up. If she didn't have the damned high-heeled boots to worry about, she'd have been making him run. "She wanted to make me look like an idiot? Why? I thought..." She didn't want to say what she had really thought. She didn't want to admit that she'd thought maybe that glamorous, sophisticated creature had actually found her interesting. "I thought she was trying to make it seem like we were friends."

"Allies," Logan corrected dryly. "She was trying to make it seem like you were allies. And I honestly don't know why she pulled that stunt in there. She—okay, Caylen, don't take this the wrong way, because it's absolutely not how I see you, at all—but maybe she didn't think you'd be smart enough to see what she was doing. She's only spent time with you in her world, so far. And in her world—well, you don't seem slow, but— the reason I know you're smart is because of what I saw in the forest, not because of what I've seen in town. Does that make sense?"

"You're saying I've been acting stupid." She wanted to argue, but had to admit that he had a point.

"No, not stupid. Just—you've mostly been kind of overwhelmed around her, right? Maybe she didn't know that you weren't always that way." She could see his smile out of the corner of her eye. "I've got to say—I like the idea of her miscalculating. She doesn't make many mistakes, that's for sure."

"But—okay, even if she thought I was too stupid to notice, why did she bother?"

"I don't know. If you were firmly in my camp, that would make sense, but she didn't seem to think that you were a lost cause—she's been trying to win you over, right?"

"I guess so, yeah."

Logan nodded. "So she thought that she had a chance with you, and then she deliberately made you look bad, and blew the chance to be your friend at the same time. I don't know, Caylen. We need Jonah; he's best at this stuff."

"Well, where is he?"

Logan stopped walking and looked around him. "Actually, where are *we*? Do you know where you're going?"

Caylen hadn't had a destination in mind, but she knew exactly where she was. Once she'd gotten used to the city, the sense of direction that had served her so well in the forest had come back into its full strength. "Are you hungry? There's an inn where I had breakfast— I don't know if they'll want you there, but I think maybe you should talk to them." It wasn't an idea she had thought about, but it made sense. If she had chosen sides, chosen Logan, then she needed to start making him be the sort of person that she'd *want* to support.

"Well, I could eat. But who are these people?"

"They're commoners." She lifted an eyebrow at him. "We don't use the names of commoners in this room."

He smiled, then, and it was the one she liked, the one that seemed real. "You'll be okay," he said softly. "You'll figure all this out, if you give it some time." The smile turned into a thoughtful frown. "And if you stay out of trouble." They were walking again, but more slowly, and he half-turned toward her and said, "Be careful, Caylen. If Rolston and Mara have decided that you're an enemy...they could be dangerous."

"Do you think that they're the ones who sent the false nomads?"

Logan looked alarmed, and glanced around quickly to see if anyone had heard her question. "We can discuss that more in private," he said.

Caylen thought he was crazy—the street was so loud, so busy, that it would surely be impossible for anyone to overhear them. But they were almost at the inn, so she didn't argue. She *did* want to hear his answer to the question, but she thought it was maybe just as important that he meet the people she had in mind.

They stepped inside the door and paused to let their eyes adjust to the gloom. Of course, those inside were already able to see, and Caylen could tell by the hush that fell over the room that she and Logan had been noticed. She had forgotten that she was dressed in Mara's fine clothes, but she had anticipated this reaction to Logan.

"Taz," she said as soon as her eyes adjusted enough to see the woman, standing by her stove and staring at them. "I still have the tokens from this morning. I thought we could have some lunch?"

Taz looked doubtful. "It's nothing fancy. Soup, and fried cheese sandwiches."

"Sounds perfect," Logan said with a smile that Caylen was sure would be charming in the circles he normally ran in. Here, it looked too big, and seemed insincere.

Caylen tried to make the best of it. There was a table free in the back corner, but that wouldn't get Logan talking to people. She gestured to the end of the large common table in the middle; there was room for them to sit at the far end, if they squeezed in. Logan looked like he wasn't sure that any of this was a good idea, but he followed Caylen's lead. She took a moment to try to imagine Mara in a room like this, but the idea was too absurd.

She and Logan settled on opposite sides of the long table. It was amazing how the people sitting further down were able to compress themselves, shrinking together so that Caylen and Logan were taking up more space than any four other people. Taz brought bowls of soup over, and Caylen nodded. "Thank you. I'm sorry if this makes people uncomfortable."

Taz's eyes were cold. "Of course not. It's an honor to be allowed to serve." She looked like she was trying to restrain herself, but she failed, and said, "I wondered if it was you. When I heard there was a nomad girl, the daughter of Lord Willem—I wondered if it was you. Something about you this morning—you just didn't seem hungry enough."

Caylen nodded. "My father—I never knew him. But I was told that he tried to change things in the city. I was told that he tried to make the Families listen to the people."

"Is that what you think you're going to do?" Taz's laugh was somewhere between bitter and disbelieving. "Better you look after yourself. Don't forget what happened to your father." She turned away and strode back to the kitchen, leaving Caylen with a frowning Logan.

"What happened to protecting the nomads and avenging Darton? You've done so well with those that you've decided to add political reform to your agenda?"

"The people here—they were afraid of speaking, this morning. They weren't doing anything bad, weren't going to hurt anyone, but they thought that if they said the wrong thing, someone might report them and they could get sent to your Dark House. And the puppy's owner—a little boy and his mother, three other kids, no father in sight, running for their lives. I have no idea what they were running from, whether it was the Dark House or something else, but they sure as hell weren't heading downtown to get help at the Great Hall. They had to take care of themselves, as best they could, because nobody else would. One more house left dark because its people ran away. Is that the sort of city you want to live in? The sort of city you want to be *in charge of?*"

"No, of course not." It wasn't until Caylen heard how loud Logan's voice was she realized that she had almost been shouting herself. "But I can't change anything without being in power, and I can't get into power if I alienate all of my supporters. It's—" He took a moment to collect himself, and when he continued his voice was quieter. "It's a careful balancing act, Caylen. I can't go charging around, making accusations—" he paused, and fixed her with a look that she supposed was meant to suggest that he was talking about Mara, "not without proof. And I can't criticize an institution that has served this city for generations, not without a damned good reason."

"Served this city? Logan, maybe it's served you, and your friends, but the *city*? The city is *these* people, afraid to speak their minds! It's the family who had to run away from their own home. Logan, the city is the people like that soldier, Sealy, forced to get involved in your stupid plots in order to keep his daughter alive. I don't see how a building dedicated to torture and terror is serving *any* of those people."

"That was a pretty good speech, Caylen." Logan sounded bitter. "Too bad you couldn't manage it when you needed in the Council room. Tell you what—you should stay in the city, and *you* can be the one to take over. Then we'll see if you still like making speeches so much, when the words you say actually matter, when they can make the difference between the city being controlled and peaceful or being chaotic and falling into civil war." He stopped talking and stared at Caylen.

She stared right back. The room was silent, all ears turned to catch their words, and they were both a little startled when a voice came from the far end of the table, almost whispering, but loud enough to be heard in the quiet inn. "They took my son. My Dann."

Caylen turned to look at the speaker, but it was Logan who replied. "I'm sorry? 'They'—do you mean the Dark House?" The man who had spoken nodded. He wasn't old, but he was too thin, and seemed exhausted. "Why?" Logan asked. "How long ago?"

"I don't know why. They never said. They just came and took him, in the middle of the night. He was just a boy—what could he have done?" The man looked down at his hands, then back up at Logan. "What could he have done?"

"I'm sorry. I don't know." Logan looked helplessly at Caylen, then back at the man. "How long ago was it?" he asked again.

"Almost three years—right at the start of the... the bad times." The man's voice was louder, now, and steadier. "I know what that means. He's gone. My wife --" He stopped, and then looked at Logan fiercely, as if daring him to judge. "I was afraid to try. We have two daughters—we couldn't—*I* couldn't risk it. But my wife wouldn't give up. She went and banged on the door of that black wall, and when they answered, she asked them right to their faces—where was Dann? Where was our boy, and what did they think he had done?"

"And what did they say?" It was Taz, drawn over from the stove, her face drawn in sympathy.

The man had to collect himself before he said, "They offered to let her see him. They said that she could ask him herself, what he'd done. They said they had a space all ready for her, right next to him, if she didn't mind her own business and stop asking questions." He was sneering by the end, and he looked at Logan not as if asking for help, but more as if he just wanted to be acknowledged.

Caylen was proud of Logan when he did just that. "I'm very sorry." He looked around the room, and Caylen felt as if he was truly *seeing* the people in it, maybe for the first time. "I—I don't know what to say. But I'll think about it, I promise. I'll try—I'll try to find..." He trailed off, and turned back to look at the man down the table. "There's nothing I can do for your son. Not after so long. But you knew that."

The man nodded slowly. "I knew that," he agreed. "But I heard what the girl said, and she's right. There needs to be changes." He looked suddenly fierce. "And if you in the Families don't make them, then maybe *we* will!"

"*Careful!*" Taz said, and turned toward Logan. "He's just upset," she hurried to explain. "He doesn't mean anything by it."

Caylen watched Logan closely, and saw him recognize her fear. "No..." he started, then tried again. "You don't need to worry about me. I appreciate..." He stopped again, and looked at Caylen, then down the table to the man who had spoken. "Words from the Time Before—'Dissent is the highest form of patriotism'." He smiled quickly at Caylen, and said quietly, "You won't hear the Chancellor quoting *that* any time soon." His smile faded as he looked at her, and his face took on a determined, almost grim expression. He raised his head and looked around the room, then spoke in a strong, loud voice. "I am Lord Logan, great-grandson of our Chancellor Lord Wiltern. Please—I can be reached through the Great Hall, or by messenger to my home in the Estates. If any harm comes to this man, or to any other citizen who has done nothing but tell the truth, please tell me. I can't—" He shook his head in disgust. "I can't do anything about the past, and I can't swear that I can do anything about the future." He looked at Caylen, and nodded slowly. "But I can try. I *will* try, I promise."

She believed him. The Chancellor had said that he'd trained any kindness out of Logan, but Caylen didn't think that was true. And if the Chancellor was wrong about that, then it made it easier to believe that he was wrong about Caylen, too. She *wouldn't* be destroyed by the city.

She had a feeling that the old man might have been right about which questions she should be asking, though. "Why would they want this? You said Lord Rolston is in charge of the Dark House—why would *he* want to do this?"

Logan looked uncomfortable. "We should talk about that later. Let's just eat, and get going."

Caylen didn't push. They both ate quickly, aware that they were being watched, the crowd's mood somewhere between curious and resentful, with a heartbreaking taste of hopefulness mixed in on top. As soon as they were done eating, Caylen pulled her wooden tokens out and left them on the table, and she and Logan were off.

They made their way through the crowded streets, and for the first time, Caylen realized that they were unaccompanied. "Where are your guards?"

Logan gave her a quick sideways look. "I expect they're still back at the Great Hall, waiting for me. We left through a different door, so they wouldn't have seen us, and you were in too much of a hurry for me to suggest we go back for them."

"Logan! Is that dangerous? I could have calmed down…"

"How could it be dangerous? I have the best bodyguard in the world right beside me, don't I?" His smile was teasing, but she felt like he'd really meant at least some of the compliment. The smile faded, though, and turned to a frown. "But you need to start being more careful. That scene this morning, and the speech at the inn—people will hear about both of them. You're making yourself into a public figure, and that means you're a potential target."

"Oh, come on, Logan. Who would care enough about me to want to hurt me?" And the Chancellor's advice came back to her again. "*Why* would they?"

"Because you're stirring things up, and making people think. And because you make me stronger." The smile was back, gentle this time. "In more ways than they know."

Caylen didn't really know how to take that. "I thought I just made you grumpier."

He nodded. "Yeah, that too." His smile turned into a grin before it faded into his more usual serious face. "We should go find Jonah. I think he and I need to figure some things out. And I think you should be part of the conversation."

CHAPTER 24

"We've always known it was someone from their camp," Jonah said. He was sitting in one of the large chairs in Caylen's apartment, where he'd been waiting for Logan and her. "Or at least suspected. Rolston wants his daughter to be the heir, so he wants Logan out of the way. Whether Rolston gave the order—*that* we still don't know. It could have been any one from his side. He might not even have known about it."

"When Mara suggested that I go talk to the Council—it was a distraction, from me trying to talk to you about who sent the false nomads," Caylen said. She tried to ignore her mortification at having been fooled so easily. She should take the lesson from it, and learn to not make the same mistake again, but it was self-indulgent to let herself wallow in misery about it; Nora would never have allowed such a luxury.

Logan nodded. "It seems that way."

"But it's a long way from proof," Jonah said resignedly. "It's not even enough to take to the Chancellor—he'd be as likely to disapprove of you making wild accusations as he would be to believe any of it."

"Well maybe it's proof enough for me. I'm here to deal with the person who caused Dart's death. If we're pretty sure that Rolston was behind it, then I have my target."

"And what about your second goal?" Jonah was watching her closely. "You want to *avert* a nomad war, don't you? Having a high-ranking noble killed by a nomad for no apparent reason isn't going to do anything to calm people down. Might push them right into an attack."

Damn. Everything was more complicated in the city. A thought bubbled into Caylen's head, the echo of words from the accusations in the Council Chamber. "The peasants hid in the forest," she said quietly.

Logan stared at her blankly. "What?"

"The peasants... Lord Balter's peasants. They hid from *nomads* in the *forest*?" She waited for him to catch up, and when she saw his frown of dawning comprehension, she said, "There are nomads who can track a squirrel through the treetops, in the forest. Hiding from a nomad in the forest makes no sense. It'd be like hiding from a fish by jumping in the river."

"So what are you saying? The nomads didn't want to kill the peasants after all?"

"Maybe. Or maybe they weren't real nomads. Just like the ones who attacked you weren't real." Caylen was starting to get excited. "Maybe this has been going on for a while! Maybe somebody's deliberately trying to make nomads look bad, for some reason."

"That's too many 'maybes,'" Jonah said quietly. "We can't make accusations based on a hunch."

"Okay, fine. But if *you* can see that Rolston's behind all this, wouldn't it be clear to the Chancellor, as well?" Caylen was still struggling to understand the system in the city.

Logan and Jonah exchanged a look. "He probably already suspects...but it's not exactly sure that he cares." Logan sounded reluctant to continue, but he did. "The Chancellor values ruthlessness. He—he loved your father, Caylen. Very much. When your father died, the Chancellor—well, this was all before my time. But I've heard it from enough people that I'm sure it's true. The Chancellor decided that Willem had been killed because he hadn't been hard enough. He'd been idealistic, trying to help people, trying to reform the system, when he should have been looking after his own interests."

Jonah nodded slowly. "It hit the old man hard. There're those that say that he's doing this on purpose, all this delay about naming an heir. He should have done it years ago, but he's dragging it out—there're those that say that he *wants* them to fight, to see which one survives. That's the one that he'd decide was tough enough to be his heir."

Caylen thought of the old man she'd met that morning. He hadn't seemed gentle, exactly, but she certainly hadn't sensed this level of cynicism. But she was still learning to understand city ways; maybe she'd misread him entirely. "So there's no point in trying to prove anything to him," she said. And that was fine. She hadn't come to the city in order for someone else to mete out justice for her. "Are *we* sure it was Rolston? Or Mara?"

"Or anyone from their faction," Logan reminded her. "It's entirely possible that they don't know anything about it. They might *suspect* that it was someone from their side, but they might not know for sure."

Caylen hit the arm of her chair in frustration, then got up to pace restlessly around the room. The puppy had been sleeping by her feet, but he got up now and walked with her, making her dodge with every turn to avoid tripping over him. "So, killing you—that could benefit anyone from their side. What about the false nomads? We can't be sure that the attacks were staged, but what if they were? If someone's trying to make nomads look bad—why? They want to start a nomad war? Who would that benefit?"

Jonah nodded thoughtfully. "It's a good question. A nomad war—what would that look like? We'd shut our doors to trade with nomads, and we'd send out more soldiers with our caravans. We'd have to try to get the other cities on board to have even a prayer of having any impact; otherwise, we'd just be hurting our own trade while the nomads would still be able to get whatever they wanted from other markets."

Caylen tried to imagine the events from the nomad perspective. "I don't know how you'd ever really win. We'd watch you, and if there were too many, we'd just melt into the forest. You'd maybe be able to hire a few guides good enough to track us, but you'd never have many soldiers well-enough trained to be able to keep up with us in our forest, and if you sent too few we'd just pick them off."

"Maybe we'd burn the forest," Logan said as if he was thinking aloud, with an apologetic look at Caylen. He stopped looking apologetic after a moment. "But we'd never be able to get rid of enough to trap you. We could clear it, slowly, but if we were at war, you'd be attacking our loggers while they worked." He shook his head and looked at Jonah. "I never really thought it through, I guess. Even if all the cities joined forces, it would be uncomfortable for the nomads, but I can't see how we could ever really win."

"And even if we did win, what would we get? There's nothing to plunder, no livestock or machinery to bring home. We'd be stuck spending a huge amount of time and energy trying to hold onto land that isn't any use to us anyhow." Jonah seemed just as confused as Logan, which wasn't too reassuring.

"So, why?" Caylen asked. "Have the people pushing for war really not thought it through, either? Or have they thought about it, and decided that they don't care? Is there some other benefit that they could get, other than winning a war?"

It was Logan's turn to stand up and move impatiently. It seemed like a waste of the luxurious furniture in the room, but the puppy loved having one more person to chase. "It can't just be..." He looked at Jonah, then Caylen, and explained, "For the last couple years, it's seemed like the nobles are moving toward Mara and Rolston's side. The military leaders are more inclined to back me. They couldn't just be trying to get the soldiers out of the city to make me more vulnerable, could they?"

Jonah nodded slowly. "Or weakening your support there. I haven't heard a lot from the generals, but the rank-and-file soldiers are all for attacking the nomads. If you spoke out against the war, maybe you'd lose military support."

"The people don't seem to like nomads," Caylen mused. "But I didn't hear any of them talking about war."

Jonah waved his hand dismissively. "The people don't matter. They're not armed, they don't speak in the Council, and they don't have money to pay for campaigns. My family, and a few others, we have enough coin to buy a voice. The other commoners are insignificant to this."

Logan didn't disagree. "So what do I do? I can't speak out against it, but if we go to war, my most powerful supporters will be out of the city." He was starting to look hunted again, the same look he'd had in the river that day, when he'd first really accepted that there were some in his band of soldiers who were trying to kill him.

"What about the Dark House?" Caylen asked.

Logan looked almost hurt. "I'll try to get to that, Caylen, but I'm not going to do anyone any good if I'm not heir, or if I'm dead in a ditch somewhere."

She wasn't really interested in soothing his self-pity, but she needed to clarify. "No, I didn't mean it like that. I meant—why is the Dark House so busy? Why are they rounding up so many people? The man at the Inn said things started getting bad a few years ago. So what does that mean?" She wasn't sure if she should be impatient with the men and their blank looks, or with herself—had she missed something obvious? "I'm saying—if we think that Rolston and his people are behind the attack on Logan, then that means that they're also behind the false nomads, right? And you said that Rolston was in charge of the Dark House. So is he trying to use *it* as a way to get at you, too? Or is the whole thing directed somewhere else? Does he have something else that he's trying to do?"

Jonah nodded slowly, and then smiled at Caylen. He looked tired, but genuine. "It's good to have fresh eyes on this. We're so used to seeing things from one direction..."

"Not that it actually helps all that much," Logan said. "It's given us more questions, but no damned answers!" He crossed to the window and looked out at the city, then spoke so quietly that he could barely be heard. "The reason I wanted to go overland...the reason I didn't take the river back from the estate, the way I was supposed to...I didn't want to come back. I just wanted to stay out there forever, out where it was simple, and I felt like I understood everything."

Caylen walked a little closer to him. "If it makes you feel any better... from what I saw, you really didn't understand all that much in the forest, either. You were just too ignorant to even know what you didn't know." She waited until his surprised look shifted to a reluctant grin, then said, "I have to stay here, until we get the nomad stuff sorted out, and until I know who had Dart killed. But after that—if you wanted to run away, I'd help. You weren't so hopeless that you couldn't learn. You could be a good nomad. If you wanted."

"Yeah?" Logan seemed to realize how much of a compliment she'd given him. "I might—damn, I might be pretty tempted to take you up on that. No chance we could just leave now, is there?"

Caylen shook her head emphatically. "Nope. Nomads don't quit."

The conversation was interrupted by a knock on the door. Logan answered it to find a team of women bearing packages, and he nodded as if he recognized them. "Caylen," he said, turning, "We've finally got some seamstresses. They'll measure you, and let you pick some designs." He looked at the woman closest to the door. "Try to find something that she'll be comfortable in—she's used to leggings."

The seamstress didn't exactly look impressed, but she nodded dutifully, and Jonah edged past the women to join Logan at the door. "We'll leave you to this, if we may. I have an appointment with the Chancellor, and Logan really should make time to see his doctor and make sure that everything's healing properly. One or both of us can come back to have dinner with you, if you like."

"In order to keep me from being seen with Mara?" Caylen asked. "I don't think you need to worry about that anymore." Logan cut his eyes toward the seamstresses and back to Caylen, the warning clear. Apparently, in Logan's mind, everyone was a potential spy. But Caylen wasn't in the city to make friends, and she wasn't afraid of stirring things up. "If she and her father are responsible for Darton's death, then they're my enemies. If they're trying to stir up a stupid war that would get a lot of people killed for no reason, then they're the enemies of my people, *and* of everyone in this city." She said it loudly enough that not only the seamstresses could hear, but anyone in the hall, as well.

Logan looked concerned, and Jonah's frown was deeper than Caylen thought she'd ever seen it. "Well stay IN, then, and ask them to bring you dinner," Logan said. "You can't go walking around town saying things like that without making yourself a prime target."

Caylen didn't bother to let Logan know that being a target would be just fine with her. As long as she was a *moving* target, she wouldn't likely get hit, and she welcomed the thought of getting a chance to see who was shooting at her. But Logan would just worry. "I'll have to go outside with the dog..."

"Take guards, and don't go far." Jonah sounded like he was getting tired of being a babysitter, and Caylen couldn't really blame him. "I'll dig around a little and see what I can come up with on what we were talking about earlier. Logan can do the same, in his circles. We'll meet back here tomorrow morning, for breakfast?" Logan and Caylen nodded agreement, but Jonah didn't look like he was sure he should trust either one of them. He left reluctantly, with Logan trailing behind.

Caylen turned to the woman who seemed to be in charge of the seamstresses. "I'm in your hands. But, please—I'm a nomad. These city clothes are too much for me. Can you find something in between?"

"A nomad, are you?" The woman said. "My mother used to always say that if I was nasty, your kind would come and steal me away."

Caylen hoped the seamstress was joking. "Why would we steal the nasty children? We usually try for the well-behaved ones. They're easier to manage."

There was a pause, and then the woman's frown relaxed, and she smiled. "Well then, I guess I was safe. Come, miss, we'll get you measured up."

Caylen submitted. The women did almost exactly the same things as Mara's seamstresses had done the night before, but this night, Caylen let herself be drawn into their conversation, and indulged her curiosity with questions about their actions. She was tired of thinking about who was trying to kill who, and *why*, especially when answers were in such short supply. Better to find some shallow amusements than deeper frustrations, at least for a while.

CHAPTER 25

The seamstresses had bustled off with promises of at least one outfit for the next morning and Caylen was just contemplating taking a trip downstairs with the puppy when there was a firm knocking on the door. The puppy almost tripped her three separate times on the ten-step trip to the door, but she managed to get there safely. She opened it to find a boy, maybe twelve years old, in the uniform that she had come to understand signified an official messenger.

He gave a slight bow, and then said, "My Lady— the Chancellor requests your presence."

"Right now? Is Jonah still with him?" It seemed unlikely; Caylen had been busy with the seamstresses for quite a while, and the Chancellor didn't seem like the sort to indulge in long meetings, especially with commoners. But she really had no idea how these things were done.

"I'm sorry, My Lady, I don't know. I was just told to come and get you."

Caylen wasn't used to being at anyone's beck and call; well, no one except Nora. But she was pretty sure it wouldn't be wise to keep the old man waiting.

She moved to follow the boy, and almost tripped over the puppy. The poor creature hadn't been outside in some time, and who knew how long Caylen would be trapped with the Chancellor. She reached behind her and found the short chunk of rope that they'd been using as a leash. The Chancellor might have the right to summon her, but surely she had the right to choose her own escort. And she reached back and pulled her bow out from its spot by the door. She'd choose her own weapon, too.

Caylen wasn't sure if the messenger boy found nothing unremarkable about the situation or if he was just too well trained to show his surprise, but he said nothing as he led the way downstairs. He paused as they neared the group of guards who were, as always, standing just outside the door. It seemed silly to her, but she could just imagine Jonah's exasperation if she showed up alone. She found a familiar face in the group, a man who she was pretty sure had been with Logan earlier. "I'm—the Chancellor wants to see me."

The guard nodded easily. "Standard or enhanced security?"

She had no idea. "Standard? Probably?"

"If you're just going to the Great Hall and back, that's probably fine," he agreed. "If you plan to go around the city afterward, though, we should take more men; it's getting dark."

"No, just to the Hall and back. Thank you." If she was going around the city, she'd come back and change her clothes, and sneak out on her own. She'd feel much safer by herself in the shadows than surrounded by guards but stuck in the light.

The trip to the Hall was simple, and Caylen found herself growing used to the stares she got from the people they passed. She still didn't like the attention, but it didn't make her cringe anymore. And she felt like it was easier, with the puppy by her side; she could pretend they were looking at him, instead of her. And his frequent stops to sniff or mark areas made their walk less like an official procession and more like an oversized and somewhat erratic window-shopping trip.

They left the guards at the main door and the messenger boy led Caylen inside. They passed right by the big doors that Caylen had gone through that morning; the boy saw Caylen's confusion and said, "I'm supposed to take you to a different room. I don't know why."

Caylen didn't want to be paranoid, but she also didn't want to be ambushed. "Was it the Chancellor himself who told you to come get me?"

The boy nodded thoughtfully. "Yeah. Usually it would be an assistant, but he told me himself. Gave me an extra token to be quick and quiet. That's what he said—'quick and quiet.'"

"And will you be? Quiet, I mean?"

The boy's eyes were a little too wide to be convincingly innocent. "Of course, my lady."

They veered off into a narrower hallway with doors on either side. The boy stopped walking when the hall turned into a narrow staircase. There was a uniformed guard on either side, but neither looked familiar to Caylen. The boy nodded his head up the stairs. "The door's at the top."

It was a strange set-up, a far cry from the grandeur of the opulent main office. Caylen scrutinized the boy. He was too young, surely, to be involved in trying to ambush her. She thought of herself at that age, and remembered some of the jobs Nora had sent her on. She might not have understood every detail, but that hadn't made her any less effective in her role. "He normally has meetings here? This is routine?"

The boy shrugged. "Not really. Usually he has his meetings in the large office. But I know he goes here, sometimes. I've taken messages to him, here."

Caylen nodded; she'd gotten all she thought she could out of the boy. "Come on, pup," she said to the dog. He was still figuring out how to climb stairs, but Caylen didn't let herself be distracted by his antics. She was on alert as she moved, ready for anything suspicious or harmful.

The door at the top of the stairs was heavy wood, and her knock was more like a thud. She kept her eyes on the bottom of the stairs; if someone appeared there, especially with a gun, she was a sitting duck. But no one appeared, and a small shutter in the door was opened enough for someone to look out at her before a bolt was slid aside and the door itself opened slowly.

The Chancellor was there, looking much the same as he had earlier in the day. "Thank you for coming, Caylen," he said, as if she'd had a choice. And who knew—maybe she had.

She stepped inside and tried not to notice the look the Chancellor gave to the puppy. It wasn't the dog's fault that Caylen still hadn't found time to bathe him. "This is a beautiful room." She meant it. The space wasn't large, but it was well-shaped, almost round, with rich wood on the floor, and dark fabric on the furniture. The walls were lined with books, more than Kaylen had ever seen in one place; there was a narrow catwalk running around the room to form a second story, with more books and a only a few windows. The effect would have been too dark, except for the huge domed skylight, and the ample electric lighting. She could see why the Chancellor would want to spend time there. "But the approach is strange."

"I supposed it is. But I like it—I think it adds clarity to the role of this room—it is my private library, not my public office. And the bolt on the door is nice, to keep my assistants at bay." He gestured toward two armchairs half-facing the unlit fire. "Please, sit down."

She did as she was told, and he sat across from her and looked at her for longer than she was comfortable with before saying, "I hear you've taken my advice to heart. Some of it, at least."

"Not the running away. But I've been asking 'why', if that's what you mean."

"It is what I mean. I must say, though—I envisioned you going about it a little more subtly. I didn't anticipate you presenting your ideas to Council, or making a spectacle of yourself in a commoners' inn. I've spent almost all day dealing with Councilors upset in one way or another, and I'm booked solid all day tomorrow, as well. I spoke to Jonah this afternoon—we had been scheduled to resolve some very important financial matters, and instead spent almost the entire meeting discussing you." The Chancellor didn't seem upset, exactly, but Caylen had the idea that he considered the whole thing to be an aggravating waste of his time. "He finally admitted that he had no way to control you, short of having you killed and thrown in a ditch. And he seemed to feel that Logan might object to that approach fairly strongly. I also got the impression that he wasn't exactly sorry to see you stirring things up a little." The Chancellor leaned forward a little, and fixed his eyes on Caylen's. "I, on the other hand, am not terribly impressed."

Caylen leaned forward herself. The puppy whined, as if sensing the tension in the room, and slinked a few steps away from them, toward the fireplace. "I'm not terribly impressed myself, sir. I know that I'm new to the city, but it's amazing to me that no one else has been asking the questions I'm asking. No one's asked whether the nomad attacks were genuine? No one's asked why the Dark House is rounding up countless citizens? And, sir, no offense, but no one has asked why their Chancellor seems content to sit back and let these things happen, instead of protecting his people?"

The Chancellor stared at her, and Caylen got the distinct feeling that she had gone much too far. The puppy whined again, and actually seemed to be trying to climb *inside* the fireplace. Caylen pulled back on his leash. "Pup, no."

But the puppy was growling now, his muzzle pointing at the unlit logs on the grate—the unlit logs that actually seemed to be smoking a little. Caylen leaned over and waved her end of the rope at the Chancellor. "Pull him back, will you? I want to take a look at that..."

The Chancellor didn't respond immediately, but eventually he took hold of the rope and pulled, and Caylen slid down to take the pup's place. There was a packet of something, with a long, slow-burning fuse leading to it, nestled into the shadows behind the logs. Caylen was trained to be observant, but she was pretty sure that she wouldn't have seen it if the dog's nose hadn't tipped her off.

"You aren't actually trying that 'having me killed' thing right now, are you, sir? There's no reason for whatever that is to be there?" She leaned forward and cautiously pulled the packet out, holding it in front of her for his inspection. From the way his eyes widened, the Chancellor was as surprised as she was to see it. She was glad she still had Dart's knife, even if it *was* a nuisance to carry it when she was all dressed up. She fished it out from her makeshift ankle sheath and carefully cut the fuse, tossing the burning part back in the fireplace before she started poking at the package it had been attached to.

She carried it over and placed it on the desk, under the brightest lamp, and the Chancellor peered over her shoulder as she made a careful slit in the outer wrapping. "I'm not sure..." She took a cautious sniff and then jerked her head away. "I'm not an expert on explosives, but I don't think that was going to have a very big blast. Not enough to kill us, not for sure. But it sure does stink." She thought back to the hall, the way it had made her skin crawl with apprehension. It was a perfect spot for an ambush. She grabbed the Chancellor's arm just as he was heading for the door. "Whoever set it wasn't planning on killing us *inside* this room. But they might have been planning to smoke us out, send us into that hallway."

Her mind was racing. "There're two guards down there. They might be crooked, and they're the ones who are supposed to do the killing; or they might be dead already. If those guards knocked on the door, sir—would you have let them in?"

The Chancellor nodded, his eyes wide. "Yes, I would have."

"So if the enemy just wanted you dead, and those guards are in on it—they could have just killed you in here. If the enemy wanted me dead, too—the guards could have attacked me as I walked by. As long as you didn't see it, you would have let them in. But you have that peephole, you might have seen it..." Again, there were a maddening number of variables to consider, and Caylen was short on time.

"I want you to stay here, sir. Keep the door barred until someone you absolutely trust comes to get you. Maybe go up on the second level, so you could climb outside if they send another bomb in."

"And what are *you* going to do?"

Caylen headed for the spiral staircase that led to the second floor. She already had a window in mind. "I'm going to try to circle around, get some guards, and trap whoever's waiting for us down there. They must have been inside those rooms off the hallway—do those rooms have other doors?" She was trying to calculate the timing in her mind. How long would the assassins wait before they aborted the mission?

"The rooms to the north don't have other doors. The rooms to the south open onto a hallway. It should be locked, though."

"Yeah, so should this library, but someone managed to get inside to plant that smoke bomb." The window wasn't designed to open, and Caylen felt a little bad for having to pull a book off a nearby shelf as a tool to break the glass. She wasn't sure which was more valuable, the window or the book; they both looked like they came from the Time Before, so they were both probably priceless. She carefully cleared the jagged edges of glass out of the window frame and then leaned outside. The ground sloped down, so rather than being on the second floor, it was more like she was on the third, but the rough stone here was similar to that of the apartments. She looked back over her shoulder. "Take care of the dog, okay?" and then she slid outside and started climbing.

The climb had been a lot easier that morning, when she'd been wearing her own clothes. Wearing her own *boots*, damn it, not these high-heeled, slippery... Her toes lost their hold and she caught herself with her fingers. She could feel the skin grating off as she tried to dig in, tried to stop the painful, scrabbling slide. Finally her feet found a grip, and she took a moment to re-center her mind before continuing down the wall. She should have taken her boots off and gone barefoot, but it was too late for that now. She'd have to learn her lesson, and keep it in mind for the next time she tried to escape a luxurious library by climbing down a sheer stone wall in formal city clothes.

She let herself drop when her feet were about five feet off the ground, landing in a crouch that turned into a roll as her boots tipped her off balance. Damn them. But she didn't have much farther to go, now. She was on a grassy lawn not far from the front doors, and she walked as briskly as she could without being obvious enough to alert a sentry, in case the assassins had one. She trotted up the stairs to the main door and found the guards that had escorted her there. But she needed as much manpower as she could get. "Is someone in charge?" She asked, her voice loud and as authoritative as she could manage. She saw her guards' confusion at her appearance from the wrong direction, but didn't have time to explain.

"I'm the Sergeant," a middle-aged man said, and his uniform *did* look a bit different from the others. She needed to pay more attention to that sort of thing. But not right then.

"I was just with the Chancellor. He's trapped in his library—he believes that there are assassins waiting in the hallway below his stairs. He wants you to set up a circumference around that hallway, and the locked hallway to the south, and then move in, catching whoever's in there." She supposed she probably should have asked for the Chancellor's permission before borrowing his authority, but there really hadn't been time. And there wasn't time now for the guards to be staring at her as if they thought she was crazy. She turned to the man in charge. "You need to get your men moving."

He looked unsure. "*You* say those are the Chancellor's orders..."

"We brought her here for a meeting with him," said her familiar guard from earlier. "She's Lady Caylen—the lost heir."

That seemed to help the Sargent decide. "Fine. Men—let's go." He jerked his head at Caylen's guard and one other. "You two stay here, and keep an eye on her. If this is a false alarm, I want her nice and handy." He jogged toward the door, shouting orders as he went. It had taken him a while to get started, but now that he was in action, he seemed efficient.

Caylen looked at her guards. "We could just go inside, a little, to see what's happening…" she started, but they both shook their heads simultaneously.

"Sorry, my lady, orders are for you to stay here."

She hated being so far from the action. What if the guards were too late, or bungled things? What if they didn't find anything? Didn't find anyone? She felt the tension starting to churn inside. What if the whole thing had just been a stupid prank, and she'd totally over-reacted? It had been a smoke bomb, that was all—nothing deadly. She didn't know these city people, didn't know their customs, and she'd barely given the Chancellor an opportunity to speak. Maybe he wouldn't have been at all concerned—maybe the orders she'd given in his name were total nonsense.

She looked down toward the street and saw a guarded procession making its way through the crowd. She caught a glimpse of the nobles inside, and sighed. Of course. Mara and Rolston. If she'd just made a huge fool of herself, she couldn't think of anyone that she'd *less* like to have witness her humiliation. They drew closer, and she saw them see her, saw them alter their course to come closer. She braced herself; there was nothing else she could do.

"Caylen!" Mara's smile was as warm as it had been when they'd first met, and Caylen had another reason to doubt her own judgment. She didn't understand these city people at *all*. Maybe Caylen had misjudged Mara's friendliness, but what if she'd actually misunderstood her actions in the Council Chamber? Mara's next words were uncomfortably close to Caylen's thoughts. "I'm so glad I ran into you—I was going to call this afternoon, but I wasn't sure if I would be welcome. I wanted to make sure you understood what happened this morning." Another smile, this one full of compassion. "You're doing so well, I keep forgetting that you're new, and you don't know the way things are done in the city. Well, in the Council especially!" She shared an amused, knowing look with her father, then turned back to Caylen, her expression shifting into confusion. "But, what are you doing standing around out here? And why with only two guards? Caylen, it's almost full dark— you need to be more careful!"

"I'm just—waiting. There's maybe a situation inside, and the guards went to check on it." Did that sound boring enough to make the others want to leave?

Apparently not. "A 'situation'?" Mara's eyes were wide. "What does that mean?"

"Uh—I'm not really sure. I don't have a lot of details." It wasn't just her pride that Caylen was protecting, now. It had occurred to her that if Rolston was the prime suspect in the attacks on Logan, then he was hardly immune from suspicion of being involved in *this* attack. And thinking of the fighting in the forest made Caylen think of Dart, and reminded her that the man in front of her might be the enemy she'd been searching for. And even if he wasn't involved in that, she *knew* he was to blame for other atrocities. She remembered the Chancellor's words about subtly, but she also remembered her own, about not sitting around and *watching* as terrible things happened. "But I'm glad I ran into you, too. Both of you. Lord Rolston, as Mara said, I'm new to town, and I don't really understand the way you do things. Can you explain to me—why are you locking up so many citizens in the Dark House? And what are you doing to them there? And do you have any information from the soldier who attacked Logan? Has he said who sent him?"

Rolston looked as if she'd spit in his face. "We don't call it that. It's the Office of Intelligence Services. And its work is *highly* confidential. It would be completely inappropriate for me to discuss its functions in this venue."

Caylen wasn't sure exactly what a 'venue' was, but she got the main idea. "So—when *could* we discuss it?"

Rolston barked out an angry, surprised laugh. "We can discuss it when you learn some manners! And when you have some actual authority to speak to me this way. Which is to say—never."

"So who *does* have the authority to ask you these questions? The Chancellor? Just him, or anyone else?"

"Your questions display your ignorance. I don't have time to tutor an uneducated child on the intricacies of the Yorkton system of government." He turned to his daughter. "Mara, we will be late if we delay." He held his elbow out and she placed her hand through it, but she seemed reluctant.

As they walked away, Mara turned back to Caylen and called, "I'll visit you tomorrow, if I may. We'll talk!"

Caylen watched them leave, and then turned back to her guards. The one from the apartments gave her a small, crooked smile. "I changed my mind," he said. "I'd recommend enhanced security for you, from now on."

The doors of the Great Hall opened then, and three messenger boys shot out, two running full speed in opposite directions down the street, the third stopping to speak to Caylen's guard. "Lady Caylen is wanted in the Chancellor's office," the boy said.

Caylen's guard nodded before glancing at her and then back at the boy. "How're things in there? Where'd those other messengers get sent to?"

The boy seemed a bit shy about speaking in front of Caylen, but her guard gestured encouragingly, and the boy finally said, "There's a lot of yelling. The Chancellor looks upset. They sent a messenger to the Dark—I mean, to the Office of Intelligence Services—and one to find Lord Rolston."

Caylen didn't really want to face all of this alone. "Do you—are you done, now? If I wanted to send a message, could you take it for me?"

The boy nodded. "Yes, my lady."

"Could you go and find Jonah, or Lord Logan? Could you tell them I need them?"

The boy looked shyly at the guard, who smiled again, encouraging the boy to speak up. "Their messengers have already gone, my lady. There are official messengers, like me and those other two, and there are the private messengers. We call them spies, but really they don't snoop much. They just run and tell their masters when something big happens. You wouldn't have seen them because they go out the back way." He grinned and looked at the guard. "It was like rats running out of a granary, when they all left."

The guard looked at Caylen. "So it sounds like they found something, then. Ready to go find out what?" He had never been *un*friendly, but he'd certainly gotten a lot warmer since she'd argued with Rolston. She wondered just how much the guards saw, and how much of it they kept to themselves.

"I guess so." She started for the door, her two guards falling in behind her. She headed for the Chancellor's main office, the one she'd been in that morning, and arrived to find a frenzy of activity. There were several clusters of well-dressed people, all talking anxiously and loudly, with a seemingly endless stream of messengers running between the groups and the back door of the hall. A squad of guards were standing outside the first set of doors to the Chancellor's office, and unlike their usual poses of casual boredom, these men seemed alert and ready.

Two of them stepped forward to bar Caylen's way, but her guard said, "She's Lady Caylen, the lost heir. She's been sent for." The guards by the door stepped aside immediately, and Caylen went through, leaving her own guards behind.

Inside, there was relative calm. There were fewer people, and those that *were* there seemed to have definite jobs; two men were sitting at a long table, writing, and an unfamiliar woman was standing by the door to the inner office. She nodded at Caylen, then opened the door and announced "Lady Caylen, my lord." She stepped aside to give Caylen access.

The Chancellor was sitting in the same chair he'd been in that morning, but he looked much different. Much older. For the first time, Caylen felt a rush of compassion for him; he might be powerful, but he was still just a man, and apparently he wasn't quite ready for death.

"Are you okay, sir?" Caylen looked around the room to be sure that they were alone. "And do you have my dog?"

The Chancellor lifted his far hand to show the chunk of rope that he was gripping, and Caylen stepped close enough to see the puppy sound asleep on the floor, just beyond the Chancellor's chair. "He smells," the Chancellor managed.

"He smells pretty well, I'd say. He's the one who caught the smoke bomb, before it went off."

"I'm surrounded by highly trained guards, and I owe my life to a smelly mutt and an untamed nomad." He turned and looked at her for the first time. "Thank you. Both of you."

"So there *were* assassins, then? I mean—I started to think that it was maybe just my imagination."

The Chancellor looked surprised. "There were. Three men. You were right. They'd killed the guards, and were waiting for us to get smoked out, from the looks of it."

Caylen tried to remember the guards—had she even looked at them, really? Or were they just two more faceless victims of the city's absurd power struggle? "Where are the killers? Did they say who sent them?"

"They're being held in one of the side rooms. Well-guarded, I assure you. We'll transfer them to the Dark House, and then we'll see who sent them."

"By torturing them? Is that the only way? Can you even be sure they'll tell the truth?" Caylen was beginning to feel like a bird with only one song, but surely she had to keep singing it until people listened. What was the alternative, to give up, and become just another city drone, going along with an atrocity just because she couldn't be bothered to think about it?

The Chancellor looked like he had an answer, although Caylen was far from sure that she was going to be satisfied by it, but then the door to the outer office opened and the efficient-looking woman stepped inside. "We have Lords Rolston and Logan to see you, sir, if you're available."

The Chancellor ran a hand over his face as if trying to wake up from a bad dream, and took a deep breath before nodding to the woman. "Show them in, please." He raised an eyebrow at Caylen. "Although I only remember sending for Rolston. Perhaps Logan has his own reasons for being here?"

The men arrived before Caylen had time to form an answer, and they both hurried over. "I heard there was an attempt on your life, my lord," Rolston said. He looked like he might be about to start crying.

"You're all right, sir? Everyone's very worried," Logan added. Then he looked at Caylen. "Can you honestly not stay out of trouble for even one evening?" His voice was light and teasing, but there was a trace of exasperation in it, and a hint of something less familiar, as well.

"Nora was right," Caylen said. "The city *is* a dangerous place."

"Not for most of us," Rolston said, and there was no hint of humor in his tone. "Perhaps the violence of the forest has followed you in to civilization."

"It seemed more like the violence of civilization invaded her forest," Logan said, his eyes locked on Rolston's. "She's only here to try to make sure it doesn't keep happening."

"And it was lucky for me that she was," the Chancellor added. He looked down at the young dog who was trying to chew his way through the rope around his neck. "Lucky that the dog was there, too." He looked at Rolston, his face a study in innocence. "I believe we have a medal for animal bravery, don't we? Wasn't it bestowed on your horse, a few years ago?"

"Midnight Star carried me through the forest in a terrible storm, when I was too fevered to even steer him," Rolston said indignantly. "He's a paragon of breeding, the pinnacle of his species..."

"But he's never saved the life of the Chancellor, has he?" The Chancellor looked down at the pup and then up at Rolston. "This dog is a hero. I think it's important that he be recognized."

"I think it's important that he be *bathed*," Logan said, "And then call him a hero if you like."

Caylen crouched down and let the puppy climb up on her knee to lick her face. "Hero," she said. "Maybe that's his name."

Rolston looked as if he'd like to send them all back into the assassins' path, but he nodded stiffly and said, "Yes, sir, of course. I'll see to it. But first, I need to address some more pressing matters. I will escort the prisoners to the Office of Intelligence Services myself."

The Chancellor gave Caylen an apologetic look before saying, "Yes, please do. And please send word as soon as any information is available."

"Of course, my lord." Rolston bowed, then turned to Logan and Caylen. "Are there enough guards left outside to escort you home? I'm sure the Chancellor needs his rest, after his difficult evening."

"You wanted to talk to me, sir. Earlier. We'd barely gotten started before we found the bomb." Caylen hoped the Chancellor didn't remember too clearly exactly the direction their conversation had been taking.

He didn't seem angry, at least. He waved an arm to dismiss Rolston, who didn't seem quite as eager to leave once he realized that Logan and Caylen would be staying behind. But he couldn't ignore the Chancellor, and he headed for the door. The Chancellor waited until he was gone, and then turned to Caylen. "I need to think about what you said, my young friend. I wonder if I was too hasty, in wanting you to settle down. Maybe you and Jonah are right—maybe we need to stir things up around here."

"Jonah thinks that?" Logan sounded surprised.

"You and your friend are not all that different, Logan." The Chancellor smiled, then waved his hand imperiously in the air. "I'll speak to you all tomorrow. Logan, make sure you arrange extra security for Lady Caylen, and perhaps for yourself. Until we know more about the attackers, everyone is a potential victim."

Logan nodded seriously. "Yes, sir, I will." He gestured toward the door. "May I escort you home, Lady Caylen?"

She reclaimed the leash from the Chancellor and let Logan guide her out the door; she'd be compliant for a while, but he'd better not get used to it. Hopefully, he was only joking. If he wasn't, she was going to have to sit him down and remind him of who had saved whose life several times in the forest. She didn't need to be *escorted* anywhere. She could escort *him*, maybe.

Logan's voice broke into her thoughts. "I think you should come home with me."

"Pardon?"

"We can arrange for chaperones, of course. Whatever will make you comfortable." he said.

"I've already shared a bed with you, Logan—I don't think I need a *chaperone*. I just don't understand what's wrong with the apartment."

"Well, with the dog, it'd be easier for you if you could just open a door and shoo him outside. But, also— it's safer in the Estates. Still not guaranteed, I suppose, but it'd be hard for anyone but a member of the families to get inside. And I can see you having trouble with a group of soldiers, or assassins...but against someone from one of the families, I like your chances."

Caylen decided to take his words as a compliment. "Well, based on what I've seen so far, I think I'd be fine. But do you have room?"

"We have twelve bedrooms. Ten of them are empty. I think we can fit you in."

Caylen thought about arguing, but then thought better of it. Logan was watching her, and he smirked. "You're thinking that you're going to guard *me*, aren't you?" He shook his head. "I'm getting to know all your tricks, Caylen."

"The Chancellor *said* you should consider extra guards."

Logan nodded. "Okay. Fair enough. We'll guard each other—okay?"

Caylen couldn't think of a way to disagree with that, and she let Logan lead her through the darkened streets, back to the gated enclave he called home.

***

Caylen spent that night in a huge, luxurious bed, the crisp white sheets feeling almost *too* smooth against her skin. She woke when the puppy started whining to go out; she and Logan had bathed him the night before, and the dog had snuggled up next to her on the bed as if he was happy to finally be living in the manner which he deserved. Caylen, on the other hand, felt like an intruder, creeping through the opulent hallways and grandiose rooms of the mansion, looking for a door to the back garden. It was hard to imagine Logan living in this house, even now, but almost impossible to imagine him as a child, running down the marble halls, laughing and tumbling on the delicate furniture. She wondered if he'd been sent outside to play, but even there, he'd have faced a carefully manicured garden, smooth lawn trimmed carefully away from pruned shrubs and regimented flower beds. It was no wonder he was a little over-cautious, she decided.

She didn't think she'd be able to get back to sleep, and she didn't want to sit alone in the huge, impersonal house, so she stayed outside with the dog and watched the sun come up over the trees at the back of the garden. Logan had sent a servant for her clothes the night before, and she'd put on her leggings and tunic without even thinking that morning. And now, she was outside, with growing things and fresh air. It felt familiar, and the trees called to her. She walked back and investigated, and found that what looked like a bit of a forest was actually a cleverly staggered double row of trees camouflaging a tall stone wall.

She tried to find the rhythm of the tiny forest, tried to let herself blend with it as she did in her own land, but she had no luck. It felt like the wall that bounded the woods also contained *her*, and wouldn't let her go. A tiny, niggling voice asked her if she was sure it was the wall that was the problem; what if it was her, losing touch with the forest because she'd spent too long in the city?

But she wouldn't let that happen; she'd get back as soon as her business was settled. And that thought gave her another voice to ignore, the one that told her that she wasn't *settling* anything, just getting dragged deeper and deeper into the muck of city politics.

She headed back to the house, and by the time she got there, the cook was up, at least, and Caylen sat in the kitchen and visited with her while she prepared breakfast.

Logan stumbled in after a while, looking bleary-eyed and confused, and Caylen had to force herself to stay where she was sitting; apparently there was something inside her that wanted to get blankets and wrap sleepy boys up snuggly until they were ready to face the world. She didn't think she'd ever had an urge quite like *that* before; it was more than a little unsettling.

Logan managed to lead the way into a small, glassed-in room overlooking the gardens, where they sat while a maid bustled back and forth bringing linens and food. Logan woke up as they ate breakfast, and played with the pup a little, and then clapped his hands together too loudly. "Okay, enough of this. It's going to be a busy day—we need to get cleaned up and get to work."

"What work? What do you think we're going to do?" It wasn't that Caylen was lazy, but she wanted to be sure she wasn't sucked into Logan's politics when she should be worrying about her own goals.

"Hard to know, for sure. But somebody tried to kill the Chancellor last night, in his own damn library. That's going to have some repercussions. I'll need to be down at the Great Hall, looking suitably concerned and aggravated; you—" He frowned. "Well, we should check with Jonah, but I wonder if you shouldn't stay out of sight, actually. Build a little mystery. And maybe make people think that you were traumatized by the terrible events—honestly, Caylen, were you not shaken up at *all*?"

She remembered the uncomfortable moments when she wondered if she'd made a mistake, and overreacted to a simple prank. "Of course. It was— upsetting? I don't know what you want me to say."

"I guess it's hopeless to expect you to say that you'll be more careful..."

"I *was* being careful! I went to meet with the Chancellor, that's all! And then it's *because* I was being careful that it occurred to me that there might be an ambush. If I was more careful than I was, I would have just sat there in the room, waiting for who-knows-what, and the guards wouldn't have caught the assassins. I think I was just the *right* level of careful."

Logan smiled thoughtfully, then nodded. "You did well. I just..." He looked out at the garden, as if trying to distance himself from the conversation, then turned back to her. "I wouldn't like it if anything happened to you. I wouldn't like it at all." His voice was quiet, but his gaze was direct and open.

It was unexpected, and it was too much. Caylen made her voice light. "Why, Logan, I think that's—well, it's the *second* sweetest thing you've ever said to me. The *first* sweetest, of course, was when you proposed marriage. But this is almost as sweet, really."

He held her gaze for a little longer, then nodded briskly and stood up. "I need to get going. Can I leave you here, and trust that you'll *stay* here, where you're safe?"

"The Chancellor was attacked 'in his own damn library' last night, Logan." Caylen stood up and faced him. "Don't assume that anywhere's safe. And don't assume that *you're* safe, either. You're taking enhanced security?"

"You're learning the language, are you? And, yes, I'll take extra guards, if there are any left—every noble in the city has probably requested a full compliment. But don't shift the question—can you at least promise me that you'll stay here, where you're as safe as possible?"

Caylen shook her head slowly. "No. But I promise to keep trying to be the right level of careful." She looked at his doubtful face and raised her chin stubbornly. "That's the best you're going to get, Logan, so you'll just have to figure out how to deal with it."

Logan took a half-step closer to her, and lifted his fingers slowly, as if he was going to touch her face. Caylen didn't move; she wondered if his fingers would be warm. Before he touched her, though, he closed his hand into a loose fist and lowered his arm. "Okay. Be safe." He stepped backward. "I'll see you here tonight for dinner, okay? Both of us, here—safe."

"Sounds like a good plan." She stood and watched him as he strode into the house, and then looked down at the puppy. "It's just you and me, Hero. But one of us isn't too much use. You liked the cook, right, Hero? You wouldn't mind staying with her for a while, if I had to go do some errands?"

The puppy didn't object, but he didn't seem to be paying full attention to Caylen, either. Instead, he was staring intently toward the little forest at the end of the garden. Caylen tried to stay relaxed, but her mind was racing. She'd laughed at the city people, earlier, for thinking that they were safe just because they were behind walls, so she needed to be sure she didn't make the same mistake. She bent to pet the dog, keeping half an eye on the forest, and there it was. Just a little flash of unnatural movement, a shadow shifting where it shouldn't have, and she knew there was a problem.

But she had no idea how big the problem was. "Come on inside, pup," she said, and she moved as quickly as she thought would be natural, scooping the dog into her arms and carrying him with her.

"Logan?" She called as soon as she was inside. He might not be a nomad, but hopefully he could fight at least a little. "Logan? I think you've got company coming."

CHAPTER 27

They didn't have much time; fortunately, Logan hadn't wasted any of it questioning Caylen's instincts. As soon as he'd heard "There's someone in the trees at the back," he'd sprung into action, herding the staff down to safety in the basement while Caylen retrieved her bow from its spot by the front door.

Logan watched the last servant scurry down the stairs before saying, "I don't supposed I could convince you to join them?" to Caylen.

"I'd rather not sit around and wait for death to find me," she said, then grinned. "And I don't want to miss the fun."

Logan had his antique gun drawn and ready, but seemed unsure of what to do with it. "Have we got a plan?" he asked sheepishly.

Caylen shrugged. "Not a good one. But they'll have to cross that stretch of lawn, unless they circle around the side, somehow. And there's no easy way to do that. So I say we go upstairs and fire at them as they cross, and if some of them make it through, we can pick them off as they come up the stairs."

"Sounds easy," Logan decided, heading for the stairs.

Caylen followed him. "It'll depend on how many of them there are. And how determined they are."

"They must be damned desperate, to attack us here. The Chancellor last night, us this morning—somebody's making his move."

"We're still calling him 'somebody', instead of 'Ralston'?"

"Anytime there's a chance of someone hearing, it's 'somebody'. We don't need the trouble for making unproven accusations," Logan gave her a serious look that turned into a smirk. "And we don't need him *knowing* that we know. Assuming that we actually *do* know..."

Caylen was glad they were at the top of the stairs and ready to find positions. Any more of Logan's talk and she was going to get a headache. "Those windows open?" She looked into the sitting room on the landing.

Logan nodded, and Caylen crossed the room and leaned carefully over from the side of the window to twist the latch and raise the glass. She was just in time; the shadows from the forest had solidified into burly men, and the first four of them were heading across the broad expanse of lawn at a quick but cautious jog.

Caylen stepped back far enough to have room to shoot, then let her arrow fly. It hit the lead man in the thigh, and as Caylen was drawing another arrow, the deafening crack of Logan's gun echoed through the room. As Caylen loosed her second arrow, there was a thunder of gunfire from outside, at least two shotguns and several rifles. She leaned against the thick wall as the glass in the window next to her shattered. The attackers were well armed, and they'd obviously found their target.

"Move," Caylen ordered, but Logan was already on his way, running fast, heading for the bedroom just down the hall. He might not be used to all this, but he wasn't stupid. Caylen thought about finding a new window for herself, too, but she decided against it. Instead, she waited until she heard the crack of Logan's gun and then pivoted, aimed, fired, and shifted across to hide behind the wall on the far side of the window, all one smooth, easy movement. There were four men lying on the lawn, and only one of them had been moving at all. But that still left several men on their way into the house...at least three, and maybe four or five. Too many.

Caylen heard glass break downstairs, and assumed that the intruders had smashed the window of the kitchen door. They would be inside, now, moving cautiously but quickly.

Logan's head appeared at the doorway to the room he'd been in. "What now?" He seemed excited, but not panicked.

"Do you have more ammunition somewhere?" Caylen asked, quietly enough that she wouldn't be heard downstairs.

"No."

There was no point in scolding him. No point in reminding him that a gun without ammunition was just a pretty bauble; his face made it clear that he'd already realized that himself. "Four more shots, then. Make them count." She jogged down the hallway toward him. "Cross the hall, go into that room, and leave the door ajar, so it looks casual. I'll draw them down to the end of the hall, then I'll yell, jump into the far bedroom, you lean out and take them down. If they turn, you yell, and jump back into your room and lock the door. I'll come back out and finish them off." It wasn't a great plan, and if Logan got overexcited and started firing wildly, he'd be shooting *toward* Caylen, which she didn't like, but she didn't have time to figure anything else out. "Go," she hissed, and Logan gave her a doubtful look but obediently headed into the bedroom.

Caylen jogged to the end of the hall and stood sideways in front of the last door, bow ready. She took a deep breath, and let it out slowly. She was half-way through her next inhalation when the man appeared at the top of the stairs. He was in the bright light from the landing windows, and she was in the shadows, so she forced herself to wait until he stepped a little further, just a little...

The twang of her bowstring wasn't loud, and the man couldn't make much noise, either, not after her arrowhead sliced through his throat. He stumbled forward, dropping his rifle in order to grab at his neck with both hands. Caylen tore her attention away from him. She'd already nocked another arrow, an instinct after countless years of endless drills. The next man would know roughly where she was, and she readied herself to dodge.

Even with that preparation, the man was so fast that she barely had time to loose her arrow before diving sideways. She heard the boom of the shotgun and felt a burning sting in her arm. She checked it out quickly, but wasn't alarmed; she'd been grazed, that was all. Still, closer than she'd have liked. And she didn't think her arrow had found its target.

She needed to keep to the plan, needed to make sure the intruders were drawn down the hall toward her. Otherwise, Logan was a sitting duck in that room. Maybe she should have reversed the roles, and sent him down the hallway while she waited, but it was too late for that. She switched her bow to her off-hand and made an awkward, ugly shot down the hall, the best she could do without stepping out into the open. Hallways were made for guns, not bows, she decided.

But she'd done what she could. She stood silently, barely breathing, straining to hear any movement, any signal of which way the intruders were moving. Instead, she heard the front door bang open, and an unfamiliar male voice yell, "The guards are on the way! Finish it!"

That seemed like a good distraction, and Caylen let herself lean out just far enough to get a cleaner shot down the hall. She was back in the room when the shots were fired toward where she had briefly been standing.

But the shots didn't stop just because she'd disappeared. Instead, the blasting continued, and she realized that the men were heading down the hall toward her, keeping a constant barrage of bullets and shot pellets flying. There was no more opportunity for her to fire back, and as soon as the men reached the door of her room, she'd be a sitting duck. Even worse, there was no way Logan would hear her yell, not over the sound of all the gunfire. Her plan stank.

There were no doors out of the room, no furniture sturdy enough to give her any real cover, but there was a window, directly opposite to the door, and she crossed to it quickly. She looked outside. She'd have no trouble surviving the fall, and would almost certainly be able to run away after landing. But that would leave Logan alone, to face three or four armed, experienced men. She couldn't do that.

She pulled the window open and then scurried back across the room, back to the wall with the door in it. There was a dresser, there, and she crouched down behind it. Far from perfect, but at least she wasn't leaving Logan behind.

It was hard to place the gunfire, all the shots echoing and shaking through the entire house, but Caylen imagined the men walking down the hall, imagined the speed they'd be moving at, and she wasn't surprised when the door swung violently into the room, and the curtains on the window were shredded by shotgun pellets.

There was a pause in the shooting, and Caylen knew the men were thinking she'd climbed out the window, and then the sound she'd been hoping for. Shorter, sharper cracks of gunfire, and clearly from further down the hall, as Logan took the initiative and did his job.

One of the men dove into Caylen's room to get away from Logan's bullets, and she was ready. Her arrow was silent in the cacophony, so anyone left in the hallway might still think she'd gone out the window...

But then the racket stopped. Caylen's ears were still ringing, but there was no new gunfire. She couldn't hear well enough to be sure no one was moving, though, and she'd hate to have made it through all that just to get shot by one lucky survivor, so she stayed put, bow ready.

"Caylen?" Logan's voice floated down the hall.

"You okay?" She called back. "Is the hallway clear?"

"I think so." But he didn't sound all that sure.

"What we were talking about before—you have any left?" She had no idea if that was clear enough to make any sense, but she didn't want to advertise his lack of bullets to anyone who might be lurking in the hallway.

"No."

"Let's just sit tight. The guards will be here any second. If there's anyone left alive out there, and they try to leave the house, just let them go. If they come into your room, blow their heads off." She hoped he'd understand that the last words had been for the enemy to hear, not for him.

And apparently he did, because he didn't bother arguing about his lack of ammunition. "Check," he said. "I'm ready for them." She should have known he'd be prepared to bluff.

So they sat there, in their separate rooms, quiet and watchful, until the guards arrived. There was a bit of tension while the guards searched through the bodies, and a little excitement when they realized that two of the men from the back yard had been healthy enough to drag themselves some distance away, but otherwise, it was all fairly civilized. Well, civilized if you ignored the destruction and gore that was scattered all over Logan's previously pristine home. An advantage of fighting in the forest, Caylen decided: much less clean-up.

But it wouldn't be her job, here, and the servants that Logan brought up from the basement seemed too glad to be alive to complain much about the mess. Logan stayed with them while Caylen answered questions from the guards. She was a little surprised to see the staff grabbing their things and heading away from the house in a nervous, excited cluster.

"Where are they going?" she asked Logan when he approached.

"I told them to go home." He looked resigned. "I can't ask them to stay here, not while I'm a target. They could have been killed, and for nothing. Nothing to do with them."

It was strange for Logan to be the one thinking about that sort of thing, while Caylen got sidetracked. She wondered if this was part of the change the Chancellor had said she'd undergo, but she didn't think so. She'd always been pretty focused on the action side of things.

"So are you going to..." Caylen broke off when she saw the messenger boys coming. There were a lot of them, splitting apart as they neared the crowd of nobles who had been watching the guards work. Each messenger worked his way through the crowd until he found his employer. Caylen recognized Logan's runner as he approached.

"They've taken Jonah, my Lord." The boy's eyes were wide with excitement. "Arrested him. He's... they're taking him to the Dark House, my Lord!"

Caylen felt an unpleasant jolt, and she could only imagine how much that emotion must have been magnified in Logan, but he responded fairly calmly. "What are the charges?"

"They say he's the one who ordered the attack last night, sir!" The messenger glanced at Caylen, as if only then becoming aware that she had been one of the intended victims the night before.

Logan shook his head as he too looked at Caylen. "Damn it! If people believe that, they'll think I put him up to it..." He caught himself. "Wait. Caylen, *you* don't believe that, do you?"

"Who has the power to order arrests? To take people to the Dark House? Is it just Rolston?" Caylen's mind was racing, and she didn't have time to soothe Logan's fears.

"Not technically," Logan said slowly. "Any noble *can* order the arrest of a commoner. But we don't. The guards act on the orders of the Chancellor, or Rolston."

"So if the Chancellor ordered it, you don't need to be worrying about what I believe—you need to be worried about what *he* thinks. And if Rolston ordered it—well, that might be the final evidence we've been looking for, right?"

Logan's face was serious, and he waved the messenger away without taking his eyes from Caylen's face. "I want to know that you trust me. I need to know that you don't think the attack came from me."

Caylen wasn't sure what to say. So instead, she reached out and smudged a little blood from Logan's face; he'd been cut by a shard of broken glass, and hadn't cleaned up yet. With her other hand, she reached to her own arm where the shot pellet had grazed her, and lifted a little blood of on her finger. Then she held the two fingers up in front of him, showing him her evidence. "We've fought together, been wounded together... I trust you." He looked mostly convinced, but not entirely. "If you'd wanted me dead, you could have just stayed in that room off the hallway. You could have jumped out the window and taken off. I trusted you when I made the plan, and you came through."

Logan held her gaze a little longer, then grinned. "To be honest, I hadn't thought about the window option. I probably should have done that, huh?"

"We both could have, and neither of us did. We're good, Logan."

"Okay. Yeah, okay." He was getting his determined look again. "So, we need to go help Jonah. We need to find the Chancellor."

Caylen nodded her agreement and fell into step beside Logan as he strode down the street. This time, he didn't even try to convince her to stay behind.

CHAPTER 28

Caylen was barely out of the gate from the Estates when she heard a familiar whistle. It sounded strange, echoing off hard stone and bricks instead of being muffled by forest undergrowth, but it was unmistakable all the same. She fought to stay casual as her eyes scanned the street, and when she saw Pim standing in the mouth of a nearby alley, she nudged Logan to walk in that direction.

"Damn; where've you been?" Pim asked, but didn't wait for an answer. "We've got trouble. Did you hear about the meeting?"

"The meeting? What? No..."

He nodded as if unsurprised. "That's what we figured. We sent one of those little messenger boys, but we figured you'd have shown if he'd gotten through."

"What meeting? Why'd you want to meet?" Caylen was getting a little frustrated by the lack of information.

"We caught the fake nomads. You should have been there—it was great. We killed a couple, and some of them escaped, but we caught four of them, brought them in. We figured they could get questioned in town."

"They escaped?" Logan asked. "I should have been notified if they'd been brought in."

Pim shrugged. "Not quite." His look at Caylen was clear. How much were they saying in front of the city boy? Caylen gestured impatiently for Pim to keep talking.

"Nora wasn't sure what the situation was in here, so she went up to the gate alone, and sent a messenger to tell you to meet us. She figured you could tell her who should get the prisoners. But when we went to the meeting, it was an ambush. City guards." He took a deep breath, and Caylen felt her stomach tighten. For the first time, she wondered why Pim was here all alone.

"Nobody got killed," he said quickly. "Our scouts did their jobs—sounded the alarm for the rest of us. But they got captured. Taken into town, we figure."

"Who?" Caylen wasn't sure she wanted to know.

Pim looked like he didn't want to tell her. "Taryn," he finally said. "And Connell."

"When?"

"Yesterday afternoon."

A day. Taryn and Connell had been captive, held in who-knew-what conditions, while Caylen had been sleeping in a clean bed and being served breakfast by a maid in a fancy house. If they were even captives at all; maybe they'd just been killed outright... Pim gave her a moment to think, then said, "Nora sent me over the wall to find you. She and the others are going to work their way in through the gates, if they can."

Caylen nodded, her mind racing. "Walk with us," she said, and Pim fell in beside her. "Logan's already planning to speak to the Chancellor; somebody arrested Jonah today, and took him to the Dark House."

"They arrested him? I thought he was pretty powerful in this town."

Caylen nodded. "He was. Is. I don't know—I think things are happening. Somebody's making a move, I think. They tried to kill the Chancellor, and Logan, and maybe me, if I wasn't just in the wrong place; they arrested Jonah; and why did they stop me from meeting with you all?" She frowned, and then started to get excited. "Do you still have the prisoners? The ambush must have been to keep them from talking! They must know something..." But did that make sense? "But we've been assuming that Rolston is the enemy. And he's in charge of the Dark House. He wouldn't have needed to ambush you; he could have just waited until you turned the prisoners over to him."

"We still have them—hopefully. Nora was going to tie them up in the forest, somewhere. But...would you have given them to this Rolston for sure?" Pim asked. "You didn't sound like you approved of the Dark House, out in the forest."

"And I was criticizing it to him earlier in the day, too. Maybe he was afraid I *wouldn't* turn them over, if I made it to the meeting." They were outside the Great Hall, now, and Caylen made it a few strides up the wide stairs before noticing the crowd outside the Dark House. It wasn't huge, and they were keeping a respectful distance, but there was clearly something going on. Caylen was torn; she wanted to investigate, but she needed to speak to the Chancellor. She turned to Pim. "Can you go see what's happening over there? Or are you supposed to meet Nora and the others?"

"We're meeting outside the Dark House, as soon as they make it in. I'll go scout, and find good spots for us; you find me when you can." And with that he was off.

Caylen hated to see him go; she felt like she'd just resumed contact with her family, and now the connection was being cut again. But she had work to do, and she and Logan jogged up the stairs and inside the building. She knew that her clothes earned her some strange looks, but she ignored them. She wasn't hiding anything.

She and Logan strode into the Chancellor's outer office and dodged through the crowds of people loitering there. They were mostly nobles, judging by their clothes, and they all seemed fairly upset. But Caylen didn't care about that. "I need to see the Chancellor," she said as soon as she found the man who'd been in charge of the door in the past. "It's urgent."

The man's face was strained, and he shook his head quickly. "I'm sorry; the Chancellor is unavailable."

"It's an emergency," Logan clarified.

"I'm sorry, my Lord. He's..." The assistant looked torn, then finally admitted, in a hushed voice, "The Chancellor isn't well. After the attack last night, and then too much excitement today..."

"So is he at home?" Caylen didn't want to harass an ill, elderly man, but they needed backup.

"He's in seclusion." The voice was rich and oily, and Caylen turned to see Rolston standing behind them. He looked as if he hadn't slept or changed clothes since the last time she'd seen him, but he was standing tall and staring her in the eye. "He cannot be disturbed."

"Well, maybe you can help me, then." She might not have proof that Rolston was holding Taryn and Connell, but Johan's arrest had been official. Caylen spoke loudly enough that she could be sure those nearby would hear. "Why is Jonah in the Dark House?"

There was a buzz in the crowd, but it subsided quickly as people strained to hear Rolston's response. He looked uncomfortable, then resolved. "That's confidential." He raised his head proudly. "I do not answer to you."

"You answer to the Council, though, Rolston." Logan sounded confident. "We can convene an emergency session, if needed. You can be called forward to explain Jonah's imprisonment, and to answer some other questions about the way the Dark House is being run."

"Well, young Lord Logan, if you insist on having your business spread around in public," Rolston said with a sneer, "I suppose I should stop trying to protect you." He raised his voice so that it could be heard by the entire room. "I'm sorry to say that the assassins who attacked our beloved Chancellor last night have identified Jonah as the man who hired them." He paused for effect, then said, "At this time, we are acting on the assumption that Jonah acted alone, without the knowledge or consent of his young friend, here." Rolston started for the door, the crowd parting to let him through. "I certainly hope that, after questioning the man, I will be able to confirm that Lord Logan was not involved. At this time, however—the matter is in doubt."

Logan shook his head. "No. That doesn't make sense. Why would Jonah do that?" He wasn't speaking to Rolston, but to the crowd. "There's no possible motive— how would Jonah benefit from the Chancellor's death? How would *I* benefit from his death?"

"Well, I will certainly ask Jonah those questions, during his interrogation," Rolston replied. He was almost at the door now, and Logan didn't seem to have any real way to stop him.

Caylen decided that it was her turn, and she had nothing but a bluff to put arrows in her quiver. "The false nomads—the ones my family captured—the ones you tried to steal away from them, so they wouldn't talk— they're talking."

Rolston barely turned toward her. "I don't know what you mean. I have no knowledge of any 'false nomads.'" He was almost out the door. Almost gone. This was happening. The Chancellor was missing, only Rolston seemed to know where he was, and Rolston wasn't talking. If everything had gone smoothly in the attack that morning, Rolston would be totally unopposed, now, free to take over the city for himself. Maybe the Council would have the guts to insist that Mara be appointed Chancellor, but would that really be any different than having Rolston in the position himself?

But everything *hadn't* gone smoothly that morning. Logan and Caylen were still there, and Rolston knew that. So either his plans had been so far into motion that he hadn't been able to stop them, or he'd decided that it didn't matter. Maybe he'd thought that Logan and Caylen would be too shocked or too intimidated to do anything. Caylen almost smiled, and she could feel her determination and ferocity rising inside; if Rolston thought that, he was just one more city-dweller who didn't know a damn thing about nomads. But when she looked over at Logan, she saw a matching look of determination on *his* face, so maybe Rolston didn't know either of them all that well.

"Hold on, Rolston," Logan said, his voice calm and full of authority. "We're not done here. Are you walking away from the Council?"

Rolston whirled. "I'm walking away from a child playing grown up games. *I'm* the Speaker of the Council, young Logan. I'm the one who calls it into session. And I have made no such call."

"The Council can be called by the Speaker, by the Chancellor, or by any group of twenty or more Councilors." Logan sounded sure of his facts, but Caylen wondered whether he was sure he could get nineteen other Councilors to support him. Well, eighteen, she supposed, because he certainly had her vote.

Rolston seemed to have picked up on the same weakness. He gestured grandly with his arms and spoke to the crowd of nobles surrounding him. "My friends, I don't know what games this pup is playing, but I have serious work to do, and cannot be delayed here any longer. We are in a crisis; the Chancellor has been attacked by one of our most prominent citizens. I know you are all concerned about that *real* issue, and do not have time to humor this youngster." He turned, and took another step for the door.

Logan stepped after him, looking back over his shoulder at Caylen. "Back me up, okay?" he hissed, then called out, "In the absence of the Chancellor, we need someone to act in his place. Obviously we anticipate his return, but until he's available, tradition dictates that the position be filled by his heir. I have the support of the only other potential heir currently available, and I therefore declare myself to be Acting Chancellor. And as such, I *order* you to stop walking and explain yourself!"

Rolston didn't even slow down. He didn't turn around, didn't flinch, didn't show any sign that he'd heard the words that had been shouted at him from five strides away in an almost silent room.

Logan yelled, "Rolston!" but the man was out the door.

Caylen jostled past. Logan had tried to do things the proper way; now it was her turn. She darted out the door and managed to get in front of Rolston before he was half-way down the steps. "The false nomads are naming *you*, Rolston. They're saying you're the one who sent them after Logan. It's over—I'll have them brought in front of the Council, and you'll be finished."

Rolston glanced around to be sure no one was close enough to overhear, then hissed, "You'd do better to worry about the *actual* nomads I have in my custody. If you behave yourself, we can arrange to have them released. If you keep this up...they're dead." He jostled her a little as he shoved past her and continued down the steps.

And that was the admission Caylen had been waiting for. If Rolston was holding Connell and Taryn, then he'd been the one to ambush the nomads outside the city, and the only reason to do that was to cover up the attacks. "You killed Dart," she said softly, and her hand fell to her dagger. It would be so easy to end all this, right there on the steps. But what would that look like? As Jonah had said, a nomad killing a noble for no apparent reason would be more likely to cause an invasion of the Wildlands than anything else.

Rolston took advantage of Caylen's indecision, turning again and pushing through the now-growing crowd of commoners. Some of them didn't get out of his way too quickly, though, and Caylen saw her chance. The people were afraid, but they were also angry. Maybe all they needed was a little spark.

"Why are so many houses dark, Rolston?" she called in her loudest voice. He kept moving, as she'd expected, and she kept after him. She could feel Logan close behind her, and she could feel the way the crowd parted to let her through. They *wanted* her to catch up, and to ask the questions they were afraid to.

"Where are all the people you've stolen? Why have you arrested innocent people?" Caylen was close behind Rolston now, but she kept her voice loud. She wasn't really speaking to him anymore. "Where is Connell? Where's Taryn?"

"Where's Jonah?" Logan added, his voice even louder than Caylen's. "Where's Mahia?" Sealy's daughter, Caylen realized. Logan *had* remembered her, just as he'd promised.

And that was when the crowd picked it up. "Where's Walt?" "Where's Dora?" "Where's Dann?" The questions rang out from all around them, and the crowd was following along, intent on finding answers to questions that they'd had for far too long.

"Where are they?" Caylen asked, and then said it again, and Logan joined in. By the time they reached the gates of the Dark House, the whole crowd was chanting the question. "Where are they? Where are they?"

Rolston pushed the gate open and eased inside the yard of the Dark House. He tried to turn to shut it behind him, but Caylen was there, and then Logan, and many others behind them. Rolston turned and ran for the door, a rat scurrying for his hole. Someone on the inside had obviously been watching for him, because the door opened immediately and Rolston dashed through.

That couldn't be all. There were too many unanswered questions, and too many missing people. They had the momentum now, the support of the crowd, and they needed to use it. Caylen dove forward and caught the door with her fingertips just before the guards pulled it closed. She moved around to push her body into the opening, and was greeted by two uniformed guards, one with a long knife pointed toward her, the other holding a pistol. The crowd was close, pushing against Caylen's back, pushing her forward toward the guards and making it impossible for her to dodge. It seemed like the world slowed down, and Caylen could see exactly what was going to happen. The guard wouldn't even have to waste a bullet; he could just watch as Caylen was pushed forward by the unthinking crowd, watch as Caylen was impaled on his partner's knife. She braced herself and tried to push backward, but she knew it was futile.

The arrows sprouted out of the guards' chests almost simultaneously, the bodies crumpling with two shafts in each torso, and Caylen didn't even take the time to turn around. She took a moment to make sure that the guards were going to stay down, and then let the crowd press her forward. There would be time later to thank her nomad family, and admire the vantage points that they had found in order to be ready for this job.

Logan was right beside her as she climbed over the guards, and the two of them saw the inside of the Dark House at the same time.

The core of the building was totally open, a space that looked at least four stories high but with no floors, just huge wooden support beams crisscrossing the expanse. Large cages lined all four walls, stacked from floor to ceiling. There was a rough walkway in front of each level, giving access to the metal-barred cell doors. The most horrifying thing was that every one of the cages seemed to be occupied, several of them by more than one person. Hundreds of prisoners, held in this dark hell for who knew how long...

Rolston stood near the middle of the space, beside a collection of furniture and tools that Caylen didn't even want to think about. There were four guards standing around him, and he drew himself up with whatever dignity was left after his quick retreat. "This is private government property. You are invading a top secret facility, one that is run under the authority of the

Council and the Chancellor himself." Caylen could feel Logan pause beside her, and it seemed like Rolston could feel his hesitation as well. "People have gotten over-excited," Rolston said, his voice dropping a little, "and mistakes have been made. Get your people back outside, and we'll try to make everything better." He shook his head. "You know better than this, Logan. You're one of us. We don't allow the rabble to control our town. *We* control *them*."

"You control them through *fear*?" Caylen asked. "You terrorize them into obedience?"

"We do what is *necessary*. We keep them safe from outside threats, and in return, we damn well expect their loyalty!"

"What outside threats?" Caylen spat out. "When's the last time Yorkton was attacked? And don't even pretend that you protect them from nomads, because we have no interest in hurting them! No reason to."

Rolston shook his head. "You cannot understand. You're an outsider." He turned his attention back to Logan. "But you're one of us, Logan. You know how it is." His voice became authoritative. "Now, get those people out of this building, immediately."

The front part of the crowd had filled in behind Logan and Caylen, but they were quiet, intimidated by the horrors of the room and the dead guards they had stepped over to get inside. And intimidated by Rolston's authority and Logan's presence. These people were used to doing what the nobles told them to do, and they were in a room filled with evidence of what happened to the disobedient. Caylen was pretty sure that if Logan tried, he could get them to turn around.

And for a few moments, she wasn't sure that he wouldn't try. He'd been raised to support the government of the city, not challenge it. But then he squared his shoulders, and said, loud and clear, "We're here for Jonah. And Connell and Taryn." He paused, then nodded to himself, and said, "And Dann. And Mahia. And all the rest. We're here for all of them, Rolston!"

Caylen felt the bitter triumph of the moment. There were many who would never leave that black space, but Logan was right; she was there for all of them, as much as she was there for the living. And the people behind her seemed to feel the same grim determination that she was feeling. "Where are they?" came from a few voices at first, but then more, and more, until the stone walls echoed and shook with the volume of the chant. "Where are they?" as commoners poured into the space, washed around Caylen and Logan and swept toward Rolston and his guards. "Where are they?" as Rolston backed up, his expression panicked, and "Where are they?" as his nerve broke completely and he turned and sprinted toward the door at the back of the room, his guards at his heels.

The chant turned into a triumphant roar, and the crowd surged forward, toward the cages. Caylen let herself be pushed along, but she felt the force of the crowd ebb as they got closer to the walls. She didn't blame them. The horror was too much to face all at once. But it wasn't her problem. Logan could find Connell and Taryn, and he'd be able to get them any help they needed. Caylen was in the city for revenge, and she'd found her target. She couldn't let him slip away now.

She loosed her bow and moved quickly along the row of cages. She kept close to the side, out of the line of easy fire. She worked the odds in her head. Rolston seemed useless, but a gun could make even a coward dangerous. And the guards from the main room, and maybe some from the room they'd gone into. She'd have to be careful, but she could do it. She was a Nomad, born and raised to fight. Her mind raced as she moved, scouting the room for advantages, tools she could use... and then a thin, filthy arm reached out from one of the cages and grabbed her ankle.

She wanted to shake it off. The fingers were swollen at the joints, just bone everywhere else. There was no strength, here, no real impediment. She thought of Logan's grip in the forest, when they'd found him. This was just the same, and she'd gotten nothing but trouble from helping him. She pulled her leg away, and the arm fell to the ground as if its last strength had been exhausted. She would have been okay if she hadn't let her eyes follow the arm into the cage, if she hadn't seen the emaciated face staring back at her with something that almost looked like hope.

She turned around. She'd alert the others. She could do that much. But when she turned, the crowd wasn't doing anything. They were standing where they'd been when she'd left, staring at the wall of cages as if the horror was too much to comprehend. Caylen thought of their safe lives, and wondered if they were realizing now that their safety had come at too high of a price.

Caylen took one last look at the doorway through which Rolston had escaped, then turned back. The room had quieted, the people in shocked awe as they saw the condition of the prisoners, and Caylen barely had to raise her voice to be heard. "Somebody check the guards at the door—see if they have keys. If they don't, bring tools that we can use to break the locks." There was movement in the direction of the guards. "And then we need to be organized, and gentle. We'll need stretchers for some."

"Lay them out in here?" a woman asked, her voice doubtful.

Caylen could understand the woman's objection— how could any good come in a place so poisoned? She looked over at Logan. "We should take them over to the Great Hall, and use it as a triage—let them see what they've done."

Logan nodded, but added, "What *I've* done." He seemed to be in a daze. Caylen would have liked to sympathize, but she didn't have the time.

"You were part of it. Absolutely." She stepped closer and grabbed him by the shoulder. "But you're part of this, now. Give your friends the same chance to make amends."

There was an alarmed shout from the doorway. "Soldiers coming! Soldiers coming!"

Caylen shook Logan's shoulder. "Logan, can you stop them? At least get a few of them to come inside, and see what's been done—then let them make up their own minds."

Logan nodded slowly, then more vigorously. By the time he started for the door, his stride was purposeful. "They say the soldiers are on my side—we'll see if that's true."

Caylen watched him for as long as she could allow herself, and then got back to work. There was a lot to do.

CHAPTER 29

Caylen forced herself to work methodically. When someone had come forward with keys from one of the guards, it had turned out to be Pim, and she set him the task of opening all the cell doors. A few of the prisoners were able to make their own way out; Caylen felt a surge of joy when Connell stumbled out of one of the cages, but it turned to fear when he reached back inside and gently lifted a still body that could only be Taryn's. Caylen could feel Darton's knife at her hip, crying out to taste blood in exchange for blood. But she was needed here. She knew for sure, now, who her target was, and that had been the hard part; she could complete her mission once this newer, more important task was finished. She could wait, and so could her knife.

Connell saw her and looked like he couldn't decide between joy and sorrow.

"Taryn..." Caylen murmured.

"They were rough on her," Connell said simply, looking down at the woman in his arms. "But she's strong. We'll make her better." His own face was bruised, and Caylen was sure there was more damage under his newly-tattered clothing, but he was standing straight and proud.

"There are nomads outside. I don't know who, but if you get her out there, I'm sure they'll find you. I need to..." she ran out of words, just gestured at the walls of cages, the work to be done.

Connell was already moving away. "I'll see to her, and then come back to help." He paused. "It's good to see you, Cay."

She didn't trust her voice, so she forced a quick smile and then let herself be distracted by the job ahead of her.

It took hours. Logan had been able to get the soldiers onside, and that helped; they were more used to carnage than the commoners, at least, but even for them, the scene in the Dark House was horrifying. Most of the prisoners were still alive, although a few were not, but any that had been there for any period of time were damaged, some in ways so horrible that Caylen couldn't let herself imagine the tools that must have been used. Jonah was found, the hood still over his head, his hands bound behind his back, but unharmed.

"You should go help out in the Great Hall, if you can," Caylen suggested gently as she massaged sensation back into his hands. The man was looking at the scene around him with wide eyes, obviously shaken by how close he had come to disaster. Caylen was sure there were enough workers in the Hall already, but she wanted Jonah out of the Dark House, and she hoped that he'd respond well to having a task.

It took a few moments for the words to penetrate his brain, and Caylen began to regret the suggestion.

Maybe she should have found a way to get him to go home. "The Chancellor?" he asked, and Caylen realized that he hadn't been in shock, he'd been thinking. "Is he safe?"

"I don't know. They said he wasn't well—said he was in seclusion. Maybe that's true, or maybe..."

"We need to find out," Jonah said. "I'll see what I can do. If he's not able to be in charge—the city needs a strong leader, now, to get everyone past this. If he can't do it..."

"If he can't do it, Logan can." Caylen was torn between disgust and admiration. "Do you never stop campaigning for him?"

"Do you think I'm wrong?" Jonah asked, his voice low and serious. "Would you rather see Rolston's daughter as the Chancellor?"

That was a good point, and Caylen didn't interfere as Jonah headed outside. She forced herself back to work, helping the soldiers empty the cells, arranging people to carry the injured prisoners across the street to safety, all the while trying to forget that she had found her enemy, had seen all this proof of the evil he had done, and had let him slip away.

Logan ran back and forth between the Dark House and the Great Hall, keeping things organized. Caylen found herself thinking about Jonah's words—the city *did* need somebody to be in charge, and maybe Logan was the best person for the job, if the Chancellor wasn't able to do it. Or if he wasn't *willing* to do it, Caylen reminded herself. For all she knew, he'd been aware of this situation all along. Maybe he approved of this Hell.

Finally, the last cell was emptied. The occupant had been an old man, starved to the point that he couldn't walk without help. Two soldiers carried him out; one could have done it without strain, but the guards seemed to feel better working in pairs. Caylen watched the guards drape a towel over the man's head to protect his eyes, made over-sensitive from too long in the dark, and then carry him through the doorway. Caylen followed them outside, then stood in the courtyard trying to convince her lungs that it was safe to take a deep breath again.

She watched the old man being carried across to the Great Hall, and she saw the small group of nobles coming in the opposite direction. Logan was with them, but Caylen's attention was caught by the Chancellor, frail and drawn, and Mara, walking determinedly beside him. Caylen was gratified to see the Chancellor stop and watch the old man carried by him; she hoped she saw some trace of guilt.

The group started walking again, and as they drew close to Caylen the Chancellor said, "You've been busy." She couldn't get a read on his emotions at all.

"Something had to be done." Caylen turned her eyes to Mara. "Rolston is a murderer—he's the one who sent the false nomads to attack Logan in the forest, and who knows how many innocent people he's killed in the Dark House?"

"I'll want to see proof of all that," Mara said, her head held high. "But if it's true...well, I'd be absolutely shocked. But if it is..." She broke off as if overcome by emotion, but her audience was small, and jaded; she didn't impress any of them. She realized that pretty quickly, and lifted her chin again, turning to the Chancellor to say, "I will continue to serve the city to the best of my abilities. If the accusations against my father prove to be true, it will only be a reason for me to work even harder to repair any damage he has done."

Caylen wanted to spit on Mara's promises. "To repair the damage? We just found..." Her voice was jagged, and she took a deep breath before she could continue. "We just found the body of a little girl. Maybe six years old. Tossed on a pile with a bunch of other corpses. How are you possibly going to *repair* that damage?"

Mara's face betrayed no emotion, but Logan looked stricken. "Mahia?" he asked.

Caylen shook her head sadly. "I have no idea. I don't know if there's anyone left to identify her. I almost hope that it *is* her—otherwise, it would mean there were *two* little girls dragged into all this..."

The Chancellor looked even older than before. "It's my fault," he said softly. "It was my job to keep an eye on things, and I didn't. I...I didn't *trust* Rolston, but I gave him power anyway."

"And he killed a lot of people," Caylen said. She'd be damned if she'd deny the old man's responsibility to make him feel better. "He killed a lot of people, and he *tried* to kill a lot more. Including you, and me and Logan, and I assume he was going to kill Jonah." And that was all true, and it was all serious, but it wasn't the reason she'd come to the city. "He killed Dart." She let her fingers play on the handle of her dagger. "This is your show, here. I have a job to do." She turned toward the door of the Dark House; she'd hunt Rolston down, track him wherever he'd gone...

"Not alone, Caylen." At first, she thought she was imagining her mother's voice, but when Caylen turned, Nora stepped out of the shadows cast by the gate post. Connell was by her side, and Pim, and most of the rest of the band, and Caylen smiled for the first time in too long.

"No. Not alone," she agreed. "But now. It's already probably too late."

"You had other work to do. Important work." It was as close to approval as Caylen thought she'd ever heard from her mother.

"And the work's not over." It was Logan, looking tired but strong as he moved between Caylen and the nomads. "I know you have to do this. I know you're going to go, but—you're coming back, right? We need you here. This is a start, but there's still a lot to do."

"Logan—you can do it by yourself. You don't need me."

He stepped toward her and spoke a little more quietly. "I don't *want* to do it by myself. I might not need you, but I want you. I want you to come back." His words reminded her of a petulant little boy, but she remembered his strength just a few hours earlier, when he'd turned his back on what he'd been taught all his life, in order to do what was right.

"We need you here," the Chancellor agreed. "There's a lot of rebuilding to be done, and your voice is invaluable. You could help finish the job your father began." He sounded sincere, and Caylen hoped he was.

"I'll come back," she agreed. "At least—at least for a while. To help." Logan looked like he wanted to ask for more, but he didn't. Caylen couldn't resist. She took a few quick steps to close the space between them, then stretched up and gave him a quick kiss. She'd been aiming for his cheek but he'd turned his head a little and she ended up catching the corner of his mouth. Not exactly graceful, but it wasn't like she'd planned it out.

And that was enough of that. "Can I be on point?" Caylen asked Nora, jerking her head toward the door.

"It's your hunt, Caylen. You call the positions." Caylen looked at her mother in disbelief, but she saw Connell's nod of quiet approval, and wondered if it could be true.

"I—" She hesitated, then decided to go for it. "Nora, you're on point with me. Connell, if you're up to it, take rear guard with Pim. We don't know what we're getting into, so take it slow and careful."

Nora didn't contradict her, and the nomads fell into position easily enough, so Caylen went with it. Her time in the city had changed her; maybe it had changed Nora, as well.

They headed back into the Dark House and found the door through which Rolston had disappeared. It didn't have a lock, so they eased through and found themselves in a long, narrow hallway, sloping down. It was poorly lit, with electric bulbs glowing dimly at irregular intervals, but at least it wasn't pitch black. They started down, quiet and alert, and Caylen let a tiny part of her brain be distracted enough to wonder where they were. They must be travelling under the city, and they were moving in a straight line, apparently ignoring the margins of the roads and buildings they were passing beneath.

It was claustrophobic, after a while, and there was no life other than the nomads, none of the plants and woodland animals that would normally give clues to Caylen. Here, the hard stone floor showed no tracks; if there had been any branches off the main tunnel, Caylen wouldn't have known which way to go.

But there were no branches, just a long expanse of tunnel and then a gradual slope upward. When they reached the rough wooden door at the end of the tunnel, Caylen checked that the nomads were ready, and then crouched down to make herself a smaller target before carefully pushing the door open. It creaked in a way that made all of their prior stealth pointless, but there was no flash of gunfire, no wicked song of arrows flying toward them.

Caylen edged her way out into an empty wooden shack. There was no furniture, no supplies or tools or weapons, and there was no sign of Rolston. So he was running, not staying to fight. That wasn't unexpected, she told herself. For all he knew, she could have been coming after him with the entire force of the city guards.

She moved cautiously across the cabin to the other door, and opened it just wide enough to listen before pushing it further open. She heard all the sounds she'd been missing in the city, the full cacophony of a peaceful forest. "He's gone," she said quietly to those behind her, and she stepped outside. She could see the glow of the city lights not far in the distance, but she was clearly outside the walls. Rolston had left the city behind.

After the stench of the Dark House and the tight, close environment in the tunnels, it was overwhelming to finally be outside. The cool night air filled Caylen's lungs, and made her feel as if she was expanding, dissolving, becoming a part of the forest. The disappointment that she'd felt when she realized that Rolston had taken advantage of his head start faded away. She was free.

She could run all night, she could see in the dark, and she could track anyone, anytime, anywhere. "You think you can hide from me in the *forest*?" she called, and she didn't feel anger, she didn't feel the hunger for revenge. She just felt joy, and triumph; she was back in the Nomads' Land, and she could do *anything*. "The forest is mine! Run all you want, hide if you can—I'll find you!" She felt like a falcon, freed from its jesses; she would hunt, and she would kill, but first she would *fly*.

"Are you about done?" Nora asked, her voice dry, but Caylen could hear the hint of amusement in it, and she could hear the understanding, the joy at their shared wildness.

"No," Caylen said, and she smiled widely. "I'm just getting started."